Hidden Depths

a&b

Hidden Depths

JOYCE HOLMS

First edition published in Great Britain in 2004 by
Allison & Busby Limited
Bon Marche Centre
241-251 Ferndale Road
London SW9 8BJ
http://www.allisonandbusby.com

10 9 8 7 6 5 4 3 2 1

ISBN 0 7490 8317 4

Printed and bound in Wales by
Creative Print & Design, Ebbw Vale

JOYCE HOLMS was born and educated in Glasgow. The victim of a low boredom threshold, she has held a variety of jobs, from teaching window dressing and managing a hotel on the Isle of Arran to working for an Edinburgh detective agency and running a B&B in the Highlands. Married with two grown up children, she lives in Edinburgh and her interests include hill walking and garden design.

Chapter One

The ball arced high into the pellucid blue of the evening sky and then descended like a miniature Icarus, exquisite, beautiful, bouncing once on the edge of the green and rolling gently to within a metre of the hole.

Buchanan watched its flight in humble amazement. An entire 273 yards! Damn near a hole in one but, with his second shot unmissable, two under par for the hole! An eagle, by God! Life could not hold a sweeter paradise. Balm for all the woes that beset him daily, the work stress, the poverty, the inhumanity of man, little miracles like this were what kept him going. He floated there for a minute or two, a couple of inches above the tee, basking in the beauty of the moment, then slid his driver back into the bag and followed his ball down the fairway to the green.

It was an added benison to know that he wasn't losing his touch, even though he'd barely managed to squeeze in more than nine holes a week for the last six months. Larry the Bastard knew how to wring the last drop of blood out of every minion in his chambers and Buchanan, currently at the bottom of the pecking order, regularly got the short end of the stick when it came to overtime. The few rounds he managed to fit in from time to time tended to be late in the evening when the light was going and the other members had retired to the clubhouse, but that had its compensations. There was no hanging around on the tee waiting for those in front to move on and, in the glow of a sunset like tonight's, the view over Edinburgh and the Firth of Forth beyond was quite remarkable.

He took his time over the putt, confident of sinking it but not wanting to abort the eagle with a careless slip, and as he lined it up he was vaguely aware of someone in the distance at the edge of his vision. He registered nothing more than a blur of movement, a flash of blue against the green of the grass, but there was something about the figure, some detail that must have rung a bell deep in his subconscious, because an obscure uneasiness took hold of him and his fingers tightened on the club.

His eyes flickered between the ball and the hole, joining them together with an almost visible line, waiting for the mental "*click*" that would tell him it was time – the gods placated, the omens favourable – to strike. Briskly, at last, and with perfect control, his wrists moved.

'*Yoo-hoo*!'

The ball leapt like a startled gazelle and shot six inches past the pin.

Buchanan remained stooped over his putter, refusing to believe the evidence of his eyes, while behind him the voice increased in volume.

'Geez! You're losing it, Buchanan. I could have sunk that one myself.'

Buchanan was speechless; gagged by the impossibility of ever expressing his anguish in words. He kept his back to her as he tapped the ball into the hole, retrieved it and replaced the pin. Only then did he swing his head round to look at her: so small, so baby-faced, so bloody abominable.

Her smile dropped from her face. 'Oooooooooo!' she sang on an ascending scale, widening her eyes in wholly bogus alarm. 'If I weren't used to your quaint little ways I'd think you weren't pleased to see me.'

'You saw what just happened?' Buchanan's hand flew out in an uncontrolled gesture towards the flag.

'No, what?' She followed the motion with a doubtful gaze and then laid a finger to her lower lip. 'Did I put you off your stroke? Oh, my God. What's the penalty for that on this course? Crucifixion? Disembowelling?'

'If I had sunk that putt,' Buchanan ground out, not even

throwing her to the ground and jumping on her, 'as I indubitably would have done if you'd had one ounce of consideration, it would have been an eagle. An *eagle*, Fizz. Two under
par for the hole. That's never going to happen to me again.'

She chortled with amusement, totally suffused with fond
delight as though he were an undying source of entertainment
to her, which of course he was. 'You're a hoot, Buchanan,
y'know that? It's not as if it were a competition, is it? What
does it matter whether you actually got it in the hole or not?
Nobody gives a monkey's chunky except you, and you know
it wasn't your fault that it missed. Tell yourself it went in.'

He swung away from her, angry with himself for letting her
see his frustration. There was no way he could ever make her
understand. Fizz wasn't the sort of person who would invest
a large amount of time and money in any project she regarded, purely and simply, as a pastime. She required immediate
gratification, commensurate with the effort applied, and/or a
considerable cash return on her investment. Not for Fizz the
fierce ecstasy he had experienced a moment ago, nor the rosy,
if forlorn hope of a repetition some time in the future.
Attempting to communicate the depth of his angst to such a
person was simply a waste of time; he could only be thankful
that it was a putter he held in his hand, not a chain saw.

It took some time to unclamp his jaw.

'Were you intending to meet me,' he growled, as they headed for the next tee, 'or are you just out for a walk?'

'A bit of both. A walk, primarily, but I thought there was a
good chance I might run into you here. Dennis mentioned
this morning that Larry the Bastard was heading off to the
Seychelles for a fortnight and I suspected that while the rat's
away the mice would be on the golf course.'

Buchanan was not entirely happy in his work but one of the
perks of the job was that Larry the Bastard, the most vile-tem-
pered and offensive member of Edinburgh's legal community,

was the one person in the world Fizz was repressed by (deny it
as she might) and she had quickly learned to give him a wide
berth. Larry's viciousness only kept her at bay during office
hours, however: at other times Buchanan was at her mercy.

'A walk … *primarily*,' he echoed, with a twinge of misgiving, a small warning light beginning to flicker at the back of
his brain. He teed-up, squinting through the low evening sunlight at the turn of the dog-leg ahead, reminding himself of
the deceptiveness of the slope, conscious of the strength of
the breeze on his cheek, but pondering largely on why Fizz
was here. She didn't make a habit of seeking out his company
unless she wanted something and, although she usually wanted something at least once a week, she didn't normally go to
the bother of hunting him down on the golf course. Nine
times out of ten all she required of him was advice about some
problem at the office. She'd been a fully fledged solicitor for
scarcely six months and since Buchanan had left the firm to
pursue a career at the bar she'd supposedly been working
under the supervision of Dennis, the junior partner.
Unfortunately, Dennis's main aim in life appeared to be to get
into her knickers so it was understandable that she should
continue to drop in at Buchanan's flat when she needed to talk
something over.

Buchanan wasn't sure how he felt about that. There were
times – quite often, if he were honest with himself – when he
was quite glad to hear her voice on the entryphone. She was,
if nothing else, cheap entertainment of a sort and cheap entertainment was the only kind of entertainment he could afford
these days. The way his bank balance had shrunk since he'd
joined Larry's chambers was nothing short of scary and it
would be another six months at the very minimum before he
could hope to start attracting briefs of his own. Suddenly he
was having to count the pennies and keeping up with the
extravagant lifestyles of his old friends was becoming some-

thing of an embarrassment, which was where Fizz became suddenly acceptable. She might now be earning considerably more than she had ever done but the old habits she had learned during the lean years died hard and she was as parsimonious as ever.

The trouble was, she was also a loose cannon: unreliable, headstrong, positively immoral in her dealings, deleterious to his hopes of promotion, and strychnine to his love life. People like Fizz had no place in the affairs of an embryo advocate whose respectability was, after all, his stock in trade, but she had a way of worming herself into the fabric of one's existence to the extent that getting shot of her was no easy matter. He had, while albeit nominally, her employer, sacked her more than once but she'd paid not a whit of notice and the fact that she was still with the firm while he was not had to say something about her talent for manipulation.

She stood well back while he was driving off, silent and motionless, displaying a concern for his concentration that was conspicuously alien to her normal indifference. Whatever she wanted from him, Buchanan deduced, it was something she didn't expect to get without making an effort.

'Okay,' he said as they walked on, 'hit me with it.'

'Sorry?'

'Hit me with it. If your primary reason for being here is fresh air and exercise, what's your secondary reason?'

'Oh, yes. I see what you mean.' She picked up a fallen branch that was lying in the rough and started swiping the heads off daisies with it. Buchanan could see she was rattled, as she always was when he saw through her, and it made him smile.

'So?'

'Oh … nothing very exciting, actually. Just something that happened in the office this morning that I thought you might find intriguing.'

'Intriguing. Uh-huh. Why does that word always give me the creeps?'

She mimed mystification with a half smile and a small shake of the head but didn't encourage him to delve any deeper into his subconscious. 'I don't suppose the name Irene Lloyd rings a bell with you but I've mentioned her to you in the past. She was —'

'I remember. She was a pal of yours at art school. Irene Lloyd was the one who went to the Gods & Goddesses party as Ganesh. Her boyfriend gave you his backpack when you took off to discover the world.'

He knew she was surprised and perhaps a little discomfited by this evidence of his pathological interest in her past life but she merely narrowed her eyes at him a little and nodded.

'That's the one. Well, I still see her from time to time. Not very often, maybe once or twice a year. She doesn't get up to Edinburgh all that often but we keep in touch: Christmas cards, the odd email. She still lives with the same guy she was going with at art school. Kerr Gilfillan. Yes, the guy who gave me my first backpack.' She shook her head, not looking at him. 'It's bizarre, the amount of trivia that clutters your memory banks, Buchanan. Anyway, he's now some sort of forest ranger cum estate manager and they have a tied cottage on a big estate somewhere between here and Dunfermline.'

'Abbeyfield House?'

She raised her brows. 'Yes, actually.'

'Well, it would be Abbeyfield, wouldn't it? It's the only sizeable estate in that area. It's open to the public.'

Buchanan wasn't much into wandering around stately homes but Janine, his ex-almost-fiancée who had exited his life shortly after Fizz had entered it, had enjoyed seeing how the other half lived. Abbeyfield, he seemed to remember, was not one of her favourite haunts, being a rather run-down and depressing pile that didn't quite make up in character what it lacked in elegance.

'Right,' Fizz said impatiently. They were approaching his ball, which was nicely placed for a five-iron, and she clearly wanted to make her point while she still had his full attention. 'The owner, Sir Douglas Fergusson, has a sizeable art collection and Irene was making some extra cash by cataloguing it and doing a bit of cleaning and restoration. So what happened was that Kerr phoned me a week or so ago to ask if Irene was staying with me. Apparently they'd had a row and she'd walked out. I hadn't seen Irene or heard from her and I told him so, however he turned up at the office last Monday morning and said Irene hadn't come back and he was really worried about her. The police weren't taking the matter seriously enough for his liking and he wanted to me to get some action going.'

'You don't want to get involved in a domestic dispute, Fizz. You'll find the two disputants end up all lovey-dovey and you get the blame for interfering.'

Fizz made a *tuh!* sound with her tongue against her teeth, indicative of mild irritation. 'I'm not simple, Buchanan. I told Kerr to get lost. It's up to Irene whether she wants to give him the elbow or not, and frankly I don't blame her. He's a nice guy but, frankly I don't know how she suffers him, he's so bloody touchy. It would drive me mad.'

'Mmm-hmm,' said Buchanan, thinking about how much loft he'd need to get him past the bunker.

She waited till he'd made the shot, her eyes following the ball as it came to rest, just a little too strongly, and rolled to the far edge of the green.

'You hit that too hard,' she said, she who didn't know one end of a golf club from the other. Buchanan looked at her and she shut up.

The sun was steadily sinking into a band of dark purple cloud along the horizon and, although the sky was still a pale and luminous turquoise, there would shortly be too little light to start another hole. Buchanan hurried up the fairway with Fizz pressing on with her story as they went.

'So, anyway, Kerr was pretty pissed off at me for refusing to interfere. He knew that you and I had stuck our noses into similar cases in the past and he thought I'd nothing else to do but talk to a few people and she'd turn up.' She swung her piece of stick at a stalk of fireweed, failing to decapitate it completely but severely discouraging it. 'Actually, he was pretty worried about her because, although they'd had bust-ups before, she'd never left it so long without at least phoning him.'

'So, she's been gone – what? – nearly a fortnight?' Buchanan said, trying to speed things up. 'She didn't leave a "dear John" note, I take it, and presumably, she hasn't so far contacted Kerr. It's time the police were starting to take an interest.'

'You hit the nail on the head, compadre. They just did. Not that Kerr thought to keep me posted on the matter – he went off in a huff and that was the last I heard from him till this morning.'

She paused, thinking, and Buchanan had to prompt her again. 'He contacted you?'

'No. I phoned him after I had a visit from the police. I suppose I should've checked up before that to see if Irene had come back but I'd planned to leave it till the weekend.' She produced a newsprint cutting from the pocket of her jeans and started to unfold it. 'You probably saw this in the *Scotsman* on Wednesday.'

Reading the morning papers with anything approaching concentration was one of the luxuries Buchanan could no longer afford. He took the piece of paper and scanned it briefly, half his mind computing the possibility of sinking his putt in one. The story was a couple of paragraphs about an art theft at Abbeyfield House where a Rubens with an estimated value of one point five million pounds had disappeared from the studio of the estate's art restorer, a certain Ms Irene Lloyd who had not been seen for ten days.

Buchanan was only mildly surprised. Fizz had some very louche friends, picked up on her travels in various corners of the world, and compared to most of them an art thief scarcely merited comment. 'Nice one,' he said. 'She'll be able to disappear for quite a while on a million and a half. Tell Kerr to check the Bahamas.'

Fizz turned her head to look at him, waiting till he met her stony gaze before saying in a clipped tone, 'I don't think you should leap to conclusions, Buchanan. Irene's no criminal, you can take my word for that. If she took that picture – and okay, maybe she did – it wasn't just because she fancied being a millionaire. Something pretty damn crucial made her do it.'

'No doubt.' Buchanan wasn't inclined to get into a discussion about motives, he was just thankful that, for once, there was no need for him to get involved. If Fizz wanted to put Kerr in touch with the firm of detectives that the partnership dealt with that was up to her and as far as he could see, it was all that was required of her in this instance.

He said, 'This was the first you knew that the painting had been stolen? Kerr didn't mention it when he told you of Irene's disappearance?'

'He didn't know the painting was gone. When I phoned him this morning he told me that he'd made Sir Douglas Fergusson open Irene's studio a couple of days ago so's he could check if she might have left any clues there to where she'd gone. That's when they discovered the Rubens had walked. He's in a terrible state. There are now cops all over the place, checking out all the buildings, and he feels as if they suspect him of being an accessory. Of course, he's also desperately worried about Irene – so am I, for that matter. She's in big trouble one way or another and, until we find her, we can't tell whether she's had some sort of a breakdown or whether somebody is putting pressure on her or whether she's facing some other emergency that made her do what she did – what she appears to have done, rather.' She stood between Buchanan and his shot and looked him in the eye. 'We have to find her quickly, you see that, don't you?'

He stepped around her. 'Presumably the local police force are doing that.'

'Allegedly. They've now checked out her family and the list of friends that Kerr gave them, including me, but he'd checked those out already. He says they seem to be more worried about the painting than the person. In fact, I get the impression they wouldn't be exerting themselves at all, so's you'd notice, if it weren't for the fact that the disappearance of a Rubens painting is worthy of media attention.'

A grey cloud of depression settled over Buchanan. He wanted to mention the private detective firm but suspected he wouldn't like her response so he decided to postpone it till after the putt. Fizz, with a comprehensive lack of interest in the outcome, took in the view as he lined it up and took three to sink it. The light was now pretty much gone and with it, evidently, his command of the game.

'So your plan,' he suggested, since it had to be said, 'is to get professional help?'

She pretended to be engrossed in the sunset as she murmured, 'Unfortunately, there's one wee tiny problemette about that.'

'Uh-huh? Let me guess. Lack of cash?'

'Kerr suggested getting professional help but he was pretty shocked when I told him what private detectives charge these days and, frankly, I'm not wild about chipping in to any great extent – though I suppose I'll cough up what I can if push comes to shove. He's going to see what financial support he can get from Irene's sister and brother-in-law in London but I suspect they'll want him to hold fire for a while in the hope the police will stumble across her. Meanwhile, God knows what could be happening to her. It has to be something serious, Buchanan, otherwise she'd have discussed it with Kerr – or at least with me.'

Buchanan tucked his putter away and fastened the bag as though the task took all his concentration. He found himself hunching his shoulders as though he suspected that something large and very heavy was about to fall on him from a great height. He cast urgently around for a change of subject.

'Might as well make that the last hole,' he said. 'If we cut back through the wood we'll be in time for a drink at the nineteenth before the bar closes.'

'You sure know how to sweet talk a girl,' she murmured, blessing him with the warmth of her angelic smile. 'I'm parched right down to my belly button.'

She set off with the briskness invariably engendered in her by the promise of hard liquor and seemed inclined, for the moment, to skirt around her friend's problems, although without entirely abandoning her theme. 'It sounds like an interesting place, this Abbeyfield House. Kerr arranges all sorts of events: forest walks, orienteering, paintball games, and all that. And there's masses of other stuff going on.'

'Yes, I visited it once with Janine. She was only interested in the paintings but I remember seeing posters advertising their other attractions. Friends of my parents had their golden wedding dinner there a couple of years back. Fantastic setting, apparently. Huge dining hall with plate glass mirrors all around the walls and crystal chandeliers.'

She stopped at the edge of the trees and looked away down the slope of the hillside to the spread of the city below them: misty violet shadows among luminescent sandstone walls; Arthur's Seat still vividly green against the sky. Then she looked up at him with eyes as clear and innocent as a baby's. 'Sir Douglas is quite happy for Kerr to bring in what help he feels necessary. He's absolutely convinced that Irene didn't take the picture and he's promised to lean on everyone around the estate to co-operate. So I reckon we'd have a clear field, don't you?'

Buchanan reckoned nothing of the sort but he had a very depressing suspicion that he might be only a short putt from finding out one way or the other. There were cogent reasons why he should tell Fizz to go to hell but the temptation to get involved was undeniably strong. Why was that? Was he becoming addicted to puzzle-solving or was he simply flattered by Fizz's determination to recruit him? She'd never admitted to appreciating his powers of deduction but the fact remained that he was bloody good at putting two and two together. Okay, she could come up with the occasional intuitive leap but she needed him for his incisive appraisal of the facts and, obviously, she knew it. Perhaps, had he still been his own boss as had been the case in the past, he might have gone down without a fight but with the ire of Larry the Bastard hanging over his career like the sword of Damocles, he kept flailing hopelessly.

'What could we do that the police can't, Fizz? Apart from anything else, I don't have the spare time I used to have. Even with Larry off my back for the moment —'

'You've got evenings,' she said gently, looking at him with a sweet expression that simulated the enchantress she'd be if she weren't the incorrigible, self-centred, manipulative harpy Buchanan had come to know. 'You've got weekends. That's all I've got myself but at least it's something. This isn't a case that's going to drag on and on, Buchanan, it's a race against time. If we don't come up with something concrete within a few days the chances are we'd be too late to do any good.'

'Fizz. We'd just be making a nuisance of ourselves,' he said, digging in for a last heroic stand. 'Don't you ever suspect that you could have an exaggerated opinion of our talents in such matters?'

'We've succeeded in the past.'

'By sheer brass neck and stupidity. Neither of us has a clue how to go about looking for a missing person.' There had to be an ultimate deterrent. He cast about desperately and then deployed, 'Irene may not want you to interfere, Fizz.'

'I won't sleep at night till I do,' Fizz said and, with a certain apologetic regret, hit him with the big one. 'I'd do it for you, Buchanan.'

Chapter Two

Fizz had expected Abbeyfield House to be big, but not this big.

It took them three or four minutes to cover the length of the main driveway to the point where the main building came distantly into view: a wide, three-storey facade bracketed by curved and cloistered two-storey extensions. Along the way they passed a gatehouse with mini turrets and crow-stepped gables, a gazebo, a dovecote, rolling lawns, formal gardens, and four peacocks. Signposts here and there directed the paying public to the rose garden, the woodland walk, the lake and various other points of interest.

'It takes a lot to satisfy some people,' she commented but Buchanan was looking for the car park and didn't answer. 'I wonder how many menials it takes to keep the Fergusson family in grandeur like that.'

'Mm-mm? Not as many as it used to, I'd wager. Not at today's wages. At one time they probably gave employment to half the surrounding countryside.'

That was the sort of thinking you could expect from Buchanan.

'Oh yeah. Very Christian of them, I'm sure,' she returned, letting him see what she thought of his mind set. 'The poor buggers were probably earning all of two pounds a year and watching their kids die of malnutrition just so the current Lord Fergusson could show his pals how much cash he had managed to claw out of the pool.'

Buchanan spared her a caustic look. 'If you're going to harp on about inequitable distribution of wealth all the time we're here —'

'I'm only saying —'

'Well don't. It's quite obvious that it's taking every penny the family can scrape together just to keep the house wind and water-tight. These ancient buildings are money guzzlers.'

'So why not hand it over to the National Trust? Parasites sitting in their castles, rent free, in perpetuity, with us poor buggers paying their maintenance costs. I wish the National Trust would offer me a deal like that for my flat.'

'You don't own your flat.'

Fizz drew a noisy sigh, intimating that she wasn't going to encourage his pedantry by replying to that remark. There were times, she thought, eyeing his austere profile, when he got right up her nose. One of those days she'd get herself a driving licence and a set of wheels and stop being dependent on him for transport to out of town areas. The trouble was, he was decidedly convenient to have around on jobs like this one, not only for transport but because he had an air of authority which she knew she lacked. Buchanan came across like the archetypal lawyer: assured, reliable, comfortingly in control of the situation, whereas she herself had to overcome the appearance of a pint-sized, Shirley Temple lookalike who shouldn't be out without her mother. As far as any practical investigating was concerned Buchanan was usually more of a curb on her creativity than anything else, but he fulfilled all the functions she asked of him.

'I don't see anything that looks like gardeners' cottages,' he said.

'They're in the old stable yard. We're to head towards the greenhouses.' She waved a hand in the direction of a tall stone wall just visible beyond a stand of topiaried bushes. 'That must be the walled garden over there so I'd expect them to be in that general direction.'

'Well, we can take a look,' he grunted. 'I don't see anyone around who looks capable of giving us directions.'

They skirted the car park, ignored a notice that read "No unauthorised vehicles beyond this point" and, around the corner of the walled garden, came to two long greenhouses facing on to the yard Kerr had described. There were three cottages, each occupying a side of a cobbled square, the fourth side being taken up by a wide stone archway flanked by horse ^LOOSE boxes, which were currently empty. The buildings were low-roofed and small-windowed but each had a neat strip of garden vivid with climbing roses and flowering perennial plants.

Kerr came out to meet them as the car drew up and Fizz was struck immediately by how ill he looked. He'd never been what you'd call tasty even in his early twenties but there was plenty about him that girls found attractive. He was always bursting with energy, constantly enthusiastic about everything. Big and fit, tanned from his outdoor life, he'd made the lads at Edinburgh College of Art look, to Fizz and Irene both, like slobs. Which rather a lot of them were, in fact, now that she came to think about it. Seen against Buchanan, who was immaculate as ever in his sharp sweater and slacks, his black hair carefully ruffled, Kerr seemed old and tired, with discouragement dragging down the corners of his eyes and mouth and his shoulders rounded like those of an old man.

He made an obvious effort to put a brave face on it while he hugged Fizz and shook hands with Buchanan. 'Its very decent of you to turn out for me, Tam,' he said, ushering them into the cottage. 'I can't tell you how much I appreciate it. Fizz – well, of course, I knew she'd rally round once she realised that Irene could be in trouble – but I must admit I wasn't counting too heavily on her promise to bring you along. It's a real comfort to know that someone with your experience is on the team, even in an advisory capacity.'

There was a nasty little pause during which Fizz could feel Buchanan's accusing stare on the back of her neck, then he said, 'Kerr, I don't know what impression you've picked up from Fizz but I'm a lawyer, not a private investigator. I don't have any relevant experience.'

They passed through a tiny lobby into the living room and

Kerr waved them into old leather armchairs as he said, 'But you have found a missing person before. Fizz said there was a little boy...'

Buchanan could say a great deal with a raised eyebrow. This one said, "Look Kerr, you've known Fizz longer than I have. Do you take everything she tells you as gospel?" which wasn't, she felt, entirely fair. There *had* been a kidnapped child, a couple of years back, and Buchanan had been more than usually instrumental in locating him. Okay, that didn't make him an expert, but it had to constitute experience of a sort. Besides, it would be she who was doing most of the work: Buchanan was merely for show.

'Frankly, I'm just very grateful to have the two of you on my side and willing to take Irene's disappearance seriously. Everyone around here seems to be more worried about the painting than about what she might be going through.' Kerr hovered erratically from door to fireplace, bulky and awkward and ill at ease, making the room seem cramped and the ceiling too low. 'What can I get you? Coffee? A drink? Have you eaten?'

Fizz had dined before leaving home, since the good old days when she might have expected Buchanan to buy her a meal *en route* were now but a memory, however she made a point of never looking a gift horse in the mouth. 'What is there to drink?'

'No gin, if that's what you were hoping,' he said without showing too much angst about disappointing her. 'There's a couple of cans of lager and a bottle of white wine. Chilean, I think.'

Fizz settled for the wine and Buchanan said he wouldn't bother, thanks all the same, as he was driving. Kerr footled around with a corkscrew, talking non-stop, and took five minutes to serve Fizz with a glass of absolutely foul liquid that almost melted her fillings. Finally he got himself a lager and sat down on the edge of a chair beside the dining table, cross-ing his legs and waggling one foot in a tense, unconscious jig.

Evidently this was the room in which he and Irene hung out, cooked, ate and had their being. The other doorway opening off the lobby had to lead to their bedroom and, as far as Fizz could see, there were no further unexplored areas apart from the lean-to scullery from where Kerr had fetched the booze. In floor space it wasn't much bigger than Fizz's flat in the High Street which was surprising since one could have expected Irene to be living in a little more luxury at this stage in her career. Unlike Fizz, she'd stuck it out at art school and graduated with a good honours degree and for the past decade or so she'd been in constant employment, most of that time at Abbeyfield. Kerr too had been doing not too badly but no doubt the house went with the job and they'd found it con-venient to live on site.

'Obviously,' Buchanan was saying, 'it would have been quite different if you hadn't mentioned to the police that you and Irene had had some sort of disagreement before she went off. Easy enough to say that, of course, with benefit of hind-sight, but when the police heard you'd —'

'Oh, of course,' Kerr said impatiently, 'It gave them the perfect excuse to do nothing, I could see that, but if I hadn't told them about the argument they'd have heard it from one of the neighbours anyway. The trouble is, it's so bloody silent around here in the evenings you can't slam a door without everyone wondering what's going on. You can see the set-up for yourself. We're living in a goldfish bowl.'

Buchanan leaned a little sideways to look out the window. 'Who are your neighbours?'

'A couple of the gardeners: Eddie Stevenson, the head gar-dener, is across the yard, Victor Curzon and his wife to the left. I'm quite sure it was Victor's wife, Grace, who blabbed.'

'Why?' Fizz asked. 'Don't you get along with her?'

Kerr shrugged, stilling his jumpy foot for a moment to scratch his ankle and then starting it up again. 'She's not a particular friend, a bit of a nag actually, but it's not that. She probably wasn't trying to make trouble, she just doesn't think. Anyone else would have realized that, if I'd wanted the police to know about the disagreement, it was up to me to tell them. Not Grace. If there's any connection between her mouth and her brain it's pretty intermittent.'

Just the sort of witness one needed in a case like this, Fizz thought. Someone who habitually spoke without thinking. If there was going to be any division of labour on that front – and one had to let Buchanan do something if only to maintain the illusion of his indispensability – she'd let him work on Eddie Stevenson and grab gabby Grace for herself. She forced down another mouthful of plonk, purely for the alcoholic content, and waited for Buchanan to say something, but he was still looking out the window so she asked the obvious question.

'Anybody else likely to have it in for Irene?'

Kerr waved his beer can in a jerky gesture that splashed a fan of droplets on his shirt. 'Of course not,' he said, squinting his eyes at her as if she had run mad. 'Who would have it in for Irene?'

Fizz returned his irritable frown with one of her own. 'Well, how would I know? Just because she's a nice person it doesn't follow that she's on everyone's Christmas card list. Maybe someone was jealous of her. Maybe she was standing in somebody's way, in some manner. Maybe she knew something about somebody. If you want to get to the bottom of this thing, Kerr, you'd better start racking your brains.'

'Racking my brains?' Suddenly he was in one of the furies Fizz had heard about from Irene but never seen. 'What do you think I've been doing for the past two weeks? Waiting for you to come along and do my thinking for me? When I asked for your help I didn't —'

'Let's not do this, Kerr,' she interrupted, loud enough for him to hear her over the noise he was making but keeping her expression determinedly non-critical. 'I'm only trying to keep you focused, right? Tell me about the painting. What size was it? Would it have been easy for someone to spirit away?'

He took a swig of his lager and made an obvious effort to calm down. 'Sorry, Fizz, I'm a bit…you know. It's been a long ten days. Want some more wine?'

She looked at the sludge in the bottom of her glass. 'I don't suppose you'd have any battery acid?'

'That bad, huh? You must be developing a palate. Would you rather have a coffee?'

'Maybe later. What about the painting?'

'The painting,' he said, and drew a long breath. 'Okay, it's a Rubens, as you probably know already. Head and shoulders of an unknown woman, circa 1620. I understand its market value is only about a million and a half.'

'Hardly worth pinching,' Fizz said flippantly. Nobody smiled.

'Compared to his major works, no. You'd probably pay anything up to forty million for one of those. The painting we're talking about is nothing like his massive allegorical works and the model apparently isn't one of his usual illustrious sponsors – which, I'm told, might have been expected to up its value a little. To my eyes, it's just an unexceptional little head and shoulders.'

'How little is little?' Fizz wondered.

'About so big.' Kerr's hands described an area about twenty-five centimetres square.

'And Irene was entrusted with its restoration?' Buchanan inserted, dragging his eyes away from whatever was going on outside which, judging from the silence, was probably nothing. 'She wasn't restoring it, she was just giving it a superficial cleaning. Lord Douglas had arranged to sell it to an American collector who was planning on flying over from New York next week to see it.'

'Another art treasure winging it's way to the New World,' Fizz commented.

'Yeah. Irene wasn't thrilled about that, I can tell you – nor were a lot of people. There was plenty of organised opposition to the sale but it looked like it was going through in the end. What can you do? Sir Douglas needs the cash and nobody in this country was willing to match the price the New York buyer was offering.'

Buchanan looked at him pointedly and spread a questioning hand. 'But you don't think there's a connection with Irene's disappearance?'

'You mean, do I think Irene would squirrel away the painting in order to keep it in the country?' Kerr stretched his lips in a humourless smile. 'No chance. She spoke her mind about it to Sir Douglas, she supported the group who were creating a stink about it, but she'd never dream of taking matters into her own hands like that. Would she, Fizz?'

'Not the Irene I know,' Fizz agreed, keeping her reservations to share with Buchanan in private. Irene wasn't the sort to do such a thing off her own bat but she could certainly have been pressurised into it so the theory couldn't be dismissed out of hand. 'What was this organised group that was trying to prevent the sale?'

'Oh, it wasn't all that organised,' Kerr amended, deleting his original adjective with a sweep of his free hand. 'In fact, they weren't so much trying to prevent the sale as touting for a better offer. They got a bit of media interest way back when the painting first went on the market but it didn't achieve much and Caitlin McCormick has been enlisting a few luminaries in an effort to keep the fight going. She's the events manager on the estate: one of these pushy women who acts like nothing would ever get done if they weren't around to chivvy everyone along.'

'I know the type,' said Buchanan, but when Fizz turned to look at him his face was bland as an egg. 'Right. So, you'd have noticed whether or not Irene had the picture with her when she walked out.'

Kerr pressed his lips together making the muscles stand out at each side of his mouth. Quite clearly, he wasn't enjoying having to bare his private life to an outsider but he didn't have a lot of choice.

'The way it happened...' he said, fiddling with the tab off his lager can. 'The way the argument ended was that Irene just marched into the bedroom and slammed the door. That was her way of ending an argument. She hated any kind of unpleasantness so she'd just shut herself away till it evaporated. I spent the night on the couch and went out early the next morning – very early, because I had a job to finish before the staff meeting at nine o'clock. When I got home in the evening Irene wasn't around but it didn't occur to me that she might still be angry. I thought she'd probably gone for a walk or maybe she was across the yard at Eddie's place. When she didn't show, of course, I knew she'd gone but even then I wasn't all that worried. Not really.' He put both feet on the ground and leaned forward with his elbows on his knees, looking earnestly at Buchanan. 'We don't fall out much, really. Maybe once a year we have a row – almost always my fault, I admit – and once before when we had a bit of a slanging match she walked out and stayed away overnight but that was ... that time she was really mad at me, okay? This time wasn't like that. It was just a discussion about our future plans which got a bit heated and, I suppose both of us said things we didn't mean, but we've had worse spats. We both knew that, by morning, we'd have forgotten what it was about. We're solid, Irene and I. You know what I mean? We love each other. No matter how mad at me she might be, she'd never do this to me. Never leave me so worried.'

Fizz would very much have liked to ask him what made the discussion escalate into a quarrel, but she had a natural delicacy about asking questions that might earn her a slap round the head. In any case she had a feeling she'd get a more forthright report from gabby Grace.

Buchanan, probably embarrassed by Kerr's visible emotion, returned to his enjoyment of the view from the window but said,

'When was this exactly, Kerr? About ten days ago, right?'

'Saturday the first of July. That makes it a fortnight today.'

'And she took the car?'

'We don't have a car of our own. I have the use of a Land Rover, which I'd taken to work that morning, but Irene ... she didn't go out much on her own but when she did she either phoned for a taxi or got a lift from one of the other staff.'

'You've checked with the taxi company whether they picked her up or not?'

'The police did, but they drew a blank. I've no idea what firm it might have been and the most likely ones had no record of her call.'

'What about the rest of the staff? Would any of them have given her a lift?'

'Evidently not.'

'So, the chances are she either walked down to the main bus route, which is a bit of a hike but quite feasible, or she got a lift from a visitor.' Buchanan nodded, managing as he always did to look calm, optimistic and totally reliable. 'Would she have been carrying a case?'

Kerr shook his head, but not with a lot of confidence. 'I can't see her doing that. It wasn't as if she could have intended to stay away so long. I'm certain she just felt she needed a break...a day in Edinburgh...something to cheer her up.

Maybe she wanted to make me suffer for upsetting her but there's no way she meant to stay away long enough to need a change of clothes or even an overnight bag.'

'Nothing missing from her wardrobe?'

'The police asked me that, but it's really impossible to tell. As far as I can see it's as full as ever.'

'What about footwear? You should be able to verify if any of her everyday shoes are gone.'

He wrapped a hand around his empty lager can and squeezed it till it caved in. 'She had a lot of shoes,' he said with a strenuous lack of expression. 'I can't say I ever noticed them particularly, except for one or two special pairs. I could see, for instance, that her favourite strappy sandals are there, but I can't tell what's missing.'

That didn't sound too good to Fizz and it very clearly didn't cheer Kerr up to have to say it. He knew as well as any of them that something·had happened to Irene and it was doing his head in. The question in Fizz's head was: had some unknown party forced Irene to steal the painting – or even forced her to make it available to be stolen – and, if so, would that person subsequently view her as surplus to requirements?

'Where was the painting prior to her disappearance?' Buchanan asked, obviously recoiling from a sensitive subject.

'Locked in Irene's studio in the big house.' Kerr nodded his head at the back wall of the cottage which, had it been glass and had the intervening woods been cut down, would doubtless have given a distant view of Abbeyfield's frontage. 'It's on the top floor and completely secure.'

'How many sets of keys?' Fizz put in.

Kerr looked uncertain. 'To the studio? Apart from Irene's, which are gone, there's probably a set in the estate office and Lord Douglas certainly has a set. But any stranger trying to get into the studio would first have to get into the big house when no one else was around and that would be damn near impossible unless you were conversant with the alarm system. The studio is right above the Yellow Bedchamber and there's always a guide at the doorway to make sure no one goes up the private staircase. It's roped off and there are "Private" notices but kids are always liable to sneak into closed off areas just for the hell of it so it's never left to chance.'

Fizz thought about taking off her Docs, or at least loosening the laces, but couldn't be bothered. 'Okay, so can we eliminate the keys in the estate office? How secure were they?'

Kerr hunched his big bony shoulders. 'I can't be certain, but I'd imagine they were pretty secure. Caitlin's based there and she's no amateur.'

'And Irene's studio keys? Is it possible that she could have left them lying around long enough for someone to make an impression, perhaps?'

'You know her better, Fizz. If she wasn't in her bed she had them on her person and she took them with her when she left. I had to get Sir Douglas to open up the studio to let me look round.'

Fizz had no difficulty in accepting that as fact. Irene never discarded a key. Every key she'd ever owned was probably still on her key ring and weighing her down at every step. They'd had discussions about it in the past but Irene was basically convinced that if she threw a key away, or even lost it accidentally, she would immediately find herself locked out of some room or some safe box or some vehicle which she'd forgotten all about. She even toted around a kangaroo key tag Fizz had sent her from Australia and which had to weigh at least two ounces so it certainly wasn't a bunch of keys that could slip accidentally down the back of a couch.

Buchanan retracted his long legs and sat up. It was almost dark outside and silent as the grave. 'Well, I think we've covered all we can for this evening, Kerr. I'd like to talk to some of your colleagues on the estate, if that's possible, just to hear their thoughts on the matter, but that'll have to wait till the weekend. I imagine some of them at least will be around on Saturday?'

'Sure.' Kerr summoned up a smile that was not much more than a grimace but, to Fizz's eye, he did seem to be heartened by the prospect of doing something positive. 'The full time gardeners – well, I told you – they live here and so does Caitlin and, of course, the guides will be on duty.'

'Right. We'll see what emerges from the neighbours.' Fizz lifted a finger to Buchanan to keep him in his chair a little longer. 'Just one thing before we go, Kerr. A photograph of Irene. We may need it.'

'Oh, sure.' He bounced up and started raking through the drawers of a writing desk. 'I found a recent one for the police but there should be something in here that would be good enough for identification purposes. What about this?'

Fizz studied the snapshot with mixed emotions. It had apparently been taken within the past year or so and showed Irene struggling with a retriever puppy that was trying to lick her face. She was throwing back her head and laughing with an abandon that seemed profligate enough to tempt Fate. She passed it to Buchanan. 'It's a bit on the small side but I suppose it'll do in the meantime. Have a rummage around when you have a minute and see if you can find a bigger one. There's no panic because we'll probably take all day Saturday to deal with the estate workers and they all know what Irene looks like. With a bit of luck we could get all we need without having to go further afield.'

Kerr took a somewhat doubtful look at the drawer, which seemed to be crammed with photographs, and then pushed it shut and came back to his seat. 'You'll find the staff very willing to help in any way they can. Even the Fergussons. In fact, when I told him yesterday that I was hoping for your help in finding Irene, Sir Douglas himself said he was more concerned about Irene than about his picture. They all find it hard to credit that Irene would do something like this. Everyone …' His voice croaked unsteadily on the word and he swallowed before persisting, 'Everyone is worried about her.'

Fizz wasn't entirely surprised to hear that Irene was held in such esteem. She was a very loving and loveable person, a life-enhancer, and people had always responded to her warmly. Unfortunately it was going to take more than warm wishes and kind words to get her out of this one.

Chapter Three

When you weighed the options objectively, Buchanan decided, there wasn't really much to choose between spending Saturday afternoon on the golf course and returning to Abbeyfield House. He had, after all, played eighteen holes in the morning so it wasn't as if he was failing to get the most out of his membership to any great extent. On the other hand he was already caught up in the mystery of Irene's disappearance and rather looking forward to the challenge of getting at the truth.

There was no denying the satisfaction he got from the slow, painstaking process of separating the wheat from the chaff, the facts from the inventions, the guilty from the innocent. At this stage in the game he felt like a child let loose in a chocolate factory. A crossword addict might get a similar buzz when he opened the *Times* in the morning: or an artist when he set up a blank canvas. None of his friends really understood why he let himself get caught up in such matters, least of all Larry the Bastard who suspected him of a hubris incommensurate with his station as a humble postulant. The sensation wasn't something he'd ever discussed with Fizz, whose own fascination with matters concealed and cryptic stemmed from an insatiable need to poke her nose into other people's secrets, but he suspected she discerned the lack of conviction in his denials. He genuinely did not want to get involved, of course, just as a confessed alcoholic genuinely does not want to drink, but when it came to the bit it didn't test Fizz's powers of persuasion to any great extent to break down his resistance.

Quite apart from his addiction, however, this case promised the odd bonus, not only in the joy of puzzle-solving, not only in gratuitous information about Fizz's time at Art College, certain aspects of which had intrigued him for some time, but in the highly delectable form of Kerr's neighbour,

Eddie. The head gardener was not, it appeared, the horny-handed artisan the title had originally conjured up in Buchanan's imagination, but a quite stunning blonde, leggy and shapely and given to wearing clingy T-shirts and endearingly cropped shorts.

Such overwhelming female pulchritude had been singularly absent from Buchanan's life for some time and such appearances as it had made over the past few years had been brief and unsatisfactory. There had been nobody he could class as permanent since Janine's departure and damn few *im*permanent, if the truth were told, so the prospect of being around the enchanting Eddie, even if nothing momentous came of the fraternisation, was pleasant to contemplate.

And why had he omitted to mention to Fizz that Eddie was not an Edward but an Edna, or possibly an Edwina? It wasn't a comfortable thing to admit, even in the privacy of his own thoughts, but he could not shake off the foolish suspicion that Fizz scared off other women. Part of him knew that to be pure superstition but the signs certainly pointed that way. He was beginning to lose count of the girlfriends he'd lost to the phenomenon: one minute they were clinging to him like Elastoplast, the next hightailing it into the sunset without as much as a cheerio. It wasn't intentional on Fizz's part – what would she have to gain by antagonising them? – but seeing her in the company of someone he was interested in always made him uneasy. Call it delusion, call it paranoia, but there was little doubt in his mind that the longer he could keep Eddie's sex out of the conversation the happier he'd feel about his prospects of establishing a more meaningful relationship.

'We'll have to try and have a word with at least the closest neighbours this afternoon,' he said when they got to the foot of the drive. 'You'd better take the Curzons. Grace and – what was it – Victor? The chances are you won't be able to speak to them separately and you're better with women than I am. I'll see what I can get out of the head gardener.'

Fizz demurred strenuously on the grounds that the head gardener, whose cottage was the closer, was likely to be the more interesting witness but caved in eventually albeit with a reluctance that was likely to cost Buchanan dearly next time they apportioned the workload.

'Okay,' she said sullenly, 'have it your own way but let's not spend too long on the neighbours today. I'd really like Kerr to show us round the big house so that we can see the layout of the place, find out where Irene's studio is in relation to the exits, start to establish just how possible it might be for someone to either break in when the place is shut for the night or smuggle the painting out during the day.'

'You're not going to accept that Irene took the picture, are you?'

'Not without studying all the alternatives, no. I'm not saying its impossible, nothing's impossible, but it's much more likely that someone nicked it from her studio some time after she took off – possibly hoping that she would get the blame.'

Buchanan looked at her sideways, wondering if she realised what she was saying. 'That would imply that whoever stole the painting knew she wasn't likely to come back for a while – maybe never.'

She thought about that for a minute, leaning an elbow out of the open window so that the breeze ruffled what was left of the outrageous mane of hair she'd recently dispensed with. Buchanan still missed that hair, which was crazy since it had irritated the hell out of him since the day she stormed into his life. In some ill-defined manner, that hair had epitomised Fizz's whole identity: unmanageable, rumbustious, in your face, up your nose. Uncomfortable to live with for any length of time but furiously *alive* in a way that you couldn't ignore. Now it was gone, replaced by a tidy crop of pale gold swirls, too short to curl, and wilful only at the crown of her head where a single autonomous lock reared up like a question mark, whatever steps she might take to subjugate it. A suspicious person might take that small sign as proof that if a leopard could never *quite* change its spots, nor could a sabre-toothed tiger.

The hair wasn't the only change that had come over her since she'd qualified. Her erstwhile amazingly meagre wardrobe of jeans, Doc Marten boots and a few Oxfam bargains had recently been extended to include a dark blue dress which she wore in the office, alternating it with a black trouser suit that made her look almost grown up. Clearly the purchase of these uncharacteristic items indicated that she was finding professional credibility a problem, as she was bound to do with a face that belonged to a sixteen year old novice nun, otherwise she would still be adhering to the old take-me-as-I-am-or-piss-off attitude she had maintained in the past and still maintained in her own time.

'It's possible, ' she said reluctantly. 'Someone could have killed her and then stolen the painting, knowing she'd be suspected of running off with it.'

'Or she could have run off with the painting herself,' Buchanan insisted, determined to keep that possibility in the frame. Fizz made no reply but merely rolled up her eyes as though checking to see if God were noting her forbearance.

They skirted the walled garden and, as the greenhouses came into view, discovered Kerr standing at the gateway of his cottage in conversation with an odd-looking character in a vintage Adidas shell suit.

'Crumbs!' Fizz muttered as they drew to a halt. 'What's going on here? The Antiques Roadshow? He looks like something out of "Grease". Dig those crazy trainers, man!'

Fashion mattered little to Fizz, such discrimination having been beyond her purse for many years, if not for ever, but not even she could have failed to comment on the sartorial style of

Kerr's companion. It wasn't just the shell suit – although that, being of a profoundly offensive and glossy turquoise, certainly caught the eye – it was the incipient belly, the Joe Stalin moustache, the bouffant, richly chestnut hair and the florid complexion that went with it that made one doubt the sanity of the wearer. Either he was en route to a themed event – which was possible given the programme of activities on offer at Abbeyfield – or he was a very sad man.

Kerr ushered him forward to greet his visitor and introduced him, to their astonishment, as Sir Douglas Fergusson, owner of Abbeyfield estate.

'I'm most delighted to meet you both,' he told them, in a rich and musical voice that sounded perfectly sane. 'Kerr has been telling me all about you.'

'Not *all*, I hope,' Fizz remarked chirpily, removing her sunglasses and assuming the baby-doll demeanour she used to tranquillise her future prey.

His lordship tipped his head to the side and gave her a kind smile, visibly fooled. His voice abruptly plummeted an octave and took on a pronounced vibrato. ''Entirely complimentary, my dear. Indeed, one might say he's extraordinarily lucky to have such friends at a time like this. We're all deeply concerned about dear Irene so do, please, feel free to go where you choose and talk to whomsoever you wish in the course of your enquiries. If there's anything at all that we can do to expedite matters you'll find all the staff, the volunteers and, of course, my sister and myself only too willing to help. Irene was – *is* – held in much affection at Abbeyfield.'

'So,' Fizz murmured, 'you don't hold to the theory that her disappearance and that of the Rubens are connected?'.

He had large and lustrous brown eyes, if somewhat too close together, and now used them on Fizz in a way that seemed to Buchanan to be deliberately flirtatious. Considering he was a good twenty-five years her senior and scarcely the stuff that dreams are made of, he had to be joking.

'Absolutely no possibility of a connection Ms Fitzpatrick. No one who ever knew Irene could conceive of such a thing, as I'm sure you'll agree. Absolutely not. I'm quite sure the two events are quite coincidental and all the more distressing for being so. As I was saying to Kerr: if I had to decide between having my painting returned to me and seeing Irene safely back in the fold I wouldn't have to think twice about my choice.' He touched her shoulder as though he were confiding something important and deeply revealing. 'I'm told that you are every bit as clever as you are pretty, Miss Fitzpatrick, so I have great hopes of your success in effecting a happy outcome.'

Fizz's guileless expression slipped a fraction, hinting that the pointer on her one hundred per cent shockproof shit detector was slipping into the red, but Buchanan just managed to forestall what could have been an ill-considered reply.

'It would be helpful,' he said briskly, 'if we might have a short chat with you, Sir Douglas, perhaps later on today, just to get an idea of how the estate operates et cetera.'

'By all means.' Sir Douglas pulled back his elasticised cuff and studied his watch for several seconds, apparently calculating when he might have a window in his schedule. 'Why don't you join my sister and me for tea? Five-ish? Five-thirty?'

'Very kind. We won't keep you long.'

'Time is not of the essence these days. They want me to present the prizes for a children's drawing competition at four thirty but that shouldn't take long. Marjory will be interested to meet you. Have you time to join us, Kerr?'

Kerr shook his head, clearly not too disappointed at missing out on the treat. 'Forest walk from two to four then the orienteering bunch will be getting back.'

'Righty-ho.' His lordship's smile encompassed both Buchanan and Fizz but lingered on the latter. 'Till later then.'

Fizz watched him as he strode vigorously across the pathway and out of sight beyond the walled garden and then
turned to Kerr with lifted brows. 'Am I hallucinating or was
that time-traveller giving me the come-on?'

Kerr just grinned and piloted them into the cottage, seeming-
ly unwilling to discuss the matter, but Fizz wasn't letting it go.

'What's with this guy? Is he nuts, or what?'

'No, he's not nuts.' Kerr shook his head with what looked
like assurance. 'Actually, he's a really decent bloke when you
get to know him. We've had some good days on the hills
together, he and I. He can be very interesting on a lot of subjects. Keen birdwatcher. Into modern jazz in a big way.'

'So how come the Seventies gear?'

Kerr started taking mugs from a corner cupboard, the
speed at which he moved and the jerkiness of his actions as
much in evidence as they had been the last time Buchanan had
seen him.

'That's just one of his little idiosyncrasies. I don't think he
bothers much about what he wears and there's no one other
than his sister who's in a position to tell him he should
smarten himself up – and even she is no fashion plate. I suppose you could call him a bit of a recluse. He and Lady
Marjory, almost never leave the estate – neither did Lady
Audrey, even when she was fit.'

'Lady Audrey?' Buchanan prompted. 'Another sister?'

'His wife. She died recently.'

'Of?' queried Fizz, always looking for suspicious circumstances.

'Heart attack,' he said, and shook his head at her, refuting
her distrust. 'It was something that had been on the cards for
a number of years so there was nothing iffy about it.'

He went into the scullery, and clattered around for a couple
of minutes while Fizz examined his bookshelves and Buchanan
eyed the cottage opposite with pleasant anticipation. It was

sunny outside and the little courtyard was empty, protected from the intrusion of the public by "No unauthorised entry" notices which limited access beyond the walled garden. Through the open window he could hear faint strains of classical music – possibly Debussey – emanating from Eddie's side of the square, an indication that she might turn out to be a soul mate as well as a sex goddess. Miracles could happen.

'I don't know about this Sir Douglas character,' Fizz said, extracting an art encyclopaedia from Kerr's bookshelf and riffling through the pages. 'Obviously he's a nutcase, whatever Kerr may say, so he'll bear watching. No sane man would walk about in public dressed like that.'

'No sane man would give you the come-on,' Buchanan mentioned. 'The guy's obviously capable of anything.'

'Oh, really?' she said pleasantly, not bothering to look up. 'Well, that's all *you* know, fartface.'

Kerr, stepping into the room at that moment, gave her an odd look. 'Am I interrupting something?'

'Just Buchanan trying to be amusing. Don't worry: I'll tell you when to laugh.' She eyed the three coffee mugs. 'No biscuits?'

'Sorry, no. Are you hungry?' He tapped his brow with the tips of his fingers. 'Silly question. You're always hungry. I could do you a cheese sandwich.'

Fizz sighed. 'Never mind. I might get lucky at the Curzons' place.' She put three spoonfuls of sugar in Buchanan's coffee and passed it over to him. 'Okay, so what's new? No developments since we were here last?'

'Nothing of any interest. I haven't seen the guy in charge, Inspector Teesdale, for over a week, and the sergeant – who isn't around much either – is an ignorant bastard who talks only to his lordship. When I do manage to buttonhole him he fobs me off with officialese.'

'What lines of enquiry have they been following?'

Buchanan asked, wishing he'd sit down and stop jittering.

'Not very many, as far as I can make out. They talked to a few of the staff who were around at the time. They've also been checking on possible buyers for the painting: known fences, I suppose. They checked airlines and ferries, of course, and other ways that Irene could have left the country, but her passport's still here so there's not much point in that. She also left her credit cards behind and there have been no withdrawals from her bank account. I keep on nagging them – practically on a daily basis – but they never look as if they're doing a damn thing, never question anyone all that closely, never show the slightest concern for Irene's safety.'

'Well, that could be a good thing,' Fizz claimed, not very convincingly. 'At least they haven't muddied the waters, so when Buchanan and I get to work we won't be going over old ground.'

'What are they saying to the fact that Irene's credit cards and passport are still here?' Buchanan asked. 'I'd have thought they'd have found that somewhat sinister, wouldn't you?'

Kerr flung out a hand in an angry gesture. 'All they can tell me is, "We're looking into that, sir. We'll let you know if anything transpires". Bloody pricks! The sergeant as good as hinted that an art thief planning to leave the country would have arranged a false passport and, as far as the credit cards go, nobody's at all surprised by the fact that she left them behind. She couldn't use them, they say, without leaving a trail that would be easy for the CID to follow.'

'Well, it's one way of looking at it, Kerr, you have to admit it,' Fizz said, and hurriedly changed the subject when he showed signs of losing his rag again. 'Anyway, Buchanan's going to speak to Eddie this afternoon and I'll be handling the Curzons so why don't you sit down and tell me what you know about Victor and Grace so I'll know what I'm dealing with. What age are they?'

Kerr seemed to experience a momentary difficulty in focusing his thoughts. 'Victor's a bit older than me,' he produced finally, 'just into his forties I think, and Grace is about the same, maybe a bit younger but not much. She's expecting a baby in September: their first, so they're pretty excited about it. I think they'd just about got used to the idea it wasn't going to happen.' He hooked a seat back from the table with one foot and sank into it wearily. 'What else can I tell you? They used to have a small market garden down Hawick way – at least Victor did, I don't think Grace had much to do with it other than at peak periods. He sold it at the beginning of the year, February or March, and came here as Eddie's assistant.'

'How many gardeners are there?' Fizz asked.

'Just the two full-timers and occasional part-timers who are really just handymen. There used to be seven gardeners, full time, so Victor and Eddie concentrate on the public areas and try, otherwise, just to keep the wilderness at bay.'

Anticipating an imminent diversion to the background of the other full time gardener, Buchanan said quickly, 'How many of the staff have accommodation on the estate?'

'Apart from the three households here in the yard there's just Caitlin, the events manager, who has the gatehouse. An old family retainer of the Fergussons' used to live there but when she got too shaky to live alone they moved her up to the big house.'

'We'll probably want to speak to everyone who was around when the picture disappeared,' Fizz said, getting up and smoothing her short skirt over her hips in an unconsciously seductive gesture.

'That shouldn't be a problem.' Kerr contemplated her legs in a manner his missing partner would not have applauded.

'Okay, we'll get to them later. Right now I'm off to see the Curzons.'

'I warned them you might drop in this afternoon,' Kerr

said, getting ready to walk her to the door. 'They'll be at home. Victor's off duty but he's not planning on going any- where. I could come with you if you like.'

'No thanks,' Fizz said and put a hand on his shoulder to push him back down into his chair. 'This sort of thing works better if the interrogators don't outnumber the interrogated, at least till they get to know you. One to one is ideal but I'll probably have to talk to both the Curzons at once.'

'We have a lot to get through this afternoon,' Buchanan warned and she nodded her agreement.

'Okay. I'll keep it brief and to the point. What'll we say – half an hour? That'll leave us time for a quick recce of the grounds before our tea party.'

'Roger.'

She left, and he watched from the window as she went striding across the yard to the Curzons' door. She strode everywhere, like a guardsman, which was cute even in her Docs but actually very sexy in the high heels she'd taken to wearing on occasions such as this, when she wanted to look businesslike. Sometimes it struck him as extremely sad that such engaging young charms should be wasted on an impossi- ble woman like Fizz.

'I have great hopes of Fizz,' Kerr said, into the silence. 'Say what you like about her, she's always had this trick of getting people to open up to her, even as a kid in her teens.'

Buchanan had been about to set forth to launch his assault on Eddie but decided that could wait for a couple of minutes. 'I didn't realise you'd known her that long.'

'Oh, sure. Irene and I got together in her first year at art school and Fizz was one of the people she was sharing a flat with.' Kerr's tense frown eased momentarily and he almost achieved a smile. 'Fizz ran that flat like a Young Offenders Institution. No music after eleven p.m., no overnight visitors, no leeway on the duty roster. Seventeen years old and already making life hell for all about her.'

Buchanan had to smile at the picture that conjured up. 'She likes things to be organised,' he said, nodding his agreement. 'I don't know if you've seen her flat in the High Street but it's like a monk's cell. She says she can do her housework in ten minutes, including the windows, inside and out.'

Kerr acknowledged that with a shrug. 'That figures. I can't see Fizz sewing fancy cushion covers or knitting tea cosies, can you? Of course, she carried all her possessions around in a backpack for seven years. I suppose that would make you accustomed to doing without inessentials.'

'I always wondered why she did that,' Buchanan said casually, 'packing in her degree course and just taking off like that to work her way around the world.'

For a moment it looked as if Kerr not only knew the answer to that one but was about to share it, but he answered only with a vague 'Yeah,' and then looked at the clock. 'I should really check how many have turned up for the forest walk. Should I take you over and introduce you to Eddie or are you okay on your own? She knows to expect a visitor.'

'I'll be fine on my own thanks, Kerr. Fizz and I will get back to you before we leave for home just to let you know if anything interesting transpires.'

He checked his hair in the hall mirror before crossing the yard to the strip of garden that fronted the cottage opposite. It looked empty from the outside but the door opened just as he raised his hand to knock and there she was, in all her glory, dressed in a cornflower blue halter necked top that matched her eyes and fiendishly tight jeans that matched Buchanan's collar. Close up she looked a little older than he had imagined, probably close to his own age, but lithe and lissom for a woman in her early thirties.

'Tam Buchanan,' she said, smiling. 'I saw you the other evening when you visited Kerr and he told me you might want to talk to me. Do come in. I'm afraid the place is a bit of a mess but I really have to get these geranium cuttings in today and I thought I might as well get on with it while we talk. You don't mind do you? I assure you I can do it without thinking, so you'll have my full attention.'

'No problem. I don't expect the few questions I want to put to you will take up more than a few minutes of your time.'

'Oh, don't worry about my time,' she protested, pulling out a second chair at the table where she'd been working and waving him into it. 'Actually, I'm only doing this because we're two part-timers short at the moment and I don't want the schedule to lag too much behind. It's not important – and neither is my time. I'll work nights if it helps to find out what's happened to Irene.'

Buchanan sat down and crossed his legs, trying not to stare. 'You're worried about her?'

'Well yes. It's been two weeks now and she hasn't even telephoned Kerr. I can't help but worry.'

'Were you...are you close to Irene?'

She looked down at the newspaper she'd spread over the table top and brushed some soil back from the edge with her fingers. Her face was smooth and heart shaped, quite wide across the cheekbones but tapering to a delicate little chin.

'Close? I'm not quite sure what that means, exactly, but I like her a lot and I imagine she quite likes me. We talk every day: she pops across for a coffee or I go over to her place, sometimes she gives me a hand with jobs like this.' Fine lines crinkled the corners of her eyes as she smiled. 'She likes getting her hands dirty – like me.'

'Does she confide in you?'

'Not often.'

'Has she spoken to you about her relationship with Kerr?' Buchanan asked and then added, 'I'm sorry to have to ask you that but, obviously, it's something I have to understand if I'm

to be at all effective in clearing up this mystery. I could ask
Kerr, of course, but could I be sure of getting an objective
answer?'

She picked up a cutting and started stripping off the lower
leaves and trimming the end of the stem. Her hands moved
fast and confidently, completing the task in seconds and moving on to the next cutting without a pause. Several cuttings
later she said, 'Yes, of course, I understand what you're saying.
You don't fully trust any of us till all the facts are in.'

Buchanan opened his mouth to apologise for that
inescapable fact but she glanced up at him and smiled again,
this time widely enough to reveal a small, but engaging space
between her two frontal incisors. Oddly enough that small
imperfection made her all the more entrancing, marking her as
the sort of person who would not bother with cosmetic den-
tistry because she was comfortable with herself as she was.

'Oh yes, I'm quite *au fait* with investigative procedure,
Tam. I haven't missed an episode of *The Bill* in years.' She
went back to her cuttings and disposed of another half dozen
before she sighed and said, 'The thing is, an outsider can't
always tell whether a relationship is a bad one or a good one.
You see only the peaks. I know that Irene got pretty brassed
off with Kerr now and then but I also know that they had
good times together. Lots of them. Whether the good out-
weighed the bad – who knows? Maybe even they themselves
couldn't tell you.'

'Kerr told me they'd had their ups and downs,' Buchanan
mentioned, just to make her feel better. 'But he wasn't specific as to the cause.'

She drew a compost-filled seed tray towards her and
whipped a cutting into each segment, firming the soil around
them with a delicate thumb. 'The cause,' she said in a dry tone,
'was Kerr's jealousy. She couldn't have a mug of coffee with a
guy in her tea break but Kerr would find out about it and start

acting like she was Messalina. Didn't matter who the guy was: the postman, the garbage collector, the plumber's apprentice, every male between sixteen and eighty who paused to pass the time of day.' She glanced up, her eyes challenging. 'That would drive any woman crazy. God knows, Irene was as placid a person as I've ever known, but you can only take so much.'

Buchanan thought about that for a minute, coming to the realisation that nobody had a bad word to say about Irene. 'You don't think he had grounds for jealousy, then? I mean, Irene wasn't the kind to encourage other men?'

'No way.' Her fingers stilled for a moment as though her attention had wandered from the task, then she said, 'She was the same to everyone, women and men: just a nice person. Someone who cared deeply about other people and showed it.' Suddenly she threw up her head. 'Dammit! Why do we keep on referring to her in the past tense?'

Buchanan was momentarily tempted to pat her shoulder but was struck by a similarity to Lord Douglas's tactics and dropped the idea like a shot. 'It's natural,' he said. 'We're talking about how she appeared a fortnight ago not how we saw her today. Don't start getting superstitious about it.'

The look she turned on him was warm and appreciative. It seemed to his drugged senses that she had moved physically closer to him but all she said was,

'Would you like a cup of coffee?'

'I'd like nothing better,' Buchanan said, which was something of an exaggeration since he could have thought of something if he'd tried, 'but I have to meet my colleague in a few minutes. We've arranged to speak to Sir Douglas and his sister this afternoon, but perhaps I could beg a few minutes more of your time tomorrow?'

Maybe he could have hung around for another couple of minutes but he didn't want to push his luck. In another few minutes he'd be running the risk of bumping into Fizz on the doorstep and anyway, past experience had taught him it was usually better to quit while you were winning.

Chapter Four

The past half hour had not, for Fizz, been the undiluted pleasure it had been for Buchanan. The moment Grace Curzon had opened the door to her she'd known that it wasn't going to be easy and, from then on, things had gone rapidly downhill.

Grace was a gaunt scarecrow of a woman – though currently somewhat distended – and her face showed none of the prenatal glow so vaunted in song and fable. On the contrary, it was putty-pale and wore an expression usually seen on someone suffering from acid indigestion. Her mean brown eyes hit Fizz like bullets, as she took instant – and quite obvious – exception to the baby-faced bimbo on her doorstep.

Fizz was familiar with that reaction and couldn't quite blame the woman for it since she rather detested the type herself when it crossed her path, but there wasn't much she could do about it. 'Mrs Curzon?' she said crisply, and frowning a little in the conviction that this lent her a certain credibility. 'My name's Fitzpatrick. I believe Kerr mentioned that I might drop in.'

As she spoke, a small hairy face appeared from the folds of Grace's voluminous cardigan: a ratty little Yorkshire terrier with a hostile expression – in fact with an entire physiognomy – oddly similar to that of its mistress. It fixed its own mean brown eyes on Fizz's and peeled back its upper lip, exposing twin rows of tiny but very sharp teeth.

Grace tsk-ed audibly, making a noise like a wet fingertip applied to a hot iron. 'It's not a good time,' she said, glancing over her shoulder into the shadows of the hallway. 'We're watching the football. Oh well, it's nearly over anyway. I suppose we can talk in the kitchen for a few minutes.'

Fizz followed her into the house making vague I-could-come-back-later noises but not with the sort of conviction that might encourage an acceptance. The kitchen was shadowed and cheerless, scented by the lumps of fish-based dog food in a dish on the floor. There was barely room, between two rows of cupboards and appliances, for a small table and two chairs and it became immediately apparent to Fizz that she should have accepted Kerr's offer of a cheese sandwich when she had the chance because her current hostess wouldn't give a toss if she starved to death.

'I don't know what you want to talk to us for anyway.' Grace seated herself at the table with the little hairy rat on her lap, still half hidden in her cardigan. She omitted to invite Fizz to sit and Fizz, with a mental "sod *you*, then", chose to remain leaning against the littered work top at a distance calculated to entail the utmost stress on the cervical vertebrae of a seated observer.

She said, 'At the moment we're just hoping to have a word with everyone on the estate who knew Irene well. We're looking for any pointers that might indicate where we could start looking for her.'

'And what if she doesn't want you to start looking for her? Had you thought of that? What if the last thing she wants is to be found?'

Fizz produced her sweetest smile. 'You have some reason for believing that to be the case, Mrs Curzon?'

The mean eyes didn't flicker. 'I'd have thought that possibility to be perfectly obvious. It certainly wasn't lost on the police.'

'You mean, you believe she could have stolen the Rubens painting?'

Grace's tongue poked the inside of her cheek for a moment while she tried to stare Fizz out. 'Is that what you've come here to find out?' she said with an insolent jerk of the chin. 'My opinion of Irene's morals?'

'Not unless they're based on direct observation, no.'

She declined to reply to that but maintained her basilisk

stare, as did Bonzo. From the other side of the hallway the excited voice of a football commentator rose to a frenzied pitch and then plummeted to a nadir of disappointment.

'I don't know if Kerr thought to mention it,' Fizz said, knowing full well that he would have done, 'but I've been a close friend of Irene's – probably her closest friend, excluding Kerr himself – for more than ten years. I think we can assume that, whatever trouble she's in, she'd prefer me to trace her rather than the police.'

'Yes, but it's not a matter of what Irene wants, is it? It's a matter of getting the painting back and the two things may not be the same.' Grace presented a prohibitive palm. 'Oh, don't start getting on your high horse. I'm not saying Irene's a thief. I'm just saying I think these things are best left to the police. They know what they're doing and enthusiastic amateurs just get in the way.'

Fizz nodded pleasantly, reflecting that she had seldom met quite such an obnoxious person. Some were born obnoxious, some had obnoxiousness thrust upon them, but some actively *went* for it, and such was Grace.

'The thing is, Mrs Curzon,' she said, 'the police aren't doing anything to find Irene other than what might lead them also to the painting. They've assumed, up till now, that the two disappearances are linked, whereas no one who knows Irene well is willing to accept that premise. That's why I believe my colleague, Tam Buchanan, and I could profitably explore areas ignored by the CID.'

'You're wasting your time,' stated Grace, managing to convey that it was her own time that was her sole concern. 'You'd be better advised not to interfere. You'll see: you won't get any thanks for it in the end.'

Fizz regarded the carving knife that lay on the work top only inches from her fingers and then decided to give it one more try.

'Actually, we're only planning on a very low-level inquiry so we won't be crossing over much with the police investigation. In fact, all I wanted to ask you about is what you remember about the evening Irene disappeared. She and Kerr had a dis-agreement, I understand. I suppose you overheard it?'

Grace tucked in the corners of her mouth and slowly shook her head, not so much in denial, Fizz inferred, as in pseudo-compassion for a pathetic no-hoper. 'Irene didn't leave that evening. Surely even Kerr could have told you that. She left the following morning.'

Fizz abandoned all thought of the carving knife. 'Kerr couldn't be sure of what time she left – but you can be? You saw her go?'

Taking her time about it, Grace took a packet of sweets from her pocket, popped one in her mouth and fed one to Bonzo who tipped up his head and crunched it with intense concentration. The strong smell of aniseed drifted across the table from his slavering jaws.

'I didn't see her leave, no,' Grace admitted. 'But she was still in the cottage the following morning. I'm sure I saw the curtain move just after Kerr left for work.'

'You didn't see Irene herself?'

'No, but I'm sure she was in the house.' For a moment her face was a war zone as her desire to appear superior strove with her resolve to be as unhelpful as possible. Conceit won. 'Victor was driving me to Edinburgh to do some shopping and she was definitely there when we left. I saw the curtain move.'

'What time was that?'

'Oh…before eight o'clock. Quarter to, maybe.'

'You didn't mention this to the police?'

'Of course I mentioned it but you know what the police are like. If you can't swear to something it's not evidence, it's just a possibility.'

She took a wad of pink toilet paper out of her pocket and

blew her nose, during which operation the dog, momentarily released from her embrace, eyed Fizz menacingly as though planning to have her arm off at the elbow if she moved a muscle.

'I don't suppose you could make a guess at what the argument was about?'

'No I could not.' Grace raised her eyebrows and lowered her lids, lending her face an expression which added condescension to her battery of offensiveness. 'In a situation such as we have here, Miss Fitzpatrick, we do our best not to intrude on each other's privacy. We see each other every day. We're familiar with almost every aspect of each others' lives and our conversations centre on what's happening around the estate: who's currently not speaking to whom, who's not pulling their weight, which department is getting an unfair slice of the budget, what Sir Douglas and Lady Marjory have been doing or saying, who might be having it off with whom.'

She broke off and started fondling the dog's ears as though she regretted having said so much but then she couldn't resist adding, 'It would drive you batty. Those with a bit of sense get off the estate as much as they can. You have to make a deliberate effort to do that because it's easy to get trapped.'

'What about Kerr and Irene?' Fizz said softly, sensing that Grace's barriers were starting to wobble. 'Did they get out much?'

'Now and then. Not enough, in my opinion. That's why they had such problems with their relationship.'

'Kerr told me their problems were really just superficial.'

Grace responded to that suggestion with a frown and an impatient twitch of her shoulders. 'Well, they didn't look all that superficial to me. I said to Victor, away back when we first came here, those two have been stuck in this concentration camp far too long. I've seen it before – the way people go when they don't get out enough and Kerr was definitely getting things all out of proportion.'

'And Irene? You think the way of life here had an affect on her as well?'

A small, secret smile bent Grace's lips. She looked down at the dog and scratched its head for a moment, once more swithering between flaunting her insider information and denying Fizz the satisfaction of getting it out of her, and once more her ego wouldn't let her be silent.

'Actually, Irene was good at escaping. If Kerr'd had his way she'd never have got out of the house, never mind the estate. I've said many the time to Victor, that's why he took the job here – because there was work in the big house for Irene and he wanted her under his eye. But Irene wasn't as submissive as he thought she was. Oh, no.' She hugged Bonzo to her bulge with a sort of smug satisfaction, clearly pleased to have found a small imperfection in someone so basically nice. 'She had him totally fooled.'

Fizz found she was clenching her teeth so tightly that her jaw ached. She took a slow breath and said steadily, 'Really?'

'None of my business, of course,' Grace acknowledged with patent insincerity, 'but we knew what went on, Victor and I. Every time Kerr went off for the day, sometimes even for an afternoon, Irene was down that drive like a rabbit down a burrow.'

'Where to?'

'You tell me. Victor saw her once, getting into a taxi at the end of the drive, so what does that say to you? That she didn't want any of us finding out what she was up to and telling Kerr about it, that's what. Easy enough to blame everything on Kerr – all the flaws in their relationship – but maybe he knew what she was like. Maybe he had cause to be jealous. There's more to people like her than the face they show the world, isn't there?'

Fizz could only hope that the murderous thoughts that were roiling in her breast were not reflected in her expression.

Buchanan was forever enjoining her to maintain a blank face but he'd been a lawyer for years and had therefore had longer to practice looking enigmatic. Even now, although he could maintain the look of a poker player with a Royal Flush, he was given to grinding his teeth on occasions like this, a dead give-away to those who knew him.

'But, you never saw Irene show an interest in another man, did you, Mrs Curzon?'

'That kind,' said Grace, with strenuously subdued venom, 'is interested in every man that crosses her path. Women like that don't have to do anything, they don't have to say anything. They send out a signal, a vibration, a blast of pheromones – whatever you like to call it – that makes every man in the vicinity sit up and beg.'

There was absolutely no truth in that allegation, Fizz was sure of that. Irene was friendly and sympathetic to men as well as women but if she had started to act like a femme fatale at this stage in her life it must have been a very sudden and totally unlikely transformation. Much more likely was the explanation that Grace was the jealous type and didn't like to see her husband responding to Irene's natural warmth. She said, 'You never mentioned any of this to Kerr?'

Grace mimed zipping her lips and assumed a holier than thou expression that wouldn't have fooled a bat. If Grace had kept her mouth shut it was because she enjoyed watching the situation develop from a seat in the front row.

'How often are we talking about here?' Fizz asked. 'Once a week? Once in a while?'

'Just about every time Kerr was away. He's on a Scottish Natural Heritage committee that meets once a month in Glasgow and that takes all day. He also visits his elderly father every Tuesday afternoon: sometimes it's well into the evening before he gets back. All through the summer he's had all-day orienteering events on the hill and once in a while he takes off up the hill with Sir Douglas. Irene never missed her chance, I can tell you. At least once a week, I'd say, for the past few months. It was only a matter of time before he caught her at it.'

Her mean little eyes locked on to Fizz's. She didn't quite have the bottle to suggest that the situation had come to the boil the night before Irene disappeared but the implication was writ large across her face. Clearly, nothing would please her more than to have her neighbours' real life drama end with a resounding climax. A hostile parting was reasonably enter-taining but – a murder? Ah now, that *would* relieve the monotony for a while.

The sounds of the frenzied TV commentary emanating from the living room ceased abruptly as the set was switched off and a couple of seconds later Victor Curzon stuck his head round the door.

'Hello,' he said, coming face to face with Fizz at a distance of three feet. 'Sorry about that. It was Celtic versus Juventus.'

Fizz nodded as though she perfectly understood that an encounter of such magnitude would take precedence over practically anything. 'Who won?'

'Juventus, two nil,' he said with a grin that came as quite a shock to Fizz as she had been subconsciously expecting another grouch like Grace. Instead – and it was quite obvious from the warmth of his regard and the affability of his out-stretched hand – he was a reasonably nice person and willing to be friends. He looked older than his wife because there was a fair bit of grey in his hair and a life in the open air had coars-ened the skin of his face, but he was probably still on the right side of forty-five and fit as a flea.

'We got on fine without you,' said his lovely wife and rose from the table in a purposeful way, indicating that, as far as she was concerned, the interview was over. 'I've told Miss Fitzpatrick everything we know about Irene so there's no point in you going through it all again.'

Victor gave her a speculative look and, as if he had asked her a direct question, Grace nodded briskly and said, 'Somebody had to be told about Irene's little secret and, after all, she's an old friend of Irene's.'

For a second or two Victor remained staring at her while the colour rose in his face. He was obviously trying not to show his anger but Fizz could feel it coming off him in waves and his voice was gritty with it as he turned to her and said,

'I hope you won't find it necessary to say anything about Irene's outings to Kerr, Miss Fitzpatrick.'

'I'd hope it wouldn't become necessary,' Fizz told him straight, 'and as long as there's a hope of Irene coming back I'll certainly keep it to myself. But there will come a time, and pretty soon, when we have to start pulling out all the stops.'

'You know what it'll do to their relationship?' Victor insisted. 'Kerr's insecure enough as it is but if he finds out that Irene was cheating on him —'

'You don't know she was cheating on him —' Fizz started to say but he cut her short.

'I don't mean cheating on him in the sense of having an affair, just that she kept a part of her life a secret from him. God knows what she did when she went out on her own, probably nothing very terrible, but it was evidently something Kerr wouldn't have sanctioned and if you know him at all you'll realise that finding out about it would only make him worse than ever. Their relationship quite possibly wouldn't survive it.'

'Irene would be better off without him anyway,' Grace opined, her reaction to her husband's displeasure being one of aggressive self-righteousness. She fed herself and Bonzo another aromatic gob-stopper and gave him back stare for stare. 'She's wasting her time with a man like that. If he hasn't learned to handle his jealousy in ten years she's never going to be free of it. You can't live like that.'

'That's a decision only Irene can make,' Fizz said gently enough but only succeeded in incurring a look if intense hostility. If Grace had disliked her on sight she was now blaming her, however unjustly, on causing this rift with her husband, and she didn't care who knew it.

'Right,' she said, squeezing around the table and starting to edge Fizz towards the door. 'If that's all we can help you with for the moment we've got things to get on with. Victor, you could hang out that washing for me while I show Miss Fitzpatrick out.'

Victor was definitely embarrassed as hell by his wife's rudeness. Fizz gave him a nice smile and said, only a little pointedly, 'It's been nice talking to you, Victor.'

On the doorstep Grace drew herself up to her full height, which wasn't all that imposing, and gave Fizz her best sneer. 'As you see,' she said with real malice, 'interfering in other peoples' business causes an endless amount of trouble to all concerned. I hope you won't find it necessary to bother us again.'

And as she spoke, Bonzo stuck his head out from under her arm and snarled as if to say, "And that goes for your cat too, missus!"

'I hope so too,' Fizz said honestly, and got the hell out of there while she could still be proud of her forbearance. In fact she was more amused than anything else by Grace's attitude. The plain truth was that she found such appalling people interesting if only for the curiosity factor: i.e.: how repulsive could they get without being actively encouraged? She couldn't wait to report to Buchanan.

She'd expected that she'd have to go and look for him but he had apparently made short work of his audience with the other gardener and was keeping an eye out for her from the doorway of one of the greenhouses.

'Come and look at this,' he said, holding the door for her.

'It's like Kew Gardens.'

Fizz, having spent her formative years on a farm where she was imbued with the belief that plants were of value only if they could be eaten, was not much moved by the pots of shrubs and climbers that filled the benches. Most of them weren't even in flower and there was a dank, earthy smell about the place that conjured up a memory of the tractor shed back at Am Bealach, misty autumn evenings, mud, chapped knuckles and manure.

'Very interesting,' she said and turned on her heel. 'Let's go walkabout. I've things to tell you. What about the other gardener? Did you find out anything?'

Buchanan followed her out into the sunshine and they turned down the path in the direction of the walled garden. He said, 'Nothing much. I decided not to push too hard right away, however it does begin to look as if Kerr's jealousy wasn't just a matter of occasional possessiveness, it was getting on towards being a phobia. Irene must have been pretty much at the end of her tether.'

'Right,' Fizz nodded. 'That's more or less the same story as I've been hearing from the fragrant Mrs Curzon – and let me tell you – if I didn't garrotte that bitch before she got it out, it was only by the grace of God. Think Hannibal Lecter with piles.'

'Nice for you. What about her husband?'

'He's okay. Comparatively human. He was blazing mad at Grace for letting out the one piece of interesting information she gave me: namely that Irene went over the wire every time Kerr turned his back for a few hours. Apparently, she was in the habit of having a taxi meet her at the end of the drive and scooting off who knows where. At least once a week: sometimes for the whole day, sometimes just for the afternoon. Apparently, Kerr had no suspicion she was doing it and the Curzons didn't tell him. I reckon Victor leaned on Grace to keep her mouth shut but she was only too happy to drop

Irene in the shit when she got the chance. A real dyed in the wool bitch, if you ask me.'

'Some women go funny when they're pregnant,' Buchanan volunteered.

'Balls. Where do you pick up these myths, Buchanan?'

'It's a hormonal thing.'

Fizz was not in a mood to argue with him. 'This particular pregnant woman was just naturally what my medical dictionary calls proctalgia fujax.'

'What's that?'

'Basically, a horrible pain in the arse. If we have to get back to the neighbours about anything you can have the pleasure of interviewing the Curzons and I'll settle for Eddie.'

'I've booked another session with Eddie tomorrow,' Buchanan said, pausing to look through the tall iron gate that led into the walled garden. 'But presumably you'll be busy then anyway, tracking down the taxi driver who picked up Irene on her mysterious escapades. That's the best lead we've got so far.'

'According to Kerr the police have already gone down that road without results.'

'Yes, that's true,' Buchanan admitted, turning his head to smile at her. 'But they were only asking about the day Irene left, not a regular once-a-week pickup that's been going on for some time. It shouldn't prove too difficult.'

'Difficult? Possibly not. Time consuming? Indubitably. Boring? Bet your sweet ass. And all you have scheduled is a half hour chat with Eddie.'

'The luck of the draw,' said Buchanan.

No doubt he had something more interesting in mind: a look at the salmon river, a man-to-man talk with Kerr or something similar, but Fizz could live with that. He needed a spoonful of sugar to help the medicine go down.

Chapter Five

By four-thirty Buchanan felt he had assimilated a fair picture of the estate, or at least of those parts of it within easy walking distance of the main building. It had never really been what you might call a renowned beauty spot, even before death duties had reduced the Fergusson family to its current level of indigence, so you couldn't claim that their exploitation of its amenities amounted to legalised rape.

There were signs everywhere that the refurbishment budget was reserved for keeping up appearances and was concentrated largely on the areas hired out for functions. Much of the original building had already passed beyond all hope of conservation and was closed to the public but even the part that remained carried an air of neglect. To Buchanan's mind there was little in the rooms presently available for inspection that merited more than a passing glance unless you were into social history, antiques, or twenty foot walls smothered in the stuffed heads of slaughtered stags. He and Fizz had time for only a ten minute survey of the ground floor but that was sufficient to convince both of them that Abbeyfield was no Balmoral.

The Fergussons' apartments were on the upper floor of one of the eighteenth-century extensions that stretched out like arms on each side of the original building and reached by means of a servants' staircase that climbed sharply from the rear of the property. In answer to their ring, they were admitted by a round-shouldered old lady wearing an ivory crucifix over a grey dress that could have been a nun's habit and apparently chewing a large wad of gum.

'See they stairs,' she complained in a Glasgow accent, 'they're gonie dae ma knees in wanny they days. Youse two ur the lawyers, ur ye? Right. C'mon.'

She turned and led them in single file up the narrow staircase, levering herself from step to step with a shaky grip on the banister. Fizz, who was right behind her, turned and made a pathetic face at Buchanan over her shoulder and, in a most unusual display of thoughtfulness, paused on the first landing, pretending an interest in a brass wall sconce to give the old dear a breather.

'I bet you've worked for the Fergusson family for a long time,' she said, leaning a shoulder against the wall as if she too were tired.

'How'd you know that?' demanded the crone, pausing in her chewing to concentrate an accusing stare on Fizz as though the answer to her question were classified information.

Buchanan was amused to see Fizz momentarily short of a handy lie. She could hardly say, *well you've been too old for at least twenty years to be a cost-efficient employee so you must have been recruited before that,* but finding an alternative justification for her remark made her stutter for a moment and, even then, all she could come up with was,

'I don't know what made me think that, really. I suppose you just appeared so…at home.'

'Well, yer right there, hen. Ah've been wi' the Fergussons since Sir Douglas wiz a wee laddie. No jist here, mind. London. Paris. South o' France in the winter. Nursery maid, Ah wiz when Ah started, then nanny to Miss Marjory and Miss Elizabeth too, her that's the Honourable Mrs Campion-Edwards now and away to New Zealand. Still sends me a card at Christmas time, but. "To Nanny with all my love." Never misses a year.'

Buchanan had encountered but few nannies in his time but he couldn't help suspecting that the accent this one exhibited had to be a-typical of the breed. On the contrary, there was a tendency among the Scottish gentry to inculcate their kids with an English accent – an issue that reduced Fizz to nausea – and Sir Douglas's diction, although not as tortured as some of his peers, was certainly proof of that practice.

'Abbeyfield must be a nice place to work,' Fizz offered.

'No whit it wiz.' The aged face twisted into a wrinkled mask of disgust. She chewed vigorously and tipped her head towards the window. 'Aw they folk hingin' aboot. Weddin' parties and business dinners. Folk bein' sick in the rose bushes. Och, it's just terrible. No whit it wiz. Ah seen the days when the toffs wid roll up in thir Rolls Royces wi' thir chauffeurs and thir ladies maids, dinner for fifty folk an' more o' them arrivin' afterwards for the dancin' in the ballroom. Changed days, eh? Thir hisnae been a do like thon since Mr Douglas's twenty-first.'

Fizz projected rapt attention, looking so impressed and shiny eyed that no one would guess what she really felt about such ostentatious over-spending. Evidently her motive in pausing here had not stemmed entirely from her consideration for their escort's fragile knees. Buchanan wondered if she expected to get anything worthwhile out of the old lady but suspected that, while she could be hoping to strike lucky with an innocent question, this was more likely to be just a softening-up operation.

'Take a look at the photies up the stair here in the drawin' room.' Nanny resumed her ascent, bringing her left foot up to join her right foot on every step. 'There's some old ones on the piano: his old lordship and lady Emily going out wi' the hunt and the wee ones at their first communion. There's a few of Sir Douglas as a young man.' She paused for breath and glanced back at Fizz. 'Ye think he's a fine looking man now? Well, jist wait till ye see him when he was in his twenties. Like a film star. Should've been in the pictures. Ah'm tellin' ye, ye nivver saw a better-lookin' —'

A head appeared over the galleried landing above her and a rich contralto voice said, 'Is that Mr Buchanan and Miss Fitzpatrick now, Nanny?'

'Aye. Ah wiz jist —'

'Good afternoon to you both.' The head grew rapidly into a somewhat foreshortened, low-bosomed figure dressed in a wine coloured jumper and skirt and sturdy, cuban-heeled shoes. 'I hope you didn't have difficulty finding the way in. Douglas said he'd forgotten to tell you it was at the back.'

'No problem,' Fizz said. 'There were plenty of people around to direct us.'

Lady Marjory shook hands with them both in turn, resolutely ignoring Nanny who hobbled away down the corridor chewing and muttering to herself.

'Of course, Douglas isn't back yet from his prize-giving. I told him it would go on and on – these things always take longer than you expect – although, I have to say, Caitlin does organise them wonderfully, but people do want to chat and Douglas is so patient and warm-hearted. I don't know how they'd go on without him really.'

Buchanan nodded and smiled, as did Fizz, but she chatted on without a break, appearing to require nothing from either of them in the way of response. The room she showed them into was aglow with the late afternoon sun, which poured in through ceiling-high windows and cast long rectangles of light across parquet flooring and pale oriental rugs. The furniture was also pale: fat beige couches and arm chairs, cream and gold ormolu side tables and cabinets, a chaise longue covered with primrose brocade and scattered with small pillows in a variety of pastel shades. Only the grand piano provided an area of contrast but even that was largely hidden by a fringed silk shawl and dotted with a couple of dozen photographs in silver frames.

It seemed to Buchanan to be an overtly feminine room but there was nothing overtly feminine about Lady Marjory. She was a big strong woman, not much under six feet and probably weighing in at something approaching fourteen stone, very little of which was superfluous fat. The calves which the hem of her skirt exposed as she sat down were as massive and solid as the legs of the piano and her hands seemed to Buchanan, covertly comparing them, to be as big as his own.

'He pretends it's such a bore, of course,' she continued without a pause, 'but really he likes meeting the public and doing his bit to make the enterprise successful. It's what he's good at: charming people. Always has been. Any time there had to be a confrontation with someone – some tradesman not doing his job properly or someone not paying their rent – father used to say to our estate manager, "send Douglas to deal with them, he'll have them eating out of his hand in no time." Not Elizabeth and I. We never excelled in that way but then we never had Douglas's looks. Oh, Caitlin asks me to do my bit now and then but Douglas is so much better at it than I am. Would you like a sherry while we're waiting for him? This is the trouble with children's events: there are always one or two little ones who finish late and, really, you can't go ahead without them. As Caitlin says, the last thing we want is to send them home in tears. And then, Douglas feels he should make a little speech about how high the standard was, just to cheer up the losers – there you go, Miss Fitzpatrick, I hope it's not too dry for your taste – and then there are always one or two of the mothers who want to chat – they do like to tell their friends that they've spoken to Sir Douglas in person you know and, of course, he's always had a way with the ladies, so it never takes just the few minutes that Caitlin estimates when she asks him to do it. I did ask him if he thought we should have tea a little later today but he felt quite sure that wouldn't be necessary so I – my goodness, is that the time? Wherever can he have got to? I dare say he has got into conversation with someone. One has to be so careful not to give offence, you know, because people are so quick to accuse us of snobbery which is absolutely ridiculous but...'

Buchanan found his concentration drifting. It was already obvious that Lady Marjory's level of silence-toleration was so far below national average as to constitute a phobia and he could see even Fizz starting to look somewhat glaze-eyed under the barrage of trivia. It took an accomplished bore to get the better of Fizz. He knew, because she had told him, that she had a secret game she played with such people, the point of which being that her conversational partner had to try and bore her while she had to resist being bored. She claimed a high success rate but right now she was clearly on a sticky wicket.

He tried to keep his eyes more or less on his hostess as she rambled on but what he could see in his peripheral vision was, if only marginally, more interesting. Apart from the photographs on the piano, which might or might not merit inspection, there were signs, just in the general aspect of the room, that hinted at lack of cash. What had appeared, at first glance, to be elegant and distinctive, showed a certain shabbiness when you looked a little closer. The scatter cushions on the chaise longue didn't quite hide the threadbare patch on the seat: a beautiful porcelain lamp base had been chipped and unskillfully mended, the fringe edging the base of one of the couches had lost half of it's silken tassels, a faint square on the wall above the fireplace showed where a painting had once hung, indelibly marking the wallpaper.

It wasn't what one would have expected, Buchanan mused, comparing it to his own place of residence. Even in his present straitened circumstances he wouldn't have left such neglect to go untreated. Well, there was the patch on the wallpaper where Janine had thrown an avocado at him the day she stormed out but that had resisted all attempts to eradicate it so it couldn't be said to count. One had to conclude that either the Fergussons didn't give a hoot for appearances – which was entirely possible – or they were strapped for cash.

Kerr, of course, had hinted at the latter explanation but when somebody told you a peer of the realm had a cash flow problem you naturally assumed he was down to his last couple of million, not actually counting the pennies.

Finally, just when Buchanan's eyelids were starting to droop, the door opened and Sir Douglas rushed in, red in the face and spewing apologies. He had changed, since last observed, into sharply creased grey flannels, navy blazer and paisley patterned cravat. First dynasty Redgrave without the charm.

'Oh, don't apologise,' Fizz told him, her face shining with relief. 'We've had a lovely time talking to Lady Marjory.' She gestured widely with her empty sherry glass and Sir Douglas reacted like Pavlov's dog.

'Let me pour you another sherry, my dear. You Marjory? Not drinking, Tam?'

'I'm driving,' Buchanan said.

Lady Marjory opened her mouth to start yammering again but her brother silenced her with a lifted forefinger, saying, 'Of course. I understand. It wouldn't do for a young man in your position to fail a breathalyser test. How long before you complete your pupilage?'

'Six months still to go, I'm afraid.'

'Not easy.' He handed Fizz her re-charged glass and delivered a slightly less generous portion to his sister. 'Very hard on a chap financially.'

Buchanan immediately spotted an opportunity to edge the conversation into productive topics and went for it. 'Very hard,' he agreed, smiling, 'and I don't have a Rubens to sell to see me over the hard patch.'

Sir Douglas threw back his head and laughed. Marjory started to speak but was forefingered again and shut up instantly, though without displaying any visible angst.

'Well, neither do I, as it turns out, Tam, and damn annoying it is too. I have a prospective buyer damn near slavering for the thing and I can't keep him dangling forever. That bloody "Save-the-Rubens" bunch have held things up long enough as it is without all this added inconvenience.'

'It must be hard to part with something that's been in the family for generations,' Fizz commented with, to Buchanan's eyes at least, a singular lack of empathy.

'Actually, I'd be very happy to sell most of the stuff that's been in the family for generations.' Sir Douglas lowered himself onto the couch beside her, being very careful of the creases in his flannels. 'I only wish I could, but it's all entailed, you know. Ridiculous, isn't it? The roof's leaking, there's dry rot in the basement, the old chapel is now completely unsafe, and I can't afford to do a damn thing about it. The Rubens was part of my late wife's estate and, of course, its sale would have financed a great deal of improvement. That's what's upsetting. I never thought much of the painting, tell you the truth, but I have to admit I was looking forward to getting the builders in. It's damned alarming to realise that someone can just walk in along with the punters, lift what they want and walk out again without anyone seeing them.'

The door opened and Nanny came in wheeling a tea trolley before her like a zimmer frame. Sir Douglas took no more notice of her than if she were painted on the scenery but her ladyship leapt muscularly into the conversational lacuna.

'Well now, what will you have, Miss Fitzpatrick? Tea? We have – oh, Nanny, where's the hot water pot? Surely Mrs Oliver set it out with everything else? You must have taken it off to fill and forgotten to put it back on. Run along and get it now so that it will be here when I'm ready for it. Milk or lemon, my dear?'

Nanny ran along, at roughly the speed of a tectonic plate, and Marjory let rip on the subject of show jumping for a few minutes till silenced by her brother's finger which acted on her with the imperiousness of an electric cattle prod. Buchanan didn't dare catch Fizz's eye but he knew she was wondering, as he certainly was, just what inducements had previously been brought to bear to warrant such total and instant obedience. That they had been humane he had no doubt since one had only to witness the lambency of her lady-ship's eyes each time they fell on her brother to know that she thought he was the bee's knees.

'And tell me,' he said, 'have your investigations moved forward any since I spoke to you this afternoon?'

The question was addressed to Buchanan, but Fizz, finding her mouth momentarily unemployed, chose to answer for him.

'We've just been making the acquaintance of Kerr's neighbours and familiarising ourselves with the layout of the estate,' she said, ogling a plate of pastries. 'Its important to build up our own picture of the situation here at Abbeyfield around the time Irene disappeared. We should also take a closer look at the layout of the main building: the parts not open to the general public, if that would be possible.'

'That's no problem,' said Sir Douglas, waving imperiously at his sister to start pushing the food. 'I'll show you round later, if you like. Damned interesting tour, though I say it myself, particularly the old chapel. Sixteenth century, y'know, but there was an ecclesiastical building on the site before that. Parts of it are getting a bit shaky now, as I was saying, which is why we keep it strictly out of bounds to visitors, but we plan to spend some money on it in the near future. I'll enjoy showing it to you.'

Buchanan saw Fizz's hesitation and felt he knew what she was thinking. Sir Douglas's company was best taken in small doses. He said, 'There's no real need to do that this afternoon: tomorrow would be fine. We probably won't need to keep you for more than a quick look round but if we could see where

Irene worked, where the painting was when it was stolen, it would be very helpful.'

'Absolutely. No problem at all.'

'Did she work regular hours?' Fizz asked, embarking on a bridge roll. 'Nine to five?'

'I believe she did, most of the time, but of course that was up to her. She seemed to be around for much of the working day.'

'You've no idea how dirty most of the paintings are,' Lady Marjory inserted while her brother paused to drink his tea. 'All those years of coal fires and tobacco smoke. Most of the valuable works are up high, you see, to keep them safe, so they don't get dusted as often as they should. It's years since we had sufficient staff to do that sort of thing – getting the ladders out and moving them from room to room. Such a chore. But Irene was making a real difference to the collection. You wouldn't believe how much brighter the colours looked after she'd worked on them. The Raeburn in the ballroom —' She caught his lordship's eye, lost impetus, and abridged, '— looks wonderful.'

Fizz looked at Sir Douglas. 'Who decided which paintings were to be cleaned? Irene or you?'

'Oh, Irene, of course. She had a free hand. She was the expert and I naturally deferred to her opinion. I might make a suggestion now and then but, generally speaking, she did what she thought best.'

'And in the case of the Rubens,' Fizz persisted, 'was it fully Irene's idea to have it cleaned?'

His lordship raised a knuckle to dust crumbs from his moustache. 'Indeed it was, my dear. I suppose I should have thought of it, since we were expecting a prospective buyer to come and appraise it, but it was Irene who decided it could be spruced up a little for the occasion. Why do you ask?'

'No particular reason,' Fizz said brightly. 'Just getting the facts straight in my head.'

'What time would suit you to show us round, Sir Douglas?' Buchanan said into the ensuing, somewhat thoughtful silence. 'We plan to spend most of the day here.'

'Any time's good for me. Some time in the morning suit you? Eleven-thirty?' He basted Fizz with a roguish eye. 'Not too early for you Miss Fitzpatrick?'

'Not at all. We have to make the most of what free time we have.'

Buchanan heard a distant grandfather clock striking six-thirty and made it his excuse to beat a retreat. Fizz looked affectionately at an untouched chocolate gateau and appeared about to ask for a doggy bag but contented herself with glowering at him when no one was looking.

Outside she sucked assiduously at her teeth, evidently relishing the residual flavour of cherry tart, and said, 'Well that was nice. Thank God the tradition of Scottish hospitality has not yet died out in the upper classes.'

'I thought you'd scorn to share in the proceeds of slave labour,' Buchanan teased but she refused to rise to that. 'Actually they're quite an inoffensive couple, I thought, didn't you?'

'He,' she said, 'is a bit oleaginous for my taste. She's okay, I suppose – or would be if someone would just cut her vocal chords.'

Buchanan thought that was a bit thick coming from Fizz, about whom he'd often entertained the same fantasy.

Chapter Six

Early on Sunday morning Fizz started work on the Dunfermline taxi drivers.

Buchanan had quibbled a bit at the idea of being dragged from the arms of Morpheus to drive her there, claiming that he could scarcely inflict himself on the head gardener much before ten, but Kerr had suggested showing him the outlying parts of the estate while the opportunity offered so he let himself be persuaded. This plan allowed time for him to interview Eddie later in the morning while Kerr drove into Dunfermline to pick up Fizz and get her back to Abbeyfield in time for the eleven-thirty rendezvous with Sir Douglas.

It was just before nine when Buchanan dropped her off and the town, at that hour on a Sunday morning, was virtually deserted. There was already heat in the sunlight and the breeze was scented with the smell of warm grass and the occasional hint of frying bacon from an open window. The few pedestrians she passed carried Sunday papers or bags of morning rolls. They ambled along, contemplating the windows of the closed shops, as though they, like Fizz, were in no hurry to be indoors.

There was always something she found enlivening about a town centre – or even better, a city centre – in the early hours of the morning when the sun was up and the populace still abed. It was akin – but only on a minor scale – to the buzz she got on top of a mountain, looking out on a panorama of peaks and high plateaux and distant horizons. In both cases she felt privileged to see a view of things denied to most and marvelled at the purity of a world without people.

By the time she had wasted half an hour on the dispatchers at her first two ports of call, however, the magic had completely gone. The traffic along the main shopping street had picked up and the increased herd of pedestrians stepped out with a purposeful briskness, sports-bound, dog-attended or chapel-hatted.

Fizz consulted the list she had compiled from the yellow pages. The biggest taxi firms – in terms of advertising space if nothing else – had already proved totally unhelpful to the extent that Fizz was confident Irene had never used them. It wasn't always easy to be sure since some people would lie rather than get involved in a police matter and others would make only the minimum effort to remember. You had to really hang on in there, prompting them with every detail that might ring a bell and, if all else failed, simply stand your ground staring wistfully at them till they started racking their brains in an effort to get rid of you. It was surprising how many people broke under this treatment but you couldn't use it effectively by telephone so it was hellishly labour intensive.

Instead of heading for the next biggest operator on her list, she zoomed in on the nearest: a medium sized business just off the high street. The building it occupied looked at least a couple of hundred years old and, in a town less copiously endowed than Dunfermline with historical property, would long ago have been converted into some rich bugger's house of character. Currently it was in need of considerable upgrading but in its day it must have been a rather smart livery stable with a broad entrance leading into a now tarmaced yard. There were two cabs parked at the kerb outside while their drivers languished in the office, partaking of coffee and bacon rolls in the company of a mature woman who was knitting up pale pink wool at something approaching the speed of light.

All three of them turned and looked at Fizz with surprise and a certain discomfiture as though they'd been doing something profoundly lubricious instead of merely having a late breakfast. Clearly they were unaccustomed to receiving customers in person.

'Can I help you?' asked the woman in an affronted tone.

She had dark blonde hair which was going grey and she had apparently tried to give herself a blue rinse ending up with a multicoloured beige/silver/pewter effect vaguely reminiscent of Grace Curzon's Yorkshire terrier. Fortunately the resemblance ended there, her face being pinkly plump and her expression not unkind.

'Hi,' said Fizz, including all three of them in a smile as she took out Irene's photograph and a business card and laid them on the counter beside the woman. 'I'm here to annoy you, I'm afraid. I know you've already had the police questioning you about Irene Lloyd, the woman who's disappeared from Abbeyfield House, but I'm also trying to find her, on behalf of her partner, and I wondered if maybe, now that you've had time to think about it, you might have remembered dealing with her.'

The woman detached one hand from her knitting needle to slip her glasses, which she wore on top of her head, down onto her nose and examine the card closely. 'Yes, I remember the police asking about her. The lassie that stole the oil painting. I remember fine, but it must have been some other taxi firm that picked her up. It wasn't us. Nothing in the book. I let them look for themselves.'

'And every booking is noted down?'

'Everything's logged, luvvie, that's right. If there'd been a call-out to Abbeyfield it would be in there.' The glasses were returned to the top of her blue/beige head and the needles started clicking again like cicadas in a tropic night.

'What about other times?' Fizz suggested. 'I'm also interested in any other journeys she might have made by taxi.'

'Well, that could take hours to find out.' All three of them exchanged disgusted glances at the suggestion, apparently hoping no one was going to suggest that such exertions might become necessary. 'You'd have to go through all the entries one by one and – how far back would you want to go?'

'Just a couple of weeks before she disappeared.'

That was greeted with outraged stares.

'A couple of weeks?' The telephone rang and the woman loosed a hand from her knitting to pick up a set of headphones and hold them to one ear. 'Jaffray Taxis...certainly...Seven Glebe Terrace...' Wedging the receiver in place with a hunched shoulder she scribbled on an old fashioned carbon copy pad, tore off the top copy and gave it to one of the drivers. 'About five minutes. He'll give you a ring on his mobile when he gets there. You're welcome.'

Getting back to her knitting she gave Fizz a "you-still-here?" look and sketched a polite smile. 'We're not able to be much help to you I'm afraid, luvvie. We just don't have the time to search back through two weeks of calls. That's hundreds of names, you know.'

'You're not computerised?'

'No luvvie, I'm a bit too old a dog to be learning new tricks.' She flicked her whizzing needles in the direction of the duplicate book. 'I've been doing it this way for thirty-two years and I won't be changing now.'

Fizz sighed and leaned against the counter in a manner that suggested she was preparing for a long haul. Looking from the receptionist to the remaining driver she said, 'So there's no other way we could check up?'

They shook their heads glumly.

'Do you get a lot of calls from Abbeyfield?'

They exchanged doubtful looks.

'I've done a few runs over there,' admitted the driver. 'Not many, just once in a while. Dropped a guy off with a stuffed fox one time.'

'Any pick-ups?' She slid the snapshot towards him, obliging him to look again.

He hesitated, apparently searching his memory while his tongue chased an errant morsel of bacon roll around his lower teeth. 'Not recently. Not that I can remember. You remember any, Mrs J?'

She came to the end of her row and paused for a second to rub the free needle against her scalp. Fizz thought she was scratching her head but then remembered seeing Auntie Duff – back in the dear dead days beyond recall – do the same thing in the belief that the faint trace of sebum thus applied made the stitches slide easier along the needle.

'I wouldn't be surprised if we've had the odd pick-up at Abbeyfield, Andy, but there's no telling *when*. It's not the sort of thing that sticks in your mind. I certainly don't think —'

The phone rang again, cutting her off, and as she attended to the call Fizz became aware that the driver was trying to catch her eye. Slowly, and keeping Mrs J in her peripheral vision, she slid her eyes around and saw Andy twitch his head a hairsbreadth, like the flicker of a snake's tongue, in the direction of the door.

'Forty-eight Kinnaird Crescent to the station,' said Mrs J, handing him the top copy and, without as much as a glance in Fizz's direction, he gulped down the rest of his coffee and took off.

Fizz retrieved Irene's snapshot but left her card lying on the counter. 'Well thanks anyway for giving me your time, Mrs J. If you or any of your drivers think of anything that might be of help to me I'd really appreciate it if you'd give me a ring.'

'I will, luvvie, don't you worry about that. I don't expect it'll happen but you never know.'

Outside there was no sign of a taxi at the kerb and Fizz's heart sank for a moment, submerged by the suspicion that she had mistaken Andy's signal or that he had not had the patience to wait for her. However, as she passed through the entrance she spotted him a few yards up the road where he was out of sight from the office windows, leaning out of the driver's door to catch her attention.

'Okay,' he said hurriedly as soon as she drew level with him. 'This is between you and me, right? I never spoke to you. I never told you a thing.'

'Sure. Absolutely.'

'Okay. Well, there's one of the other drivers – I'm not telling you his name so don't ask – he does the odd run on the side. It's his job on the line if he's caught so I'm going out on a limb here just telling you, right?'

'I swear to God —'

'Aye, right. So there's this woman he picks up regular. Abbeyfield gates to the town. That's all I know.'

Fizz leaned closer, scared he might escape her before she could milk him dry. 'Can you get him to talk to me?'

'No way. Absolutely no way, so forget it.' He retracted his head and shoulders into the car and slammed the door shut. 'He doesn't even know that I know. I should have shopped him when I found out but the guy needs the money or he wouldn't be doing it. Old Mrs Jaffray can afford it – she's rolling in the stuff – but I wouldn't want her to find out I knew what was going on and didn't tell her.'

He started to switch on his engine but Fizz hung on to the edge of the window. It occurred to her that she was now in a position to blackmail him into coming clean but she quickly dismissed the thought. For the present anyway. If push came to shove poor old Andy's future with Jaffray Taxis was doomed.

'Where did he drop her off?' she demanded.

'Listen, miss, don't push your luck, okay? I tried to help you but, like I told you, that's all I know.'

'You said he took her into town. You must know whereabouts in town.'

'You're never bloody satisfied, are you? I wish to God I'd kept my mouth shut. Listen, I only once saw him dropping her off. It was outside the Bridge café in Belleview Road. Now, piss off.'

The car shot forward, jerking Fizz's hand off the window and making her stagger, but she was too gratified to object. At least she had a lead. Maybe someone in the Bridge café would recognise the photograph. Maybe Irene met someone there for coffee. Maybe someone waited there for her to arrive and then went off with her to some other venue. But even if this lead led nowhere at all there was still Andy, who could still be squeezed a little harder. There was little doubt in Fizz's mind that his naughty friend was a figment of his imagination, a variation of the "another-boy-did-it-and-ran-away" defence and it would soon topple if she leaned on it hard enough. Admittedly, it did appear very much as though Andy knew little more than he had already revealed, there being no reason why he should conceal Irene's destination if he knew it, but that wouldn't save him from a no-holds-barred grilling if the need arose.

It was still only twenty past ten which gave her three quarters of an hour before she'd arranged to meet Kerr, so there was still plenty of time to locate the Bridge café. She hadn't a clue where Belleview Road was but it couldn't be all that far away.

Finding someone to direct her to Belleview Road was easy. It was only five minutes from the high street, on the main road that circled the shopping centre but, on inspection, it was difficult to imagine why Irene, or anyone else, would choose the Bridge café as a meeting place. Although it was currently empty of customers, except for a man reading his *Scotland on Sunday* over a cappuccino, there were enough tables and chairs to accommodate at least thirty people in surroundings of minimal comfort and no privacy whatsoever. The music was intrusive, the furnishings basic and the ambience failed to persuade Fizz to order as much as a coffee. She walked straight up to the counter and smiled at the young woman behind it, a sleepy-eyed twenty-something presently engaged in carrying out a quality control test on the Tunnock's caramel wafers.

She looked at Fizz's business card and the snapshot of Irene with a marked lack of animation and continued to munch the caramel wafer while she listened to her spiel. Then she shook her head.

'Never seen her. See, it's right busy in here most of the time with the school up the road and the office workers coming in for their takeaways. If she was in every day maybe I'd get to recognise her but, really, you don't get time to look at folk if they come in in the middle of the day.'

'Maybe one of the other waitresses might remember her?'

The tip of her tongue emerged from the corner of her mouth and managed, by dint of an extraordinary mobility, to capture a crumb of wafer from the inner edge of her cheek. 'There's just Susan and me and she's not in till eleven. Anyway, she's only been here a fortnight.'

'Take another look at the photograph. She'd have arrived by taxi. Doesn't that ring a bell?'

'No, sorry.'

It seemed like a dead end. Fizz hung on for another few minutes in the hope of annoying her into some creative think-ing, but that didn't work either. By then she was so hungry from watching everyone else stuffing their faces that she suc-cumbed to the temptation of a coffee and a caramel wafer and consumed them glumly at the window, staring out at the traf-fic and wondering what to do next.

The view was obscured partly by a bus shelter which, over the next ten minutes or so, began to fill up with people. Fizz watched them listlessly, her mind on other things, and it was-n't until the bus came along that she realised the significance of what she was seeing. Irene could well have been dropped off here so that she could complete her journey by bus. She jumped up and ran outside just in time to read the indicator board before the bus pulled away. 41a. Kilmartin. Limited Stop.

The discovery seemed like a breakthrough of sorts for the few seconds it took her to return to her table but the elation soon ebbed away. Only one bus stopped there, according to the notice on the shelter, but even a limited stop bus had to call at half a dozen places *en route* to Kilmartin – wherever that might be – so it wouldn't be easy to pinpoint Irene's destination. However, the likelihood of her taking the bus in the first place was a persuasive one – there was nothing else around here that could possibly have attracted her – and perhaps a clandestine pillaging of Kerr's memory banks might narrow the field of inquiry a little. If Irene knew someone who lived in that direction so might he.

With this intention in mind she took the long way round to the car park where she had arranged to meet Kerr so that she could call in at the bus station and pick up a timetable for the 41a. She had time for only a glance at the listed destinations because she was already running behind time but that gave her enough material to start picking Kerr's brain on the way home.

Of course he was impatient to hear if she'd had any success with the taxi firms so she had to lie to him, claiming she'd covered them all and drawn a blank. He was bitterly disappointed, although he had no right to be since the police had already ploughed that field, but evidently he had been hoping against hope nonetheless.

'If she didn't take a taxi then someone must have given her a lift,' he said miserably, wrestling the Land Rover round the twisty road in an effort to make up time and get Fizz to Abbeyfield House for eleven-thirty. Personally, she wasn't too panicked about keeping Sir Douglas waiting for five minutes but it seemed important to him.

'There's public transport,' she pointed out.

'Two buses a day. The Merkhouse bus passes at seven-thirty in the morning and five forty-five in the evening but Irene didn't get either of those. She couldn't have. I'd have seen her leave in the morning and I was home by five that evening. Besides, the police checked with the driver just to make sure. It's not often he picks up passengers at that stop so he'd probably have remembered seeing her.'

'Which direction is Merkhouse?' Fizz asked, purely to keep him on the subject of public transport till she could contrive a way to introduce the route of the 41a. Luckily he went into a fairly intensive description of the surrounding district so she had a minute to think before she said,

'I read somewhere about an archaeological dig that's going on over towards Kilmartin. A Roman villa. I'd quite like to see what they're doing. D'you know that area at all?'

'No, not really. I've probably passed through it but there's not much of interest out that way.'

'Pretty, though,' Fizz remarked, watching him sideways. 'I seem to remember Irene and I went on a sketching trip out that way when we were at college.'

'Really?' he glanced at her in apparent surprise. 'She never mentioned that to me.'

'Well, it was out that direction. Borland. Mearns. Darron Bridge. One of those old mining villages.'

He shrugged, slowing for the turn into the drive. 'Your geography's better than mine, Fizz. I never heard of any of those places.'

And that, Fizz decided, was about as closely as she could question him without his getting suspicious, but the day was approaching when they'd have to stop playing silly buggers and then the shit would really hit the fan.

Chapter Seven

Fizz, of course, was late back from her survey of Dunfermline's taxi firms and, while that wouldn't normally have irritated Buchanan to any great extent, today it got right up his nose. He had curtailed his tête à tête with Eddie (Edwina!) Stevenson ten minutes earlier than necessary rather than risk having to introduce her to Fizz but twenty minutes later he was still hanging about watching for the Land Rover coming up the drive.

The really bitter bit was that Eddie had been, quite conspicuously, more than willing for him to stay. She was an extremely intelligent and self-assured woman, certainly not shy about letting him know she was interested in him and, while Buchanan was old fashioned enough to feel a trifle threatened by women who were too pushy, he found her subtle advances pleasantly encouraging. She was quite straightforward about determining whether there was another woman in his life at present and in making it clear that she too was emotionally free and, that being established, her attitude appeared to be "well, shall we take this thing further or not? I'm up for it if you are."

Buchanan was definitely up for it, his sole doubt being whether he could actually afford to wine and dine this woman in the manner to which he, if not she, was accustomed. Given the choice – and he'd had the choice for many years – he preferred to pamper his girlfriends. A date meant – to him – a really good dinner in a well chosen restaurant or the best seats at the theatre with supper to follow, or even, at a later stage in the relationship, a weekend at a five star hotel or a brief jaunt to Paris or Amsterdam. A keen student of human nature such as Fizz might discern a lack of confidence in that trait, submitting that he doubted his own intrinsic worth, his own ability to charm, so much that he had to offer all manner of extra inducements to make up for his inferiority. But he knew that not to be the case. In fact he estimated his own intrinsic worth – at least when it came to pulling birds – pretty damn high, and even hanging onto them, once pulled, had been no problem till comparatively recently. No, he just enjoyed the whole seduction process and liked to augment the pleasure in every way possible. He'd found it expensive, sure, but while the money was coming in and while he had nothing compelling to save for, why deny himself what was, in effect, a fairly innocuous hobby? Of course, if he'd known that the opportunity of being called to the Bar would turn up when it did, if he'd realised just how fast his meagre savings would dwindle once the mother lode dried up, he'd have been more prudent. Now he was having to choose his luxuries carefully, to weigh golf club fees against the purchase of a new suit, and already there was little he could sacrifice in order to spoil Eddie for any length of time.

However, Eddie didn't hang about waiting for him to make the first move and her choice of entertainment (fortunately, since her emancipation didn't stretch to footing the bill) didn't look likely to entail the remortgaging of his flat.

'I'm driving over to Anstruther Castle this afternoon,' she told him, within minutes of his arrival. 'I want to kick-start some ideas for next year's summer bedding and I've been hearing good reports about what they've been doing over there so I'm hoping their display might give me a little inspiration. Want to come? There's a really nice snack bar there so we could grab a quick lunch.'

'Sure,' said Buchanan without missing a beat.

She looked pleased. 'I hate to be indoors on a sunny day and we can talk just as easily there as here. I'm not precisely sure what help I can be to your search for Irene but you're welcome to pick my brains as much as you like.'

Buchanan too was unsure what questions he wanted to ask

her – not in relation to the current inquiry, anyway – but he was confident that he'd think of something. Fizz would almost certainly want to know why he judged it worthwhile to devote an entire afternoon to the interrogation of the head gardener so it would be nice if he could elicit enough valuable information to convince her – and hopefully himself – that it had been be time well spent.

'You're Irene's closest friend on the estate,' he said, enjoying the graceful picture she made as she moved around the room assembling coffee mugs and doughnuts. 'She confided in you. You probably know more about her than anyone here, except Kerr. The trouble is, you don't necessarily know what information would be of use to me and I don't know the right questions to ask you. We just have to give it time and hope the connections occur spontaneously.'

'Well, here's to spontaneous connections,' she said, giving him a look that would have burned the sugar off a man's doughnut.

Buchanan returned her toast with his own mug. 'God bless them.'

'So, have you discovered anything so far that might point to where Irene's gone?'

'Nothing specific,' he said, launching on a tortuous route around the information he needed to glean but couldn't demand outright. 'We've just been trying to get an impression of Irene's background, her state of mind around the time she disappeared, the sort of life she led here on the estate. I get the picture of Abbeyfield as rather a close community. Perhaps unnaturally close.'

She gave a short laugh, flicking her hair back from her forehead with one tanned finger. 'It didn't take you long to establish that! I dare say it's par for the course in this sort of place. I wouldn't know. I've only worked on civic projects in the past and they're a completely different kettle of fish. But, yes, you're quite right: Abbeyfield is particularly insular, probably because it's so isolated but also because there's plenty to do on the estate itself. If you don't have friends or relations in the area – like the Curzon's do – it's quite easy to slide into the habit of spending your free time socialising with your colleagues.'

'Did Irene have any friends or other interests off the estate?'

'Not that I know of.' Eddie's answer came forth with neither hesitation nor doubt. 'Kerr's a bit of a loner, as you probably know. It's not that he's antisocial, he just happens to enjoy pastimes that are basically solitary. Like hill walking. I know you can do that in a group but he doesn't. I think he's quite content with Irene's company and, I must admit, she always seems quite content in his but the truth is, she didn't have much choice. Kerr didn't like to share her.'

'You think he prevented her from making friends of her own?'

'Not intentionally, no.' She shook her head and looked out the window for a moment, thinking. 'You could easily get the wrong picture of Kerr, you know. He's inclined to be a little…a little, well, possessive and that doesn't make for a perfect relationship, but then, what relationship was ever perfect? I don't like to sound like I'm running him down – he's a really nice guy – and I know that he made a real effort to overcome his jealous feelings or at least hide them from Irene. She told me that and I think she believed it. He didn't bully her – not intentionally. I mean, he never actually forbade her to go out without him or nagged at her when she did. I'm sure he tried to play it down but Irene knew what he suffered so she was just as…coerced, I suppose you'd call it, as if he'd taken a whip to her. Actually, she told me more than once that it was no big deal. She had her own interests here on the estate and she wasn't much interested in swanning around on her own. I

suppose, after ten years, she'd got used to Kerr's idiosyncrasies.'

'What interests did she pursue here on the estate?'
Buchanan asked.

'Well actually, her only interest – at least the only one I
know about – is her painting. Any spare time she had she
spent in her studio, getting on with her own work. That's one
of hers over there above the bookcase.'

Buchanan got up and walked over to look at the small canvas but wasn't overly impressed. Modern art rarely spoke to
him in any meaningful way and this piece struck him as just a
swirl of nebulous shapes against a dull background. It did
glow with a peculiar luminosity and the colours were attractive but he couldn't imagine anyone getting excited about it.

He turned back to Eddie. 'I imagine,' he said casually, 'that
if Irene wanted to go off somewhere on her own she'd try to
do it at a time Kerr was busy elsewhere so that he wouldn't get
upset.'

Eddie popped the last morsel of her doughnut into her
mouth and licked her fingertip. 'Mmmm,' she said, making it
sound like an agreement of sorts.

'Were you aware of her doing that?'

'Me? No, but I'm not around for most of the day.' She saw
by his face that he wanted her to think about it and obliged,
turning again to the window as if she could see Irene out in
the yard. 'I don't think she would risk that, Tam, not unless it
was something she really needed to do, you know? She tried
all the time to build up Kerr's confidence in her – personally I
think it was a waste of effort, he's never going to change, but
there you go – so I can't see her taking a chance on his finding out she'd been pulling the wool over his eyes.'

'Would he have been angry?'

She looked at him carefully, her cornflower blue eyes suddenly intent. 'This is a hypothetical question, right?'

'Of course. Absolutely,' Buchanan said easily. 'I've no reason to suspect Kerr of anything, believe me. I'm just covering all the angles, that's all.'

He couldn't tell if she were fooled or not but she nodded quite compliantly and said, 'I don't know about angry. He'd be hurt – bitterly hurt, that's for sure and Irene would simply hate that. Quite apart from hating to distress him she'd know that it would set their relationship right back to square one. He'd probably never trust her again. That's why I'm sure she wouldn't take the chance.'

Buchanan nodded and changed the subject since he now had all the confirmation he needed to be sure that, whatever Irene had been up to over the last few months, it must have been something pretty pressing.

His mind returned to the issue as he sat on a bench outside the walled garden waiting for Fizz. The most obvious reason for absenting oneself so surreptitiously was, of course, some sort of extra-marital fling. That seemed unlikely, in view of the effort Irene appeared to put into her relationship with Kerr, but it wasn't impossible. Sex was a common cause of insanity. He'd seen plenty of evidence of that in his years as a solicitor so he was unwilling to dismiss that explanation out of hand. However, it was also possible that Irene had been under some sort of external compulsion and that potentiality seemed to offer a more promising line of enquiry. In the restricted and, to a large extent, protected environment Irene lived in it should be easy to pinpoint the source of such a compulsion, but if it came from outside – perhaps from someone from her past – he and Fizz would have their work cut out for them.

It was already eleven-thirty when the Land Rover finally appeared so there was no time for more than a word or two with Kerr before heading for the big house and their rendezvous with Sir Douglas.

'You know I don't like to keep people waiting, Fizz,' he

said when Kerr had dropped them off outside the big house.

'I know, I know,' she said, dragging on his sleeve to slow him down, 'but I didn't strike pay dirt till the last minute. I was sitting in a café – just killing twenty minutes till it was time to meet Kerr – when I had a brainwave so then I had to dash round to the bus station for a timetable.'

Buchanan shortened his stride. 'What did you want with a bus timetable?'

'I'm sure Irene was in the habit of catching the Kilmartin bus in Bellevue Road.'

When Fizz said she was sure about something it actually meant she thought it quite likely but after listening to her story of how she had come to that conclusion, Buchanan was inclined to agree with her. 'How many stops?'

'Ah, there's the rub. Six stops. Borland, Mearns, Clayton, Torby, Darron Bridge, and Banavan. I've already sounded out Kerr on two or three of these names and he didn't twitch. He claims he doesn't know that area at all and I believe him.'

Buchanan walked on in silence for a minute, thinking about it. Then he said, 'Trouble is, it doesn't exactly tell us a whole lot, does it? Unless you've thought of some way we can follow on from that information?'

'Nope,' she said glumly, marching along like a pint-sized storm trooper. 'I suppose we could take a run along that route and see if anything catches our eye. I wouldn't know what to look for but if there's some sort of visible clue we might know it if we saw it. Anyway, we can keep our ears open for any mention of those places. You never know when you'll get a connection.'

Buchanan's still somewhat overheated brain translated that as "spontaneous connection" which brought Eddie forcibly to mind, prompting him to say, 'Oh, by the way, I want to talk further with the head gardener – who turns out to be Irene's main friend and confidant on the estate. We didn't get very far this morning so there could be quite a bit of ground to cover. It could take me most of the afternoon so I hope you have other plans.'

'I could come with you,' she suggested, looking – rather intently, he thought – at his face.

He shrugged lightly. 'If you like. You know what I feel about two-against-one approaches, particularly in the early stages of an enquiry, but if there's nothing more promising you feel able to do I suppose we could chance it.'

Fizz made no reply. She was either reviewing the alternatives or wondering what he was up to, but the arrival of Sir Douglas prevented her from sharing her conclusions so he had to worry about it for the next half hour.

'Hello, hello, hello,' said his lordship jovially, advancing on them with his usual energetic stride. 'I thought I'd just come down and meet you – save you climbing these awful stairs of ours. All ready for the grand tour?'

'You bet.' Fizz eyed his drainpipe-trousered, electric blue suit with ill-concealed awe. 'At least I wish it could be the grand tour but we've a lot to pack into this afternoon. Irene's studio is a must, I'm afraid, but it would be a pity to rush seeing the old part of the house. Maybe we could do that another day?'

'Of course. No problem about that.' He put an arm momentarily about her shoulders, shepherding her in the direction of the main entrance. 'We can just take a peek into one or two of the grander apartments as we pass. Those are the windows of the banqueting hall, for instance, but you can see that next time. They hire it out for weddings and corporate dinners these days but it's still very beautiful. The chandeliers are quite a feature and there are one or two good paintings. Raeburn. Cornelius Jansen.'

They passed through the 'hall of heads', as Fizz had christened it, his lordship proudly indicating which sets of antlers had been added to the collection by himself, and proceeded up the grand staircase, through various interconnecting ante-chambers and along the Long Gallery to the attics. In almost every room there was a guide in attendance, most of which were middle-aged women, and these his lordship greeted with a warm affability which was universally returned.

Much of the interior was familiar to Buchanan from his previous visit – although he couldn't have called a single feature to mind without a visual prompt – but he made all the appropriately appreciative noises that appeared to be beyond Fizz. She, predictably, stalked from floor to floor, doing her best to appear neutral but refusing to flatter his lordship by pretending to be in awe of his riches. It wasn't lost on Buchanan that she had perceivable double standards when it came to inherited wealth. Her closest friend from her child-hood days owned much of the land around Am Bealach and was certainly worth a bob or two. Admittedly, Abbeyfield was on a somewhat grander scale than Rowena's place but the principle was the same.

Irene's workspace was at the end of a long corridor of what had once, their guide informed them, been servants' quarters. He didn't say what they were used for now but there was loud jazz music coming from one of them and an intermittent hammering coming from another so they were evidently still in use. The studio turned out to be a long, brightly lit room with a sloping ceiling. Two wide windows extended the length of one wall giving a view across a shabby looking tennis court and some matted shrubbery to a glimpse of distant rooftops that marked the outskirts of Dunfermline. There was an empty easel at an angle to the windows and, beside it, an old table littered with paints and brushes and rags and bottles of oil and spirits. The centre of the room was taken up by a much bigger table which was covered by what appeared to be an old carpet and strewn, like the other, with a collection of arcane implements and materials. An office chair with a paint-stained fleece jacket draped across its back was placed halfway down one side of the table facing a large sketch pad that was lying open at a colourful page.

Sir Douglas propped a hip on the edge of the table and waved an arm expansively. 'Well, there you have it, people. This is Irene's little nest. The police have already taken a look round, as you're no doubt aware, but I don't believe they found anything at all that was of any use to them. The Rubens was on the easel over there, last time I saw it.'

'When was that exactly?' Fizz wanted to know.

'Around three-thirty on the day before she disappeared.' He'd obviously established that fairly accurately when questioned by the police and didn't have to think about it.

Fizz went over to the table and bent down to look at the sketch pad. 'Was there some special reason you came to the studio that day?'

'No, not really,' said his lordship but, after chewing the edge of his moustache for a moment, he amended that to, 'I suppose I wanted to see how she was getting on with the Rubens.'

'You were in a hurry for it?' murmured Fizz, starting to turn pages.

Sir Douglas looked at her a little curiously, plainly wondering, as indeed was Buchanan, what that had to do with anything. 'Not in a hurry, no. A little impatient – no, hardly that even – let's say, interested, because as I told you, a prospective buyer was hoping to inspect it within a few days, but I certainly didn't anticipate a problem with that and neither did Irene. She assured me that her work on the painting was nearly finished.'

'Was she working on the Rubens when you saw her?' said Fizz looking up. 'Or on this?'

'Well now, I have to say I'm not entirely sure, Miss

Fitzpatrick.' His confused eyes flicked to Buchanan's and back to Fizz as he thought about it. It took him a moment to decide. 'If I had to make a guess at it I'd say she was sketching when I looked in, but I don't really have any clear memory of what work she was engaged in. She often worked on two or three projects at the same time. Stopped her from getting stale, she said.'

Fizz nodded and waved a finger at the sketch book. 'This is her own work?'

'I believe so,' said his lordship without getting up to check. 'In fact, I know it is. As I told you yesterday, she made her own time. During the daylight hours she would work on those jobs that needed plenty of light and any other work was attended to when the light was poor.'

Buchanan walked over and looked over Fizz's shoulder as she flicked through the pages. What he saw was a collection of studies similar to the one he'd seen in Eddie's cottage earlier: the same formless colours, vaguely pleasing to the eye but unexceptional except for the Turneresque proficiency in capturing light. He doubted very much whether Fizz's study of the sketchbook was likely to tell them anything but he left her to it and spoke to Sir Douglas.

'Would you mind if we had a rummage around?'

'Not at all. Nor would the police, I imagine, otherwise they'd have told me to leave things alone.' He looked about him uncertainly. 'If you'd care to tell me what you're looking for I'd be happy to help you.'

'It's kind of you to offer, but in fact I don't know what I'm looking for till I find it,' Buchanan told him with a smile. 'In fact, I'm not really expecting to find anything, just going through the motions and hoping to get lucky.'

'In that case, if you're quite sure I can't be of any help to you, I'll leave you to it for a few minutes. My little hobby lobby – my music room – is up here and I can attend to a few things while I keep out of your way.'

Buchanan sped him on his way with voluble assurances, and started poking into various cupboards and chests that stood around the walls. Fizz listened to the decreasing sounds of his lordship's departing footfalls and then said,

'Take a look at this, Buchanan. It's like the bloody Marie Celeste. Look at this sketch – it's unfinished. Look at that brush – it hasn't been cleaned or put away. Look at that jar of dirty water. Look at the tube of colour lying there with the cap off.' She turned to stare up into his face as he leaned over the table beside her. 'What does that tell you, Watson?'

'I dunno, Holmes. That she was called away in a hurry, per-haps?'

'Elementary, I'd say, wouldn't you? Either called away or struck down where she sat working.'

Buchanan examined the floor and the arrangement of the tools on the table. 'No blood. No sign of a struggle.'

Fizz transferred her attention to the fleece jacket. She held it up to the light and scanned it carefully, back and front, then went through the pockets, pulling them inside-out to search the seams. 'Nada,' she said. 'Looks like she could well have left here under her own steam but I'll lay you any money she was in a fair old panic. I know her and she's not the kind to leave an expensive sable brush lying around caked with paint.'

'Okay,' Buchanan nodded. 'That's worth knowing. It puts a whole new slant on things but let's think about it later. Right now I want to have a thorough hunt around this place before Sir Douglas comes back and starts to quibble about the extent of our search. That could give us only a few minutes so let's get a move on.'

The distant sound of jazz music stopped suddenly and then started up again: a different tune and even louder. It helped to cover the noise of slamming drawers and creaking cupboard doors as they tore through every storage place in the room –

and there were plenty. It was difficult to marry speed to thoroughness but, when he came to the last drawer, Buchanan was fairly certain he hadn't missed anything of significance. He'd have noticed a bus ticket or a promotional book of matches had there been any such clue among the junk he uncovered, which was mostly scraps of canvas, empty tubes of glue, bits of wood, and other esoteri of that genus.

Fizz too had drawn a blank and progressed to an examination of the pictures stacked against the walls. Some of these were clearly Irene's own work – even Buchanan could recognise her style by now – and it was those that appeared to hold Fizz's attention but whatever it was that intrigued her about them she didn't choose to share it with Buchanan and before he could suggest she do so Sir Douglas was back in their midst and clearly in a mood to be rid of them.

'Seen all you need to see, Tam?'

'Yes, thank you, Sir Douglas. It's been very helpful.'

'Any further on with your inquiry?'

'Not really,' Buchanan smiled, 'but one can never tell what could turn out to be significant.'

In fact, he thought as they followed their guide down the stairs, considering they were only a couple of days into the case they had made quite reasonable progress. Things were already beginning to look less obscure than they'd originally appeared and, if they didn't have any wildly promising leads to follow, at least there were certain eccentricities that could profitably be explored.

Chapter Eight

Sir Douglas left them in the hall of heads and went back upstairs, covering the first flight like a gazelle and the second flight – probably unaware that Fizz was watching him up the stairwell – like the unfit and slightly overweight middle-aged man he was.

Fizz couldn't help feeling there was something pathetic about a person who needed to pretend like that to gain approval. She didn't really dislike him personally, even if he were a bit too touchy-feely for her taste, it was just what he represented that got her hackles up.

She turned to Buchanan and caught him looking at his watch. 'Lunch?' she said hopefully and he looked just a little discomfited as if he'd guessed he'd be stuck with the bill.

'It's a bit early for me,' he said, walking over to the door and holding it open for her to pass through. 'I'd rather get started on the head gardener. Why don't you go round and grab something at the cafeteria and I'll catch up with you later.'

Fizz swithered, pausing uncertainly on the steps outside while she tried to make up her mind. She was certainly starving but she also felt she should make an effort to meet the head gardener now that Buchanan had broken the ice with him to some extent.

'I don't know…' she was starting to say when she turned her head and spotted old Nanny pacing sedately past at the edge of the driveway. The sight decided her.

'Look,' she said. 'There's somebody I want to speak to again. I'll grab her while I get the chance and then I'll grab myself a soup and sandwich. You can meet me in the snack bar if you're finished with Eddie in a reasonable amount of time or, if not, I'll walk back to Kerr's cottage and see you there.'

Buchanan raising no objection to that itinerary, she ran

down the steps and caught up with Nanny as she turned in at a small doorway in the angle of the porte cochere. The old lady was deep in some thought of her own and appeared a little startled to be approached so suddenly, but she recognised Fizz immediately.

'I wondered if we could have a wee chat,' Fizz said.

'Whit aboot?'

'Not about anything in particular, just your general reminiscences I suppose. You've been here at Abbeyfield longer than anyone else, other than Sir Douglas and Lady Marjory themselves, and I like hearing your stories.'

Nanny's pinched expression softened visibly and she gestured at the stone steps that led downwards from the open doorway. 'Well, you'd better come away in then. Ah'm no standin' here when ah could be sittin' doon.'

Fizz followed her down a steep and ill-lit stone stairway into the servants' quarters, only parts of which were open to the public. They passed through a vast Victorian kitchen where a guide was demonstrating the workings of an array of archaic equipment, and penetrated into a 'Strictly Private' area which consisted of nothing more than a small utility room containing an ironing board, a collection of vases, an electric kettle, some boxes of industrial cleaners, an ancient couch and two mismatched armchairs.

'This here's ma wee howff,' said Nanny, using an old Scots word for a hideaway that Fizz hadn't heard in years. 'Ah've ma own room, mind, but Ah like a bit of company. This here's supposed tae be fur the guides tae hiv thir teabreaks but naebody'll be bye fur a while. Sit yersel' doon.'

Her bony hands gripped the arms of one of the chairs as she lowered herself gently into it and, twisting herself sideways, she opened the double doors of an adjacent cupboard. From this she slid out a wooden tray on which was a jigsaw puzzle so close to completion that Fizz could recognise the picture as the Falls of Dochart. She'd grown up within three miles of those falls and had seen enough of them but they still turned up on every 'Glories of Scotland' calendar, every tin of shortbread and every piece of tartan trash she'd come across between here and Australia.

'Her ladyship...' Nanny remarked, chewing contentedly as she settled the tray across her lap. 'Her ladyship wiz tellin' me you an' that young gentleman are friends o' the art lassie that vanished last week.'

'Actually it was the week before last but, yes, Tam Buchanan and I are trying to find her. You didn't know her personally?'

'Oh aye, I knew her fine. She sometimes had her tea breaks in here wi' the rest o' us. A nice smilin' lassie she wiz. Eileen Something.'

'Irene Lloyd.'

'Irene? Aye, that's right enough. I get those two names mixed up...' Her voice tailed away as she scanned her puzzle, then resumed. 'Sir Douglas an' her ladyship were right fond o' her though. They'll be awfy pit oot if it turns oot it wiz hir that took thir picture.'

'Well, so will I,' Fizz agreed. 'But I really don't think there's any chance of that. It's much more likely that someone broke into the house and took it from Irene's studio.'

'What's the world coming tae?' Nanny murmured, studying a parti-coloured piece of puzzle from a variety of angles. 'If they could get in past all they burglar alarms they could get in anywhere. We could be murdered in wir beds.'

The possibility didn't seem to be causing her any particular angst so Fizz didn't bother to deny it. She said, 'Is there a connecting door between the private apartments and the main part of the house?'

'No. There's naebody but his lordship goes in the big house much now. Lady Audrey, God rest her, used to take a daunner round sometimes, when she was able, but this last wee while back she couldn't take the stairs, the poor soul. Just shuffled from bed to chair, chair to bed. Then she got that she just stayed in her bed all day. It was that sad to see her.'

She tried the same bit of puzzle up the other way. Fizz could see that it wasn't ever going to fit in that hole but felt that Nanny would welcome no assistance so she held her tongue and said, 'What was wrong with Lady Audrey?'

'Her heart, poor lassie. The worse it got the less she could move around and the less she could move around the worse it got. A vicious circle, the doctor said. Ah well, in the midst of life we are in death.' She fell silent, chewing thoughtfully and mumbling over a particularly recalcitrant piece of river. Her dry old hands moved over the surface of the picture almost as though she were feeling her way across it and her face slackened in concentration.

'You must miss her ladyship,' Fizz prompted, seeing her gradually submerging in the Falls of Dochart.

'Oh, aye. We all miss her. Poor Sir Douglas is fair devastated.' She glanced up and must have seen the disbelief on Fizz's face because she added, 'He doesn't go around wi' his face trippin' him, making everyone else as unhappy as himsel', but Ah've known the laddie longer than anyone and Ah ken when his heart is sore.'

Fizz was willing to concur with that assumption, given his lordship's apparent need to appear on top of things. 'It hasn't been all that long since Lady Audrey passed away, has it?'

'It's been a few weeks.' She shuffled a few bits of sky and picked out one with a straight edge. 'A month, maybe. More like six weeks. See sky? Ah hate sky. Why d'they hiv tae put in so much sky?'

Fizz listened for a moment to the distant drone of the guide's voice. She couldn't make out the words but she could recognise the strange modulations of lecture–speak and hear the polite ripples of laughter at the probably well-worn witticisms.

'Sir Douglas has his hobbies, though,' she suggested.

'His music, are you talkin' about? Oh aye, he has his music, and a fine noise he makes with it. It would've drove a body mad, the racket of it, before he moved it all away up to the attics to give Lady Audrey a bit of peace, but Ah don't think he has much heart for that either any more. Same wi' his fishin'. Just can't be bothered, he says. Break your heart, so it would.'

'It's early days,' Fizz said, seeing she was genuinely distressed. 'I'm sure he'll come back to it in time.'

'Oh aye,' Nanny said strongly, chewing her gum (or gums) with vigour. 'He'll get over it. He's a young man yet and it'll be no surprise to me if he marries again wan o' they days, the way he has wi' the lassies.'

'Really?' Nanny's admiration for her erstwhile charge was, as far as Fizz was concerned, definitely over the top. The guy was not bad looking for his age, she supposed, but he wasn't exactly the answer to a maiden's prayer. 'Is there someone waiting in the wings do you think?'

'Eh?' Nanny lifted her head with a jerk, the pinched expression back around her mouth. 'No there is *nut!*' she snapped. 'And don't you go tellin' folk Ah said any such thing. There wiz never nuthin' like that wi' Sir Douglas from the day Lady Audrey came to this house. None o' your hanky-panky. Ah'm no' sayin' the lassies didny give *him* the eye but he never encouraged them. No, no. He's no' that kind at all. Just a home-bird, his lordship. Perfectly happy with what he's got.'

Fizz wondered if that were true and decided it probably was. He had some peculiar traits, no doubt about that, but his flirtatious manner seemed totally one-dimensional. A juvenile habit he'd forgotten to give up. Poke it and it would turn out to be thinner than tissue paper.

Nanny went on for a few minutes about what a sweet and

beautiful child Douglas had been, how constantly in demand as a teenager for tennis parties and dances, how widely admired as a man. Fizz hit her snooze button and waited for an opportunity to introduce a topic that had more likelihood of proving useful.

'Was Lady Marjory ever married?' she asked, eventually.

'No, dearie, she never was. There was a young man at one time, used to come for the shooting every year. A military gentleman. Colquhoun, his name was, and a fine upstanding figure of a man he was too. We all thought there would be an engagement but it never happened. He went off and married someone else.' She made a sudden breakthrough with one corner and fitted in several straight-edged pieces in one go. 'That's better. Now we can see where we're goin'.'

'How did Lady Marjory take it?' Fizz asked. She had no idea where she was going with this line of questioning but she was of the belief that servants invariably knew more of what went on in a big house than anyone else and one never knew at this stage in a case which information would turn out to be useful and which wouldn't.

Nanny's face darkened again. 'She took it bad,' she said, chewing her words. 'I don't know the truth of it – there's that much gossip goes round you don't know what to believe – but there was talk she'd tried to harm herself.'

'You mean, she tried to commit suicide?'

'I don't know.' She waved a gnarled hand, the thin fingers bent like twigs, pushing away the question. 'There's always folk'll say things like that just to make it more interesting. But her ladyship was sent away for a wee while, some folk said it was to Switzerland but it was never spoken aboot and Ah knew better than to ask. You kept your place in my day, no' like it is wi' this generation. Six months she was away, near enough, and she was fine when she came back. But there was never anyone else for the lassie after that.'

'What a shame,' Fizz murmured, although such mental frailty was so foreign to her as to be incomprehensible. Men were like buses: there'd be another along in a minute and if there wasn't, that still wasn't the end of the world. Lady Marjory should have had Grampa there to tell her to shut her greetin' face and get on with the ironing. She pondered the oddity of Lady Marjory's reaction to being dumped, wondering if it had really been so severe or whether her parents had chosen to spoil her, while Nanny segued into the history of the younger sister, Agnes, who had flown the family nest twenty-five years ago and never returned. None of this was of any interest to Fizz and she was watching for an opportunity to cut and run when she heard the click of heels on the stone flags of the passageway and the door opened to admit a small, red faced woman in impressive heels and a power suit.

'Hullo, hen,' said Nanny, glancing up only momentarily from her puzzle and apparently considering introductions unnecessary.

The woman halted in mid-stride, one hand inserting a cigarette between scarlet lips, the other applying a lighter to the end. Registering the presence of a stranger, she drew in a lungful of nicotine before she spoke and the smoke emerged with the words.

'Hello! Friend of yours, Nanny?'

Nanny emerged from a fog of concentration and glanced from face to face, re-orienting herself slowly. 'Oh, aye. This wee lassie is a friend o' Eileen's. She's helpin' the police tae find her. Miss...Fitzwilliam.'

'Fitzpatrick, actually. Fizz to those who find it a mouthful.'

'Caitlan McCormick. I'm the events manager.' As she sank into the free armchair a waft of perfume hit Fizz's nostrils, strong but not strong enough to overpower the smell of her cigarette. 'God, what a morning!' she said, addressing her remarks primarily to Nanny, who ignored her, but also to anyone else who would listen, which meant Fizz. 'Why is it that some events are so bloody determined to go pear-shaped? We've got the annual dinner of the Camera Club on Friday night – with some sort of prize-giving event, Fund Raiser of the Year or something – and it's taking up more of my time than everything else on the calendar put together. I've had the director's secretary on the phone every day this week and now she's complaining that there'll be no one to cheer the winners because the members are all too mean to fork out thirty quid for a ticket. What does she expect *me* to do, for God's sake? Provide canned applause? Hire extras? Christ!'

Her chest heaved as she sucked smoke into it, barely allowing the glow to subside in her cigarette before rekindling it with another drag. Watching her, it seemed to Fizz that she looked too smart to do something so self-destructive. She was no rebellious teenager, in fact she was forty-five or older, and she had the sort of decisive, no-nonsense face that belonged to someone who wouldn't allow themselves to be hag-ridden by a habit.

Getting only the minimum response to her woes from Fizz and no sympathy at all from Nanny, who was completing the top edge of her puzzle as though racing against time, she soon abandoned that tack and asked Fizz how she came to be involved in the search for Irene. Clearly, she knew all the details of the matter already so it wasn't difficult to put her in the picture.

'How do you go about something like that?' she asked when Fizz had finished giving her the background. 'Looking for someone who has disappeared. I wouldn't know where to start.'

'Well, the boys in blue have already done all the groundwork for us. They've checked up on all her friends and relations to find out if they've seen her or heard from her, they've established that her bank card hasn't been used, they've talked to all the taxi operators who might have taken her somewhere, as well as covering all the places she might be expected to turn up if she had, in fact, taken the Rubens.'

'Airports...shady art dealers...' Caitlin supplied, nodding. 'But you don't think she actually took the painting?'

Fizz found herself hesitating in the realisation that Caitlin wouldn't be fooled by flannelling. 'It would be hugely out of character,' was all she could honestly offer.

'So you believe that she simply got pissed off, either with her job or with Kerr or whatever, and decided to make a swift exit. People do that all the time.'

'That's true,' Fizz agreed, 'but when they do that they usually let somebody know: leave a note or telephone the person who's going to be most worried. Also, they pack a bag, they take their passport, they empty their bank account. Irene did none of these things, as far as can be established, nor can we find any sign that she'd made any prior preparation whatsoever.'

Without removing her gaze from Fizz's face Caitlin stubbed out her cigarette in an ashtray that already held half a dozen scarlet-ringed butts. 'I didn't know that. So, you're saying...what? That she could be lying in the woods somewhere with a broken leg? Or...' She seemed unwilling to say the words. 'Or...that whoever took the picture has...done away with her?'

'I don't see any other possibilities, do you?'

Visibly shocked, Caitlin glanced round to see Nanny's reaction but the old lady had not been listening. She seemed to feel someone's eyes on her, however, because she glanced up and muttered, 'See aw this sky? It's terrible. No even a wee cloud in it.'

Caitlin didn't answer, indeed she seemed unaware that Nanny had spoken. After a minute she lit up another cigarette and, squinting at Fizz through a cloud of smoke, said, 'The police don't suspect foul play, do they? At least they haven't said anything to his lordship about it or he'd have told me. The last I heard, they were working on the assumption that

Irene had stolen the painting.'

'That's still the case,' Fizz told her. 'And you felt happy with that assumption. Did you?'

Caitlin opened her eyes in feigned innocence. 'Who am I to argue with the police?'

'But you must have known Irene fairly well. Didn't you think —'

'Let me tell you something, kid. Dozens of people – including the CID – knew the Yorkshire Ripper a lot better than I knew Irene. Neither of those two had the word 'baddie' tattooed across their foreheads.'

Fizz had to smile at that and Caitlin smiled back, some of the strain slipping away from her face. She drew on her cigarette with less urgency than she'd shown before and leaned her shoulders back against her chair.

'What's left for you to do, then, if the police have covered all the possibilities?'

'We're starting from the opposite viewpoint to theirs: that Irene *didn't* take the painting, but right now it's just a matter of scraping around for leads. All we can do for the moment is to talk to as many people as possible and keep on picking brains till something turns up that will point us in the right direction.'

A faint shadow of amusement passed over Caitlin's face and she threw a quick glance at Nanny who was chewing thoughtfully over a sliver of blue.

'That's what you're doing here? Picking brains?' Her lips twitched. 'Well, you'll get some colourful stuff from this lady. We let her loose on the punters sometimes to tell her ghost stories. Isn't that right, Nanny?'

But Nanny had discovered where a completed section of the Tarmachan Ridge fitted into the skyline and could only spare a vague, 'Aye, ye may laugh, but aw these old places hir ghosts.'

In any case, Fizz felt that she had just about scraped the

bottom of Nanny's barrel and was more interested in what Caitlin could tell her. She said, 'Were you upset by the theft of the painting?'

Caitlin tipped back her head and regarded Fizz down her nose, a half smile curving her red mouth. 'Personally speaking, you mean?'

'Yes. Personally.'

The smile widened. 'I take it you already know I was moving heaven and earth to make sure it stayed in the country? Yes, obviously, or you wouldn't have asked the question. So, what you're asking is: am I glad that it has vanished – hopefully on a temporary basis – so that I have a bit more time to find a UK buyer?' She drew on her cigarette and then said, on the exhale, 'Or maybe you think I had something to do with it's disappearance myself?'

Fizz met her eye steadily, knowing that this woman could take the truth without also taking offence. 'I'd have to be simple not to take that aspect of things into consideration, wouldn't I? Whether you engineered it or not, the loss of the painting allows you a breathing space. You can still continue to tout for support on the assumption that it'll be recovered sooner or later. Am I right?'

There was silence for a moment or two while Caitlin let her eyes dwell at length on Fizz's face, then she said, 'You're tougher than you look, kid, I'll say that for you, though you hide it well. Okay, let me say this, just for the record: I don't know a damn thing about the theft of the Rubens. I may feel very strongly about art treasures being bought for the nation but I'm not the sort of person to put my job on the line for an ideal. I never tried to stop the sale. All I've been doing is looking for alternative money, which is what I'm good at. Anything further than that I'm happy to leave to those with more commitment to the cause.'

'And who might they be?' Fizz responded neutrally. 'I

believe several people were involved with the campaign.'

Caitlin got to her feet and leaned down to grind out her half-smoked cigarette in the ash tray. 'None of them had either the will nor the opportunity to take matters into their own hands,' she said. 'We're talking about well-known, influential people, not fanatics. I can give you their names if you feel it's absolutely necessary but I'll guarantee you'll find them above suspicion.'

'Nobody,' Fizz said, looking up at her, 'is above suspicion.'

Caitlin took a long look at Fizz, smiled at some thought of her own, then shook her head. 'I'll be in my office if you need me. It's in what used to be the tennis pavilion.'

'Maybe I could see the maps of the estate while I'm there,' Fizz suggested. 'I'd just like to see if there are any handy places for hiding a work of art – or a body, for that matter.'

'Oh, there are plenty of those,' Caitlin said with a snort. 'Sir Graham – Sir Douglas's father – fancied himself as a builder. They say he caught the bug from Sir Winston Churchill who used to lay bricks in his spare time, would you believe? Anyway, the estate is littered with gazebo's and belvideres and dovecotes and God only knows what else. They've all been searched already, either by Kerr or by the police, but you're welcome to have another look whenever it suits you. Right now I have to go and kick ass or we won't see our laundry before the weekend.'

She whisked herself out the door without waiting for a reply, but Fizz was far from finished with Ms McCormick.

'Right, Caitlin,' Fizz muttered to the closed door. 'See you later.'

Chapter Nine

Buchanan wasn't a Monday person. Even when he'd been his own boss, in the brief interval between his father's retirement as senior partner and his own apprenticeship to Larry the Bastard, he'd been a martyr to that Monday morning feeling and nine times out of ten it had lasted all day. It struck him as odd now, looking back, that he had never realised quite how much he'd hated his job: stuck behind a desk all day, dealing, a lot of the time, with worried or angry people in depressing situations, the office politics, the nit-picking attention to detail. The Buchanan's were a legal tradition in Edinburgh, of course. For the last hundred and fifteen years one son at least in every generation had joined the profession and when his elder brother balked at the first hurdle Tam had simply bowed to the inevitable and entered upon a career that threatened to freeze-dry him into a wasted husk before his time. If it hadn't been for Larry the Bastard's offer of pupillage (and that unique act of generosity was still a mystery to all who knew the man) there would still be no light at the end of the tunnel. The last few months had not been easy but as long as there was the hope of a less boring future to look forward to he could take Larry's constant carping and insane rages with a pinch of salt.

Today, however, which had been officially Monday all day, had been almost a Thursday most of the time, with prolonged Friday touches coming in late in the afternoon. Part of this effect had been due to Larry's absence but the main reason was that Buchanan had a hot date lined up with Eddie that evening. Seven-thirty at The Arena for drinks and then on to Poseidon for dinner. It would make yet another hole in his already well-perforated bank balance but, hell, it was an investment and one which, if he had read Eddie's body-language correctly – and it was pretty articulate – would pay handsome dividends.

Her recce of Anstruther Castle gardens the previous afternoon had, he was quite certain, been quite unnecessary since
she had shown only the most superficial interest in the flower
beds. In fact, they had spent much of the first part of the
afternoon on a long lunch and only then bethought themselves to make a pretence of carrying out the research that was
their ostensible reason for being there: the perusal of the gardens, as far as Eddie was concerned and, in Buchanan's case,
the question of Irene's disappearance.

It took a deliberate conscience-driven effort for him to
start asking Eddie about recent events and their impact on the
staff at Abbeyfield especially as, since meeting Kerr and hearing what was said about his disposition, he was halfway to
believing that Irene had simply upped stakes and left him.
Certainly there were suspicious circumstances but he'd often
enough in the past seen similar suspicious circumstances turn
out to be innocuous, so he wasn't quite as worried as Fizz
appeared to be. However, he'd claimed he'd be questioning
Eddie so he felt he ought to make at least a stab at it.

'Tell me,' he said, 'How did the Fergussons take the loss of
the Rubens? Was Sir Douglas seriously upset?'

She seemed as willing to talk about that as about anything
else. 'I think he was pretty devastated, actually,' she said, passing by a magnificent bed of roses and lavender without so
much as a glance. 'He seemed to be of the opinion, at first,
that it would be only a matter of days before the police got it
back for him but, once the reality sank in it hit him badly. He
tries to put a brave face on it, you know – stiff upper lip and
all that – like he does with everything but everyone knows
he's pretty down about the whole business. The word is, he's
desperate for the money, but how any of the staff would know
that I can't imagine. Abbeyfield's a hotbed of rumours. You
learn to let them go in one ear and out the other.'

'Presumably he has servants of his own,' Buchanan suggested. 'Perhaps one of those overheard something they shouldn't have.'

'I doubt it. There's only the daily woman, Jess Oliver, who's there for a couple of hours every weekday morning, and old Nanny who's really not a servant at all, although she likes to think she is.'

'We met Nanny yesterday. She showed us in when we went for tea.'

Eddie smiled. 'She refuses to retire but, in fact, I don't think she does very much – apart from mollycoddling her wonderful Sir Douglas and telling him what a treasure he is. She's such a sweetie and we all adore her but honestly, between Nanny's smother-loving and Lady Marjory's hero worship, it's like watching an Ealing comedy. Victor Curzon does a good take-off of them both when he's had a drink or two.'

'I get the impression that both Sir Douglas and Lady Marjory are fairly easy to get along with.'

'That's probably true,' she said, after a momentary hesitation. 'They're both very egalitarian in their views and they like to be liked, if you know what I mean.'

Buchanan waited for the codicil that was implicit in her tone and, when it didn't come, he prompted,

'But?'

She glanced round at him and laughed. 'How do you know there's a but?'

'I'm psychic. Tell me.'

She hooked an elbow through his arm and hugged it to her side. 'It's nothing serious,' she said with a little impatient shake of her head. 'Sir Douglas I can put up with – he's a bit of a nutter but basically harmless – but Lady Marjory is someone I just can't take to. It's not that I've ever crossed swords with her personally – I think she knows who'd come off worse in that sort of encounter – but she's very good at getting her little knife into those who she suspects are defenceless. And always when she thinks no one else will notice.'

'Did Irene have trouble with her?'

That seemed to amuse her. 'Irene had trouble with no one,' she said, giving his arm a squeeze. 'She wouldn't dream of hurting anyone's feelings so she just swayed with every wind that blew on her and waited till it went away. No, her ladyship never tried it on with Irene as far as I'm aware – never needed to – but I've heard her giving Nanny a rough time. More than once. And, of course, the poor old dear wouldn't dream of answering her back or trying to defend herself. She just dotes on both her ex-babies to the point of obsession.'

'Who else does Lady Marjory pick on?'

'Anyone she can, basically. Jess, the cleaning woman, any of the volunteers who don't have the bottle to tell her to shove off; but with everyone else she's as sweet as honey. A lot of the staff think she's wonderful but that's because all the dirty jobs, like telling someone to pull his socks up, are left to Caitlin.'

They took a woodchip-covered path through a wooded area and came upon a large pool filled with water lilies. An old wooden bridge crossed the miniature waterfall that fell into it and they stopped there for a moment with their elbows on the rail, listening to the splash of water against leaves.

'I haven't seen your colleague yet,' she said. 'She's a solicitor, Kerr said.'

Buchanan nodded, getting immediately twitchy. 'Just graduated,' he said while he formed a question that would return the conversation to safer subjects.

'She was lucky to get the offer of a job so quickly,' Eddie said, before he could deflect her. 'My mother has a friend whose son graduated this year and he's having to go down south to get work because there are so many Edinburgh graduates on the job market.'

'Fizz has been working part-time for my old firm all the way through her course,' he said shortly and took her hand to draw her onwards along the path. 'As things worked out, I left the firm just when she was ready to fill my place.'

'Really? Lucky for her.'

It had occurred to Buchanan more than once that happy coincidences such as this one seemed to fall regularly into Fizz's lap but some things were best not inquired into too closely. He said, 'Yes, I suppose it was. So, tell me, are there any rumours about why Sir Douglas needs the money so urgently?'

'None that deserve any credence. In any case, lack of money isn't the only reason for selling a painting, is it? I don't know if you've seen the photographs that have been on the TV recently, but frankly the Rubens is not the sort of thing I'd particularly want to hang above *my* fireplace. Irene could see it's finer points of composition and brushwork or whatever but to me its simply a gloomy and very boring piece of work and if I inherited it I'd do the same as Sir Douglas – turn it into ready cash and buy something I could live with. Or spend the money on shoring up the worst parts of the big house, which would probably be his priority.'

Buchanan was inclined to agree with that reading of the facts. After all, his wife's death had doubtless brought Sir Douglas a good deal more than the painting. 'Lady Audrey also owned an estate in Hampshire, I believe.'

'No, she didn't own it,' Eddie murmured in a sleepy voice, her thumb caressing the back of Buchanan's hand. 'That was the family estate and it went to her brother.'

'But presumably Sir Douglas inherited the bulk of her property, which must have been fairly substantial.'

'I wouldn't know.'

There was a certain shortness in her tone that hinted at impatience, as though the subject had lost it's flavour and

Buchanan was not surprised when she set off on a different track, both physically and conversationally, drawing him deeper into the wood.

'I must show you the arboretum,' she said, with an enthusiasm he was unable to match, 'and I want you to see the Bavarian summerhouse. You'll be amazed. It's really beautiful but it's so tucked away in the trees that most people miss it.'

Buchanan felt it would be churlish to demur. After all, he'd had his crack of the whip, he could scarcely refuse Eddie hers.

The Bavarian summerhouse, however, proved every bit as amazing as promised. Architecturally it was scarcely worth a glance, but as a venue for a spot of advanced snogging, virtually unsurpassed. Unfortunately, one could have wished it a tad less accessible to the public. The arrival of a group of bird-watchers brought their communion to an abrupt end but the memory of those few minutes was torrid enough to light the blackest Monday with a rosy glow.

With more of Eddie's benevolence in the offing Buchanan arrived back at his flat that evening full of happy expectation and *joie de vivre*. He laid out his last good Boss suit and his lilac shirt together with a judicial choice of underwear and dived, singing, into a hot bath but he had barely got his knees wet when the phone rang.

'Buchanan,' he barked, sure it would be Fizz.

'Tam, it's Eddie.'

His heart stopped singing. It wasn't likely that she was phoning to confirm the arrangements.

'Hi. What's up?'

He heard her draw a ragged breath. 'Oh, Tam, something terrible's happened.'

'What?' he said impatiently, his mind racing around possibilities.

'It's Nanny...she's dead. She fell down the servant's staircase up at the House.'

Buchanan's immediate reaction was relief. Compared to the awful catastrophes his imagination had presented to him in the last three seconds Nanny's demise – regrettable as it was – paled to insignificance. She was a nice old lady but he scarcely knew her and at least it had been quick and unexpected, which was as much as any very elderly person could ask.

'I'm so sorry, Eddie,' he said although, anticipating her next words, he was sorrier for himself than for her. 'I know you were fond of her.'

'We all were. It's just…it's so sudden. I just heard the news and I'm totally —' Her voice wavered. 'I really don't feel like going out and enjoying myself tonight, Tam, I —'

'No, of course you don't. I wouldn't expect you to. Do you need company? Should I come over?'

'Oh, Tam…that's so sweet of you but I think I'd rather be alone. I may go over and cry on Kerr's shoulder for five minutes but, really, I'm not in the mood for company.'

'Sure. I understand. We'll do it some other time.'

'You'll phone me?'

'Unquestionably. Later in the week.'

'Talk to you then.'

'Bye.'

Buchanan stood in the middle of the bathroom towelling himself dry and watching the last hopeful dregs of his evening go swirling down the plughole with his bath water. He wondered how he could reasonably blame Fizz for this fiasco but decided that in this particular case she had to be innocent of involvement. Even at her most reprehensible, shoving Nanny down the stairs was surely beyond her. The thought barely surfaced from his subconscious but it was enough to halt his towelling and jolt him onto a fresh line of thought: could Nanny's fall have been assisted? And if so, by whom?

He was wary about allowing such a suspicion to take root, largely because he had no evidence to suggest that foul play could have been involved. If Irene's body had been found it would have been a different matter since – as Fizz was forever pointing out to him – one suspicious death following upon another was a coincidence and coincidences hardly ever happened. Therefore, if one cared to assume that Irene had been done away with, that would throw an entirely different light on Nanny's alleged accident.

Vague uneasiness stayed with him while he finished dressing. For a while the pangs of hunger diverted him into a search for sustenance but, when a survey of the refrigerator and his meagre food store revealed nothing more appetising than tinned tomato soup and a somewhat dehydrated lump of cheddar cheese, his misgivings became convictions. At the very least, Fizz ought to be informed of this development. Quite apart from anything else, she could easily decide to pay a return visit to Abbeyfield on her own instead of waiting till Wednesday, when they had arranged to go together, and he didn't want her running that risk without being aware of what she might be getting into. If people were being offed wholesale around that neck of the woods they were into a whole new ball game.

Besides, Fizz could – and did – cook.

'What do you want?' she said when she heard his voice on her entry phone. She didn't like it when people dropped by uninvited. That didn't deter her in the least from turning up on his doorstep at all hours of the day and night but she refused to see the inequity in that, alleging that he liked visitors while she did not. Which was rubbish on both counts.

'Let me in and I'll tell you.'

She muttered something incoherent and probably rude and he heard the lock being sprung. As he climbed the hundred steps to her high roost the smell of something spicy and appetising came to meet him, drifting down from her open door. He found her at the working surface in the kitchen/living room beating the hell out of something in a pot with a potato masher.

'I seem to have called at a bad time,' he said politely and she answered him with a look that encompassed the simmering pots, the table ready set for one, and her own less than formal attire which appeared to be one of those Egyptian *djallabas* that several people he knew had brought back – together with an apparently unavoidable case of gastroenteritis – from Nile cruises.

'Not ideal. What's up?'

He edged forward to see what she was mashing and she elbowed him away.

'State your business, Buchanan, and get on your bike. This isn't a soup kitchen.'

'Looks to me like you've made too much for one.'

She clashed eyes with him and then seemed to relent, probably reminded that he had fed her on a regular basis all the time she was at university.

'Get out of my way and I'll think about it.'

He went and stood at the window looking out across the rooftops of the Old Town to the Firth of Forth and the hills of Fife beyond. The two room flat held little in the way of creature comforts but it had one of the best views in the city.

'Eddie phoned me earlier,' he said.

She turned to look at him. 'With new information?'

'Nanny died today. Apparently she fell down the servants' staircase at Abbeyfield House.'

'Fell?' she said right away. 'Or was pushed?'

'Let's not start leaping to conclusions.'

'It quacks like a duck, Buchanan.'

'That doesn't always mean it is a duck. Maybe we just have nasty suspicious minds.'

'Well, if we have, it's never done us any harm in the past.' She leaned a hip against the edge of the counter top and thought about it for a minute. 'Poor old Nanny. I hope it was over before she knew what was happening.'

Buchanan nodded. 'She may have taken a dizzy turn or even blacked out before she fell.'

'Sure,' said Fizz but he could tell she was only pretending to contemplate that possibility. 'She could have been just unlucky that it happened when she was right where a fall would prove fatal. Alternatively, somebody could have wanted her silenced. What possible danger could she be to anybody?'

'Depends what she knew, what she might start talking about. It could even turn out that someone saw you talking to her yesterday and started to worry about what she might tell you. Are you sure you told me everything she said?'

Fizz didn't answer straight away but returned to hammering whatever was in the pot. The kettle boiled and switched itself off with a click and she transferred its contents to a saucepan and threw in bundles of tagliatelli. 'What we should be asking ourselves is: who knew she was talking to me in the first place?'

'But, it was a spur of the moment thing, wasn't it? You didn't mention to anyone that you wanted to chat to her, did you?'

'No, but some of the volunteers may have seen us together. And the events manageress.' Fizz put more cutlery on the table and gestured to him to take his place. 'Caitlin McCormick. I more or less admitted to her that I'd been picking Nanny's brains but I have to say she didn't look too worried about it. More or less told me I was wasting my time. There was a guide talking to some punters in the kitchen as we passed through – and, of course, anyone could have spotted me going into the staff quarters with Nanny, either from the garden or from the house itself.'

Buchanan thought back. 'You didn't hang around much. A

couple of minutes maybe, then you went inside.'

'So if someone did see us talking there's a chance you might have noticed that person as you left. Remember anyone?'

Buchanan put his elbows on the table and cupped his hands over his eyes as an aid to concentration. There had been people about, certainly, but none he'd recognised as estate workers. When he looked up there was a plate of golden soup in front of him. A breadboard holding a knife and half a loaf clattered down beside it.

'Sorry, no croutons,' Fizz said.

'Half a loaf is better than no bread.'

'Only when there's no pudding. And there isn't, so dig in.'

The soup was lentil flavoured with ham and had the constituency of porridge with a slush of mashed carrots floating around in it but it was thick and filling and went well with the wholemeal bread. Buchanan's mother would have liquidised it but Fizz was too mean to buy a liquidiser. Or maybe she was still resisting spending money on anything that couldn't be thrown into a backpack at a moment's notice should she decide to resume her nomadic life again.

He let his eyes drift deviously around the room but could see little sign that she was putting down roots. He knew what the partnership was paying her these days and, although it wasn't a fortune, she could have afforded a little more luxury: a better quality carpet, maybe some nice curtains or a couple of comfortable armchairs. But as far as he could see she was still using the few sticks of utilitarian furniture her landlord had provided and had added nothing of her own apart from some photographs of her grandparents and the farm at Am Bealach, which were propped unframed on the mantlepiece. Either she was keeping her exits clear or the frugality she'd practiced for the last decade or so had become ingrained.

She ate with her usual speed and concentration for a

minute and then paused to cut herself a slice of bread and said, 'Supposing Nanny was removed because she knew something, who would be the most likely people for her to know something about?'

Buchanan considered that briefly. 'The Fergussons.'

'That's what I thought.' Fizz looked pleased, which surprised Buchanan not at all. If she had anyone from the upper classes on her list of suspects all the others were rated as also-rans. She explained this as a logical progression from the assumption that he who had the most to lose proved invariably to be the culprit and upper-class people usually had the most to lose in terms of both money and reputation. Events had proved her wrong on numerous occasions without denting this superstition in the least.

'Lady Marjory's twice Nanny's size,' Fizz elaborated. 'She could have picked Nanny up and chucked her down the stairs without breaking sweat. And Sir Douglas? I wouldn't put anything past him. He's as nutty as a fruitcake.'

'He's not nutty,' Buchanan said, in the interest of fairness. 'He's just a little...unique. And I don't see the need to look for someone particularly strong to cast as Nanny's alleged killer. Practically anyone could have dislodged her from the top step.' He almost added, "even you" but managed to bite off the words in time, adding to cover his stutter, 'She probably didn't weigh more than ninety or a hundred pounds.'

'We'll see.' Fizz gave him a sharp look, probably reading his mind, but couldn't accuse him of anything without evidence. 'I'll be interested to find out what the forensic people have to say.'

Buchanan foresaw what was coming and tried to deflect her. 'Is there more of this soup?'

'Not for you, Buchanan. I'm feeding you: I'm not fattening you up.' She went back to the cooker and drained the tagliatelli. 'So you'll have to phone Ian Fleming and find out what the forensic report says. Is he speaking to us these days?'

'He's not speaking to you, Fizz. He's never going to be speaking to you again if he can help it, and I can't blame him. He thinks you're insane.'

'He's such a wimp. He wouldn't be a DCI if it weren't for our help in more than one of his cases.'

Buchanan watched her ladling sauce over the pasta and decided not to cite past misdeeds in case her reaction was reflected in the size of his helping. She didn't need him to tell her that her methods were not DCI Fleming's methods and if she'd given the boys in blue a valuable clue now and then she had also come – more than once – rather too close to getting that particular boy in blue drummed out of the force altogether. The days of his willing co-operation were now unarguably in the past but Buchanan knew that wouldn't stop Fizz from nagging at him till he broke down and phoned the guy for information.

Chapter Ten

There was no way Fizz was going to wait till Wednesday before returning to Abbeyfield. She had expected, when she made that arrangement with Buchanan, that it might take her a couple of days to follow up the few leads she'd gleaned over the weekend, but by Tuesday afternoon she'd already done as much of that as she could.

Not that she'd made much progress, but at least she'd managed to determine, by telephone, that there was no organised activity available along the 41a bus route from Dunfermline to Kilmartin: no car boot sales, no art galleries, no practitioners of complimentary medicine, nothing that could conceivably have drawn Irene there on a regular basis. According to the postman she managed to locate, the whole route of the 41a was sparsely populated: farmland and spruce plantations interspersed by small villages of one or two hundred souls or less, which meant that Irene had probably been visiting someone at his or her home. One could draw disturbing conclusions from that, if one had a mind to do so, but Fizz was unwilling to view Irene as a philanderer, at least till she had more evidence to back up the allegation.

She'd also managed to check up on the market garden formerly owned by the Curzons. It turned out to have been, in their time as well as at present, a nice little earner and it had sold, according to the solicitor who had brokered the deal and who was a crony of Fizz's, for well over the expected price. Whether that fact had any place in the jigsaw of Irene's disappearance Fizz could not guess but she logged it in her notes along with a raft of similar extraneous and probably useless pieces of information and hoped for the best.

Now she was at a standstill, downcast and worried by the implications of Nanny's sudden death and irked by the possibility – fast fading but still viable – that Irene could be alive and in trouble. Obviously, every day that passed could turn out to be of vital importance so she was itching to get back to Abbeyfield and talk to some more people – and to some people some more. Caitlin, for one, would merit a second visit, as would the Curzons, but even the part-time staff were worth spending time on if no better source of information could be found.

Buchanan, who had probably envisaged putting in some work on his golf handicap, balked at the idea of going back so soon, claiming that (a) he had work to do on Larry's impending cases, (b) they had no specific lines of questioning to pursue and (c) their time would be better spent on mulling over the information they had already gleaned. Fortunately, it took less than five minutes to disabuse him of all these assumptions, or at least to beat down his objections, so they were on their way by six-thirty.

Fizz was scarcely at her most effervescent, being weighed down by an incipient depression and even an occasional qualm of conscience. Until the news of Nanny's sudden demise had reached her last night she'd been convinced that everything would work out all right in the end: now she wasn't so sure. Looked at in isolation Nanny's mishap would have raised no eyebrows. Old ladies fell down stairs on practically a daily basis, or so one was led to believe, so why not Nanny? But when seen against the background of Irene's disappearance and the theft of the Rubens the accident took on a much more ambiguous light. And if somebody around Abbeyfield was the murdering kind, the chances of finding Irene alive didn't look quite so rosy.

What really niggled her was the thought that, the first time Kerr had tried to enlist her help, she had turned him down. Maybe Irene had been alive at that point. Maybe, if she had just listened a little more closely to what Kerr was telling her, read between the lines, been less dogmatic about not interfering in something that seemed to be none of her business —

'You're very quiet tonight,' Buchanan commented, break-ing her train of concentration. 'What are you thinking about?'

'Nanny,' Fizz told him, settling for half the truth. She focused on the scenery around her and discovered that they were only a couple of miles from Abbeyfield.

He stretched out a hand to flip down his eyeshade against the low rays of the sun. 'What about her?'

'Just that her murder – and I'm damn sure it was murder whatever the autopsy comes up with – makes me wonder if we really have much chance of finding Irene alive.' She glanced at him. 'But you never believed we would do that anyway, did you?'

'I don't know about that,' he said, looking defensive. 'Sometimes I did, sometimes I didn't but, either way, it's just a gut feeling. It's far too early to start making assumptions, even if Nanny's death does…well…concentrate the mind a little. There are plenty of implications to be drawn from that inci-dent without rushing to the conclusion that one *possibly* suspi-cious death points to another. We could be trying to make a mountain out of a molehill.' He tapped his fingers on the driv-ing wheel for a moment and then added, with a certain hesita-tion, 'I reckon, if Kerr were to come to me, even now, with the story he told you, I'd do precisely what you did: tell him to go away and work out his personal problems for himself.'

Fizz gave him a hard look. There were times when she could almost feel him poking around inside her head, ransack-ing her private thoughts like a looter. The idea that he knew when she was depressed and worried was bad enough, that he knew *precisely* what was getting to her was worse, but what was really scarey was that he actually cared enough to try and comfort her. That was a whole new experience for her and it felt like the worst invasion of all.

Grampa cared about her, of course, in his own way. She was pretty sure about that although she couldn't remember ever seeing him show it. In Grampa's lexicon, caring – or at least *showing* you cared – encouraged weakness in both the donor and the recipient and his sole aim in raising his two orphaned grandchildren had been to make them strong, rational and self-sufficient. If you had a stick to lean on, according to his doctrine, someone could kick it away. Stand on your own feet. Accept pity from no one, least of all yourself. Life's tough for everybody so there's no point in bleating about it. Shut up and get on with the ironing.

In fact, she thought, she hadn't actually found life all that tough but, of course, that could be due to Grampa's schooling. When you didn't expect too much you were rarely disappointed and when disaster struck, as it had once or twice, you knew deep down that it wasn't really the end of the world. Grampa could, perhaps, be said to have been motivated too much by the fear that, at sixty-four, he was unlikely to see his two pre-school charges through to maturity, but as far as Fizz was concerned, he hadn't gone too far wrong with the training he'd given her brother and herself. She'd never yet been faced with a situation she couldn't handle on her own, never needed a shoulder to cry on, never been tempted to part with her free-dom in exchange for emotional support. Let down your guard for any length of time and you could go soft. All the mental muscles you'd built up over thirty years would start to atrophy and you'd find yourself dependent on some fallible chimera, unable to function on your own and ripe for betrayal.

'You're not my mother, Buchanan,' she said crisply, bring-ing a certain rosiness to his cheekbones, 'so don't start trying to shield me from every wind that blows. I don't need you to tell me whether I made the right decision about —'

'All right, all right! I was just trying to —'

'Well, sodding don't, okay? When I need you to dandle me on your knee I'll tell you. Or slit my wrists.'

'Fine.'

It was impossible to have a decent fight with the bastard. He couldn't even glower effectively for any length of time, just wiped all expression from his face, did a few minutes deep breathing and then started talking about something else like a perfect gentleman: a response guaranteed to make a girl feel like a dyed-in-the-wool bitch.

'Are you planning to share your suspicions about Nanny's accident with Kerr?' he asked as they turned into the B road that led to Abbeyfield.

'You think I shouldn't?'

He moved a shoulder in a token shrug but said nothing, inviting her to think about it.

'I suppose there's not much point in putting thoughts in his head that aren't already there,' she said. 'Is that what you mean?'

'God knows he's worried enough. Or seems to be.'

Before she could respond to that remark Fizz's attention was caught by a police car heading towards them. It wasn't making with the siren or flashing light but even the sight of it, coming at them from the direction of Abbeyfield, was not a little disquieting. Both of them craned to see if there were a handcuffed passenger in the back but it appeared that whatever business the constabulary had been attending to at the estate had been of a more routine nature. When last heard of, Edinburgh's finest had not been taking such an interest in the case as to involve a lot of overtime but it was at least possible that they were regarding Nanny's death as suspicious.

She said as much to Buchanan but he refused to be drawn into a discussion into the pros and cons of that eventuality and it was only when they reached the stable yard that they received any confirmation that there had, indeed been a development – though not one either of them could have predicted.

There was a small crowd just outside Eddie's cottage consisting of Grace, Victor and Bonzo Curzon, Kerr, Lady

Marjory, and a tanned woman wearing dirty jeans and gardening gloves and carrying a lawn rake. All of them surged across
the yard towards the car as Buchanan slowed to a halt, Lady
Marjory leading by a short head.

'What d'you think, my dear people? We've just had word of
Irene!'

Several other voices joined in, all of them talking at once,
and Fizz could grasp only the bare fact that someone had contacted someone in America. She swung open the car door, cutting a swathe through the throng, and got out.

'Hang on. Could we just scroll back a bit here. Who heard
from her and how?'

There was a confusion of replies, some people concentrating on the who part of the question and others on the how.
They were all over-excited except a sullen-faced Kerr who
seemed in two minds whether to be ecstatic or depressed.

Buchanan got out and came round to Fizz's side. 'Someone
has heard from Irene?' he said and held up a restraining hand
as Grace tried to speak over Lady Marjory.

'The police have just left,' her ladyship was saying, Grace's
screech no real match for her booming delivery. '*Such* an afternoon we've had! Douglas is totally exhausted with all the
excitement, poor dear.'

'What happened?' Fizz asked tersely.

'I told you, my dear. Didn't you catch it? Douglas received
a phone-call this afternoon from Theo Vassileiou, the
American art collector who was interested in buying the
Rubens. Apparently, someone had just contacted Mr
Vassileiou, by telephone, offering to sell him the Rubens at a
considerably reduced price.'

Fizz looked around the circle of faces and they all nodded
in confirmation, with the exception of Bonzo who, although
clearly ready to draw blood if the opportunity arose, appeared
for the moment content to maintain his observer status. She

said, 'You mean, the call appeared to be from Irene?'

'Not *from* Irene, no – it was a man who spoke to Mr Vassileiou – but Douglas informed the police right away and they've now established exactly what was said. I'm afraid it does lead one to the conclusion that dear Irene was, in some way, implicated.' Lady Marjory's heavy face was puce with excitement, leading Fizz to the conclusion that she should be looking after her heart a bit better.

Buchanan glanced uncomfortably at Kerr and then back to her ladyship. 'Is that what the police are thinking?'

'I'm afraid so. I'm afraid there's no other explanation. You see, Mr Vassileiou was given details about the painting that only Irene knew about – outside the family, that is. A very small imperfection that didn't really affect it's value but —'

'That's the point,' Grace burst in eagerly. 'Vassileiou didn't believe that the thieves really had the Rubens, you see, but the caller had proof. He told Mr Vassileiou to ask Sir Douglas if the picture had ever been repaired – which it had, of course, in an area hidden by the frame. He knew the exact spot, which he couldn't have unless Irene had told him. Didn't I tell you right at the beginning that she was —'

'You don't know that!' Kerr said, in a voice that was hoarse with anger. 'They can't prove it was Irene, nobody can. She could have mentioned the damage to anyone. Maybe she told Vassileiou herself – weeks ago – because she felt he should know about the damage before he bought the picture. Maybe he's lying about receiving the phone-call. It could have been he himself who arranged for the theft in the first place.'

Victor Curzon sent a fulminating glare at his wife, who shrugged and fed Bonzo a sweetie. Then he stepped round Fizz to get to Kerr and put an arm around his shoulders, gripping him hard. 'I don't believe Irene had anything to do with this business, Kerr,' he said, trying perhaps a little too hard to sound convincing, 'but, even if she did, even if she helped the thieves in some way, at least this could prove that she's alive, so it's not all bad.'

'Absolutely, Kerr,' said Lady Marjory, moving up on his other side. 'You must try not to let this dreadful business drag you down, y'know. Chin up and all that, y'know? *Nil desperandum.* The police will get to the bottom of it, you can be sure of that. It'll all work out in the end.'

If Kerr appreciated that final assurance he managed to hide it well. He shrugged off Victor's arm and opened his mouth to make a remark to her ladyship that was so patently something he would regret that Fizz had to forestall him with the first thing that came to mind.

'I think a drink's called for.'

There was a moment while they all adjusted to this change of tack and then the tanned woman spoke for the first time. 'You're right. We're all a bit upset. I have a bottle of cava if that would fit the bill.'

'Sounds good to me.' Fizz warmed to her instantly. She seemed the sort of quiet but sensible person that one could get along with. She stuck out her hand. 'I don't think we've met. Fizz Fitzpatrick. You must be Eddie's wife.'

She looked surprised and flicked a sideways glance at Buchanan as she answered, 'Actually, no. I'm Eddie.'

Fizz felt the smile slipping off her face but caught it in time. 'Really?' she said, thinking, you wily bastard Buchanan. She took care not to glance in his direction as she said, 'Nobody thought to mention – in my hearing at least – that the head gardener was a woman.'

'Happens all the time,' Eddie said, stripping off her gardening gloves. She propped her lawn rake against the hedge and led the way through her garden gate while the others debated whether to accept the invitation or not. 'It's a nuisance of course but – honestly, you wouldn't expect anyone to go through life with a name like Edwina, would you? And, actually, I've been asked to a lot more job interviews as Eddie than I'd have been if I'd used my own name. Female horticulturists don't rise to the top, these days, without using their heads.'

Behind them Fizz could hear Kerr introducing Buchanan to Grace and Victor but they quickly broke away from the group and followed on into the cottage. Inside, it was cool and dim, scented with the spicy smell from the pots of pelargoniums on the two window sills. The living room was probably exactly the same size as Kerr's but it looked bigger because there was less clutter. Apart from a couple of glass-fronted bookcases and a neat array of audio equipment there was only a table and four chairs plus a single armchair by the fireplace, piled with cushions. A bachelor-pad, Fizz surmised, geared to the needs of a single busy and very organised person.

Kerr didn't sit down but stood in front of the window looking out at the Curzons and Lady Marjory who were preparing to go their separate ways. He was obviously pretty sicked off by the new evidence against Irene, and Fizz couldn't really blame him. She was pretty sicked off herself even though, whatever she'd forced herself to believe, she'd actually been half expecting something like this since day one. She was still – just about – able to hang on to the theory that Irene had been under some sort of compulsion to do what she appeared to have done but she could quite see that even that thought would be little comfort to Kerr.

'I'm never going to believe what they're saying about Irene,' he said. 'I know her better than anybody and nobody's going to make me believe she did this thing.'

'Nobody's saying she did it apart from silly old Grace,' Eddie said lightly, handing Buchanan the bottle of cava and a bottle opener, 'and nobody listens to her nonsense. Everyone else is at least keeping an open mind on the matter. I've not the slightest doubt that if the person who contacted the art collector, whoever that was, really has the painting they'll phone him again and the police will be there waiting to trace the call.'

'If Vassileiou didn't slam the door on the negotiations, the vendors will certainly be getting back to him,' Buchanan said. He eased the cork out of the bottle with his thumbs and handed it back to Eddie, barely glancing at her as he did so. 'But not necessarily by telephone, of course. I suppose they could email him and set up a meeting.'

Eddie handed out the drinks, even Buchanan accepting a half glass of bubbly which he rarely did when he was planning to drive. 'If they did that, surely Vassileiou would tell the police and they'd be able to trace the sender?'

'There are ways around that,' Buchanan said.

'I'd simply send it though an Internet café.' Kerr sank half his glassful in two gulps and screwed up his face as though he'd had a mouthful of vinegar. 'In which case the police would spend days watching the place in case someone tried to send another message from there. But that's not likely to happen, is it? This whole business – it's a complete waste of police time. It's not going to lead us to Irene and, when you get right down to the nitty-gritty, the police don't give a damn about finding her anyway; all they care about is getting the Rubens back. If it turns out – which it bloody well will – that the thieves are some professional syndicate, or whatever, they won't waste another day on Irene's case, mark my words. They'll go after the thieves all right but Irene's name will be just one item on a long list of unsolved cases.'

'Look,' Fizz said impatiently. 'None of us want to believe that Irene did this thing but even if she did do it —'

'She didn't!'

'Kerr, listen to me, will you? You have to face the possibility that she may have been forced to do something she didn't want to do —'

'She'd never have stolen from Sir Douglas. Never!'

Fizz knew without looking at him that Buchanan was frowning at her but she was totally pissed off by Kerr's dogmatic refusal to look at the facts and she wasn't going to be gagged. She might also, if the truth were told, have been still smarting at Buchanan's deviousness on the subject of Eddie's gender.

'That attitude is simply non-productive,' she told Kerr flatly. 'You have to accept that, for whatever reason, Irene appears at the moment to have done what she —'

A sound halfway between a growl and a roar escaped Kerr and his face flushed ruby red. Whipping open the door with such force that it banged back against the wall, he marched out of the house, leaving behind him a tense, embarrassed silence.

Fizz looked at the two pairs of accusing eyes directed at her face. 'Oops.'

Buchanan apparently couldn't bring himself to respond but Eddie stood up to get the bottle of cava and topped up Fizz's glass. 'He's been wound up like a spring for two weeks. It had to happen sooner or later.'

'You should go after him, Fizz,' Buchanan said.

'No way. I don't want a punch in the face.'

'Well, I will, then. He shouldn't be left in that state.'

He gave Fizz a long look as though hoping she would change her mind and do the decent thing but she stared him out. She'd had enough of Kerr's hysterics for one day and besides, there was no way she was going to leave Buchanan alone with Eddie. Not till she'd poured a little napalm on their budding relationship.

Eddie watched him go with a strange expression in her eyes and then turned to Fizz. 'I'm afraid we're all a little on edge these days. It's been a tough couple of weeks what with the business of Irene's disappearance and the theft of the painting and then Nanny's death yesterday. They say bad luck comes in threes and it sure did this time. Let's hope there's no more unpleasantness in store.'

Fizz nodded, glad of a change of subject. 'Looks like Nanny was a big favourite with everyone around the estate.'

'She was a darling old soul. His lordship adored her, of course.'

'Well he would, I suppose. People get very fond of their nanny's, don't they?'

'So they say, but of course Nanny wasn't ever the official nanny: that was only a courtesy title they gave her later – in lieu of a decent wage, I suspect. In practice she was never anything but a nursery maid.'

Eddie smiled at Fizz's suddenly inquisitive face and reached for the bottle again. Say what you like about the woman, she had her priorities right.

'No. Sally Barton, who was the real nanny to the family, died just after Lady Agnes went off to boarding school. That was, like, thirty-odd years ago and the other two were already into their teens at that point so she was never replaced. The Nanny we knew was promoted to the title and kept on in a variety of roles but basically just to look after the youngsters' needs when they were home for the holidays. I don't think she ever did much more than sort their laundry and see they brushed their teeth but they were fond of her – the younger generation at least – so they never quite got around to paying her off.'

Fizz was curious enough to ask, 'You don't think her death could be connected in some way with the other business?'

Eddie met her look without blinking. 'I wondered if you'd consider that,' she said and shrugged. 'It's a question that did occur to me, I must admit, but it seems too far fetched to take seriously. The others would laugh at me, I'm sure, because there's no reason in the world to even consider such a thing but...it's silly but...well, it did seem something of a coincidence. What do you think? Should we be concerned?'

'Your guess is as good as mine. Probably better than mine.'

'But you have experience of criminal matters, haven't you? Kerr said that you and Tam had been involved in a lot of criminal cases.'

'Not a lot,' Fizz said. 'One or two.'

Eddie leaned an elbow on the table and propped her chin on her hand. 'You've worked together a long time?'

Fizz had been waiting for the interrogation to start and had already worked out how to handle it. It was no big deal. Buchanan quite often believed himself to be enamoured of quite unsuitable women but that was purely because he wasn't comfortable with the idea of himself as a sexual predator. In his own mind, he only slept with women he loved, or at the very least, women he could envisage loving if things worked out right. However, in practice this was not much of a problem because he could convince himself quite easily that he was in love with practically any woman who gave him the come-on. That, of course, was precisely how so many men found themselves married to the wrong woman but Buchanan was fortunate indeed in that he had Fizz to look after him. There had been several wrong women in recent years but, so far, she had been able to see to it that such dangerous liaisons never progressed beyond the preliminaries.

This time, however, something was different: something she could not quite put her finger on. Putting the skids under Eddie just didn't feel right. Why was that? Was it because, in spite of herself, she really liked the woman? Or was it – God forbid! – that Buchanan's righteousness, his unflagging refusal to stoop to underhand dealing of any form had somehow infiltrated her own psyche?

The thought totally undermined her focus and she found herself saying weakly, 'Yes, we go back a long way, Tam and I. He gave me a job way back before I'd even started at university and kept me going with part-time work all the time I was a student. Luckily, he started his pupillage just after I qualified so he left a vacancy in his practice at precisely the time I was ready to start my traineeship.'

'But he still stays in contact with the practice?'

'Not officially, no, but he's always around when I need advice.'

'So...' Eddie probed delicately, 'It's a business relationship?'

It would have been so easy to hint at something deeper, more consequential between them. Even to claim close friendship wouldn't have been so very far from the truth but something held her tongue. Sod you, Buchanan, she found herself thinking, if she's what you want, have her and be damned.

'Oh, purely business.' She finished her drink and had it replenished with a generosity that made her suspect Eddie was trying to loosen her tongue. There wasn't enough left in the bottle to achieve that but full marks to her for trying.

Chapter Eleven

Buchanan was halfway across the yard before Kerr reached his doorway.

'Hang on a minute, Kerr,' he called and hurried to catch up before the door was slammed in his face. For a couple of seconds it looked as if that was what was going to happen but, after a momentary hesitation Kerr turned on the doorstep and waited for him to walk up the path.

'What is it?'

'I just wanted to say...' Buchanan hesitated. What did he want to say? 'I don't know, I suppose I just wanted you to know that I'm listening to you. Fizz...well, you know what she's like...sometimes she gets the bit between her teeth and...I wouldn't say it's always a bad thing but...but anyway, when she slows down and thinks for a minute or two she'll realise there's more ways than one of looking at things. She's totally committed to getting to the bottom of this business – we both are – and one thing we've learned is to keep an open mind. Between us, I promise you, we'll be following up every lead we can get our hands on.'

Kerr's grim expression slackened only a fraction but he nodded as though he accepted the half-apology. He turned away to enter his cottage but then muttered almost unwillingly, 'I was looking for the photo of Irene I said I'd sort out. Come in and I'll get it for you.'

Buchanan was in no hurry for the photograph but he did feel that Kerr was in need of company so he followed him into the lounge. It was now seriously untidy: the table littered with dirty crockery, junk mail and odds and ends of food, the floor in front of the writing desk was littered with snapshots, and discarded clothing was draped over every chair. Buchanan wasn't all that houseproud himself but he could recognise a pigsty when he saw one. If Irene were to walk in at this moment Kerr was in big trouble.

Kerr scooped a couple of jackets off the back of a chair and threw them on the floor. 'Sit yourself down. I think it's in the pocket of my other jeans. Won't be a minute.'

He headed for the bedroom leaving Buchanan's attention irresistibly drawn to the drift of photographs about his feet. There must have been a couple of hundred of them at the very least, holiday snaps, graduation portraits, dog-eared black-and-white mementoes of past generations. He picked up a three-quarters shot of Kerr with a brace of wood pigeon in one hand and a sporting rifle in the other and was looking at it when the subject came back into the room.

'I just spotted this in the pile,' Buchanan excused himself. 'I hope you don't mind.'

'Feel free. There's not much of interest in that lot, in fact most of them should've been chucked out long ago. It's Irene who hangs on to them.' He sat down on top of the junk on the chair opposite and held out a small studio print in a card-board frame. 'How's this? She had it taken to send to her father in South Africa a couple of years ago.'

Buchanan looked at the now familiar face, matching it to the likeness he'd seen earlier. It was pale and freckled, square jawed and pointy nosed, surrounded by waist length brown hair that looked thick and healthy, but if it wasn't a conventionally pretty face it was enormously attractive. This photograph showed what the other had failed to capture: the perkiness of the smile and what appeared to be genuine affection in the eyes. It was the sort of face you'd smile at in the street, knowing it would smile back with a warmth that would brighten your day. You could tell why she was so popular with her colleagues.

'There are more recent ones somewhere,' Kerr said, stirring the litter of prints with one ineffectual finger. 'Most of them are of me, you'll notice, because it's Irene who's the photographer, but there ought to be some of her among the ones we took up in Sutherland last autumn.'

A group shot slid into view: a bunch of bizarre characters with multicoloured hair and clothes that looked as if they'd been rescued from a theatrical garbage bin after a pantomime. Buchanan leaned forward and picked it up.

'Art school,' Kerr said, looking over his shoulder. 'God, how young they look. And nutty. I guess they were all trying to show how creative they were, catch the tutor's eye. That's Irene there, with the streaked hair and eyeliner.'

'And Fizz,' Buchanan pointed out, his attention sharpened.

She looked exactly as she did today except for her hair. Alone in the group, she was dressed unpretentiously in jeans and T-shirt, but to Buchanan's eyes at least, she presented more of a presence than any of the others. How could some-one with a baby face and golden ringlets look like the only adult in a bunch of immature piss-artists?

'Right,' Kerr nodded. 'She never went in for all that stuff. Never gave a hoot in hell what anyone thought of her but, as far as I'm concerned anyway, she was the most creative one of the whole bunch. Not the best draughtsman – Irene was way out in front in that line – but she knew what she wanted to say and she could put it across. I suppose you've seen some of her stuff?'

Buchanan shook his head. He'd seen the doodles with which Fizz – often unconsciously – covered any bare scrap of paper that happened to be lying around the office but the idea of her ever producing something meaningful was very differ-ent from the picture he had of her.

Kerr stood up. 'Come and take a look at this.'

They went through to the bedroom which was only mar-ginally less untidy than the other room. The floor beside the unmade bed was littered with magazines and coffee mugs, there were oily dungarees hanging from the handle of the wardrobe and a wispy tartan garment draped across the bed light. To Buchanan it looked like a house fire awaiting a match.

Above the bed was a biggish oil painting and at first glance it seemed to Buchanan, his spirit sinking, to be one of those formless, meaningless, soulless pieces of modern art which he so disliked. But before he could abandon it in disgust the blotches of colour suddenly coalesced into roofs and walls, shiny wet pavements and the gleam of distant water. It was unmistakably Edinburgh: a dark, forbidding and faintly spooky Edinburgh where the tenement walls leaned at threatening angles and faces hovered, ghoul-like in the doorways. What had deceived the eye at first was a tracery of transparent colour interspersed with a network of dark lines which overlaid the whole scene, mellowing it to some extent and lending a faint glow, even in the darkest areas of paint.

'God…' Buchanan heard his voice crack with some unidentifiable emotion as he realised that the colours formed a design he had seen before. 'When did she do this?'

'Oh, way back,' Kerr said carelessly, making a token attempt to tidy up some rubbish. 'It used to hang in the flat she and Irene were in when I met them. It must have been one of the first things she did at art school, but it always spoke to me somehow. I came from the sticks, like Fizz did, and I suppose this was the way Edinburgh looked to me when I first saw it – you know, big and scarey. I swopped her my backpack for it when she left.'

'Right,' Buchanan nodded, mostly to himself, as a familiar, arrow-sharp pain stabbed him in the chest. He touched the rough surface of the painting with one forefinger, tracing the veined patchwork of colour that veiled the city. 'You know what this is?'

Kerr straightened to look closer. He had a pile of clothes and newspaper under one arm and a mug hung from each finger. 'No, I never asked. Is it something specific?'

Buchanan cleared the frog from his throat. 'It's the stained glass window in the front door of her Grampa's farm at Am Bealach. The house she was brought up in. She's saying something about the strength she gets from her memories of home. She's scared and lonely but she has that to fall back on – that lens, if you like, through which she can get a perspective on things.'

They stood and looked at it for a couple of minutes. Then Kerr said,

'I see what you mean. It's not what you'd expect of Fizz, is it?'

'No, it isn't,' Buchanan agreed. The face Fizz showed the world was diamond hard, insouciant, one hundred per cent impervious to every weakness known to man but there was a small vulnerable creature underneath that Buchanan glimpsed but rarely and, when he did, it really hit him where he lived.

'That's what I mean about Fizz's stuff,' Kerr said. He looked at Buchanan's face and smiled. 'This one really got to you, didn't it? Tell you what: if you find Irene for me I'll make you a present of it.'

'No, really, Kerr, that's not necessary.' Buchanan turned away, embarrassed. 'I wouldn't dream of —'

'Listen, I'd like you to have it. It should be appreciated… understood. And I want to show how grateful I am for all you're doing.'

'I couldn't possibly —'

'*Yoo-hoo!*'

Fizz's voice, sounding as if it came from right behind him, shocked him into silence. He beat Kerr to the door and managed to intercept Fizz on the doorstep, before she could have cause to suspect that her work – that she herself, in fact – was the subject of their discussion.

'Sorry to interrupt the boys' night in but we gotta go go go,' she said, and Buchanan could discern about her a faint air of satisfaction that filled him with foreboding. He had been barely ten minutes out of her company, surely the devil couldn't have found work for her willing hands in so short a time?

She caught a paper that was slipping from Kerr's load and replaced it under his arm with a solicitude that implied she had forgotten their spat. 'We have to see Caitlin before we go because I want the names of everyone who was in the "Save the Rubens" bunch. I know it's a long shot but it has to be checked.'

'Absolutely,' said Buchanan briskly, half suspecting she could tell by his face that he'd been feeling sorry for her again. 'She's in the gatehouse – right? – so we might as well take the car. Kerr, we'll be in touch right away if we have anything to report.'

'And I'll do the same. Thanks, both of you.'

'You managed to cool him down, anyway,' Fizz said as they pulled away. 'He doesn't half get himself into a tizzy about nothing sometimes.'

Sympathy had never been Fizz's long suit but this, to Buchanan's mind, took the biscuit. He decided not to comment but apparently his face gave him away.

'What?' said Fizz. 'You don't agree?'

'I just think the disappearance and possible – probable – death of the woman one loves can't really be described as nothing, that all. The guy must be hurting, Fizz, and he's been on the rack for nearly a fortnight. Okay, you're going to say this new information proves she's alive but if Kerr goes along with that assumption he's forced to accept that she's also a thief and he obviously can't do that. I think you have to cut him a little slack.'

'Well, maybe,' she said lightly, which was as close as she'd ever get to admitting she was wrong. 'I'm hanging on to the idea that there may be extraneous facts that could yet come to light or that there must have been a compelling reason for

Irene doing what she did but, I have to tell you, I'm steeling myself for the worst. Let's face it, how else do you explain the insider information on the phone-call?'

Buchanan had a vague, imperfectly formed theory about that at the back of his mind but there were facts to check before he was ready to share it with Fizz, facts that perhaps Caitlin could confirm. He said, 'Well, as Victor pointed out —'

'Tuh!' said Fizz, cutting off that line of discussion with contempt. 'Possible, but not really probable, admit it. Irene wasn't the sort to undermine the sale by telling the buyer that the picture had suffered damage in the past. Not if the value was unaffected, as Lady Marjory claimed. Nor would she have mentioned such a trivial fact to anyone else on the estate. Who'd have been interested? Nobody. Kerr's just snatching at straws.'

'We can't afford to accept Irene's involvement till we've eliminated all the other possibilities,' Buchanan insisted.

'Okay, sure, but what have we got? I mean, if Irene didn't assist in the theft – willingly or unwillingly – someone else took the Rubens and, since they knew about the damage, that means it was someone from the estate. So who do we have? In first place, my old favourites, the Fergussons. Coming up on the rails, Victor and Grace, the lovely Eddie, and Caitlin. Bonzo's in the clear for the moment.'

'If you're referring to Grace's dog,' said Buchanan, 'it's called Indie. I was introduced earlier. However, there's some-one you're omitting.'

'Uh-huh?'

'The person Irene was visiting behind Kerr's back.'

'Right,' Fizz acknowledged, looking suddenly sober. 'But there's no way we can pursue that lead without doing a door-to-door search, which would mean a helluva lot of doors and I'd have to be a lot more convinced that Irene was in trouble before I'd attempt that.'

'I don't know,' Buchanan said, pulling in to the small parking bay beside the gatehouse. 'I'm beginning to think we should make some attempt to trace the mysterious friend. Not by doing a door-to-door search – as you say, that would take weeks – but we could at least try talking to a few people in each village. There's just a chance that Irene could have been seen – she does look fairly distinctive with that long hair of hers – or we might uncover some unadvertised activity, a resident who could have something in common with Irene, maybe. Who knows? We've sat on the story of her trips for two days now and we can't keep it from Kerr for much longer, especially in view of current developments. Personally, I'm willing to gamble a morning in a quick recce if you are.'

Fizz had a hand on the door handle ready to get out but she turned and looked at him seriously. 'You'd take a morning off? You think it could be worthwhile?'

'I'll be working in the signet library tomorrow and, with Larry away, no one will be looking for me.' Buchanan shrugged. 'I won't be getting excited by the possibility of a breakthrough but I reckon it's something we have to do.'

She got out and he locked the car and followed her round to the door of the cottage.

'Okay,' she said, leaning on the bell. 'We can always give it a try.'

The door was opened by a short woman in a green silk housecoat carrying a long spliff and peering at them short-sightedly. 'Yes?' she said, and then, 'Fizz? Sorry I don't have my contact lenses in.'

'Can we come in and talk to you for a few minutes, Caitlin?' Fizz asked. 'This is Tam Buchanan, and there's a couple of things we want to ask you.'

'Well, actually...' She looked up at the sky for inspiration but couldn't think of an immediate excuse. 'All right, if it's that important.'

'We won't keep you long,' Buchanan told her, following her wobbling bottom into a small but comfortable lounge, 'but in the light of today's developments there are one or two points that need to be clarified.'

'You heard about the phone-call, did you?' She settled herself in the corner of a couch and leaned over to switch off the television set. 'Can't say it shook me rigid, exactly, but it did seem a bit of a turn up for the books. Just goes to show: you never really know the people you work with.'

'Did you have much interaction with Irene during the working day?' Buchanan asked.

'Not really. She liked to come down to the staff room for coffee – I suppose she found it boring up there in her studio all day by herself – so I saw her most days, but there was no cross-over in our daily routine.' She took a long toke of her spliff and offered it to Fizz who was closest to her.

'No thanks,' said she cheerfully. 'I prefer not to pollute the temple of my body with anything other than pure spirits and it's no use offering it to Buchanan. He's a well brought up, middle class Edinburgh boy and thinks such things are the work of the devil. What you could do for me, though, is dig out that list of people who contributed to the "Save the Rubens" fund.'

Caitlin sighed and clutched her housecoat closer around her generous and unsupported bosom. 'You're not still interested in that lot are you? I told you, they're all pillars of the establishment and London-based virtually to a man. You'd be wasting your time.'

'I know,' Fizz admitted. 'That's the trouble with this work. Ninety per cent of it is a waste of time, but it has to be done never the less.'

'It's probably over at the office,' Caitlin muttered, but hauled herself upright and shambled, barefoot, across to a desk in the window bay. 'I know I've seen it since I spoke to you but whether it was here or in the office...'

While they waited Fizz went over and stood beside her to look at the photocopied map of the estate pinned to the wall above the desk. 'What's this building down by the river?'

Caitlin spared a brief glance. 'A fisherman's rest. One of old Sir Graham's constructions. Well, you're lucky. Here's the list, and much good may it do you.'

She handed a sheet of typing paper to Fizz who scanned it briefly and passed it over to Buchanan. He recognised almost all of the names and saw immediately that there would be little to be gained by pursuing that line of inquiry any further. 'Were you actively involved with the sale of the picture?' he asked. 'In communication with Mr Vassileiou, for instance?'

She smiled with the beatific calm of the seriously spaced out. 'Sir Douglas discussed the sale with me a few times,' she said, 'but only after he'd set the wheels in motion, not before. It was Irene who found the picture among a batch of comparatively worthless canvasses and persuaded Sir Douglas to have it valued. It was Irene who arranged for it to be put on the open market and as far as I know, up till that point Sir Douglas had no idea that it was worth so much money.'

'He must have known how much it was insured for?' Buchanan asked.

Caitlin gave an inelegant snort. 'The silly old fart ballsed that up as well. If he doesn't get it back he'll be claiming the princely sum of forty thousand pounds. How's that for congenital stupidity?'

Buchanan didn't find that hard to believe, having dealt with many clients who had seriously underinsured their property, but it certainly knocked his little theory on the head. There wasn't much point in Sir Douglas stealing his own picture for the insurance money if he stood to gain only a small fraction of its real worth.

'But Irene can't have been happy to see it go out of the

country,' Fizz suggested.

'No way.' Caitlin waved her spliff, trailing a wisp of fragrant smoke across Fizz's nose. 'She hated the idea but by that point Sir Douglas had the bit between his teeth and – Irene being Irene – she just went along with his wishes like she always did.'

'She got on well with his lordship?' Fizz asked.

Caitlin smiled a slow pussy-cat smile and held out crossed fingers. 'The two of them were like that. But Irene was good at getting along with people. Even Lady Marjory thought the sun shone out of her left ear, and that's not just unusual, it's unique.'

'Not unique, surely?' Buchanan suggested. 'Lady Marjory speaks very appreciatively of you.'

That amused her. 'Lady Marjory,' she said, slurring the words lazily, 'is all sugar and spice on the surface but a bit of a cow when she thinks she can get away with it. She's like a jealous wife with Sir D, you know, and she can't stand to see him enjoying a conversation with another woman. Sick, wouldn't you say? But that's the aristocracy for you. Too much in-breeding, if you want my opinion.'

Buchanan considered mentioning that, if that was her opinion of the aristocracy she was in the wrong job but decided it was none of his business. Instead he said, 'Was she jealous of your association with Sir Douglas?'

Caitlin took a moment to answer, blinking slowly at his face as though she was missing her contact lenses. Then she said, 'My association with Sir Douglas?'

'You and he must have had many a long conversation in the course of your work. Did that bother her ladyship?'

She relaxed back against her cushions and gave herself another hit of marijuana. 'I wouldn't know,' she said, 'and frankly I couldn't care less. I'm out of this dump anyway as soon as I find something better. Another season here and I'll be as nutty as the rest of them.'

'Are they all nutty?' Fizz asked, with the smile of one who had no possible interest in the answer.

'You've met them: what do you think? Douglas thinks he's the Young Lochinvar, Marjory backs him up – and so, for that matter, did Nanny – Grace hates everybody without exception, Victor puts up with her where any sane man would put a bullet through her head. There's not one of them but should be in therapy.'

Buchanan noticed the one omission in this list but didn't like to point it out. Not so Fizz.

'And what about Eddie?'

'Eddie?' Caitlin's wandering gaze fell on Buchanan's sunglasses which he had laid down on the arm of his chair and became fixed on them in a contemplative reverie. They were nice sunglasses, purchased when he could afford such small luxuries, but they hardly merited the awed admiration they were clearly inspiring.

'Yes. Eddie,' said Fizz when they had waited some seconds for an answer and Caitlin lolled her head around to look at her.

'Unnh? Oh...Eddie. Well, what's a girl like her doing here? Degree in horticulture. Top dog for five years in the city parks department. Working for a fraction of what she's worth. That's not just nutty, it's insane.'

Buchanan found Fizz looking at him with a question in her eyes and was glad to be able to mime total surprise at this revelation. He looked at his watch.

'We've taken up enough of your time,' he told Caitlin and got to his feet, prompting Fizz to do the same. 'If there's anything we want to clarify with regard to the "Save the Rubens" fund, I imagine you'll be in the office tomorrow?'

She smiled at him dreamily. 'There won't be anything.'

'No,' said Buchanan, knowing it was the truth. 'I don't suppose there will.'

Fizz had spent every morning for the last month staring out of her office window wishing she were outside in the sunshine so, naturally, the first chance she got to escape for a few hours, it had to be raining.

Even so, she thought, as Buchanan drove her sedately across the Forth road bridge to Fife, it felt good to shrug off the pressures of "real" work, or at least to swap them for those she had voluntarily assumed. Her hopes of seeing a satisfactory conclusion to Irene's case were at an all time low but she could comfort herself with the thought that even if it ended in a jail sentence for her old chum the blame could scarcely be laid at her own door. She had made as much of an effort to be of help as could be expected of the most faithful friend. There was the small, conscience-stabbing matter of her refusal to respond to Kerr's first appeal for help but, if Irene was still alive and well and larging it on the Costa del Sol or wherever, the heat was off as far as that was concerned. There were, of course, still a few alternative possibilities to be checked out, more or less for the sake of auld lang syne, but this morning should take care of one of them and the others could be fitted in when time permitted.

'Have you decided on a plan of action?' she asked Buchanan.

'Nothing very creative, I'm afraid. I imagine the best bet would be to call in at the post office or maybe the police station in each village and see if we can get someone chatting about the local householders. That is, assuming any of the villages are big enough to possess either establishment. Failing that, the only thing we can do is to buttonhole a shopkeeper or one of the locals. We're looking for a needle in a haystack, I know that, but at least we can say we tried.'

'Nothing succeeds like trying,' Fizz said, quoting one of

Grampa's home grown maxim's. 'How long will it take us to get to the first bus stop?'

'It depends what the traffic's like in Dunfermline at this hour of the morning. Maybe ten or fifteen minutes after we clear the edge of town.' He took a hand off the steering wheel to pass her a road map. 'Actually, the villages are well spaced out. There must be at least a ten minute drive between each of them, which is good.'

'Why good?' Fizz asked, finding the right page.

'Apparently it was worth Irene's while – at least occasionally – to make the journey there and back in the space of an afternoon. If she'd been going to the end of the route she'd have barely arrived before it was time to catch the bus back.'

'That's a point. We should definitely put in most of our effort on the first couple of stops and, you never know, we might spot a 41a along the way. If we do I'll get on and quiz the driver. He might just remember Irene.'

She was feeling almost positive by the time they reached their first port of call, a straggle of unexceptional country properties that were grouped, on the map, under the title: Wellwood. No post office, no police station and only one shop, a general store manned by two blue-overalled ladies. Buchanan bought a bar of chocolate and chatted them up for a few minutes, there being no other customers awaiting their attention. They were both on the wrong side of fifty but evidently still had an eye for a pretty face and Buchanan soon had them eating out of his hand. Fizz stood back and left him to it as he said,

'Now I have a puzzle for you ladies. I'm looking for someone who lives around these parts but, the thing is, I don't exactly know who it is I'm looking for.'

'Ooooo!' they cried, camping it up like mad. 'You're in a bit of a pickle then, aren't you?'

'But I'll bet you know everyone in the village so it should

be no trouble at all for you to work it out.'

'Go on then, give us a clue.'

'Well, it could be a man or a woman I'm looking for.' He produced Irene's mug shot. 'All I know is that he or she used to be visited regularly by this nice young lady. Her name's Irene. She used to come, about once or twice a week, on the bus from Dunfermline and always went back the same day.'

'That's all the help you can give us? Oh dear, it's not much, is it? We never see who gets on and off the bus, do we, Ruthie? We're in here all day, see. Nice photo, but no. Doesn't ring a bell. Sorry.'

'This lady was an artist. Would that mean anything to you? Are any painting courses held in the vicinity? Anything at all that would interest a painter?'

They looked at each other, their faces blank. 'No. Nothing like that, son. There used to be a woman did pottery down at the old mill but she packed up and went back to England after her man went off with the district nurse.'

'Can you think of anything at all that would bring someone out from Dunfermline on a regular basis?'

'No. Really, son, there's nothing here you couldn't get in Dunfermline. Certainly nothing for artists.'

'There's that man who makes glass things out at Hillfoot,' said one of them to the other. 'He might know if there's anything on.'

'Where's Hillfoot?' Fizz asked. 'It's not on the map.'

'No it won't be on the map. It used to be a farm but there's someone making glass lampshades and stuff living there now. It's about a mile down the road – or you could take the short-cut down the wee lane across the road there and through the wood. Five minutes and you're there. He'll be the man to ask right enough. Mac-something his name is. He hasn't been there any length of time and he doesn't come in here much.'

That seemed to be about as much as they were likely to

come up with and it didn't sound all that exciting but there was nothing to be done but set off on foot, in the drizzling rain, down a dog-shit alley and across a sodden field towards a morose-looking stone building on the skyline. Buchanan had a golf umbrella but if he held it over his head it was too high to do Fizz much good so he was pretty wet by the time they got there, poor sod.

The barking of dogs greeted their approach but none arrived to hassle them as they splashed across a cobbled yard and banged on the door. There was a long silence before footsteps sounded from within and the door swung open to reveal one of the most gorgeous men Fizz had ever seen in the flesh. He was maybe a couple of inches over six feet, copper-brown hair, dark eyes, designer stubble, and a tiny silver hoop piercing one ear. He just stood there, in jeans and a tartan shirt over a white T-shirt, and Fizz could do nothing but stare in disbelief.

'Sorry to bother you,' Buchanan said, as if he hadn't noticed he was addressing a phenomenon, 'but we're trying to trace someone who might know an artist called Irene Lloyd. We wondered if you might know of any —'

'Irene? Sure, I know her. Is there a problem?'

The goggled at him.

'You know her?' Buchanan said.

'Sure. I haven't seen her for a week or so but, sure I know her. How can I help you?' He glanced from Buchanan to Fizz and back again. 'You'd better step in out of the rain.'

In response to a nudge from Buchanan, Fizz closed her mouth and stepped through the doorway into a big kitchen not unlike the one at Am Bealach except that this one was stone floored and cheerless while the other was the warm and comforting heart of her family home. The walls had once been painted white but they were now stained with mould and starred with holes where shelving and cupboards had been removed. The vast iron range that occupied a niche in the end wall was pitted with rust and the door that led to the rest of the apartments grated on the flags as they passed through it into a passageway lit only by the daylight coming through an open doorway. The room beyond, however, was warm – almost too warm.

It had once been two rooms, that much was obvious from the beam that ran across the high ceiling and from the faint trace of the old wall that still showed through the plaster, but it was now a hot-glass studio. At one end were the cooling ovens and a small kiln bracketed on one side by a rack of blowing tubes and on the other, by long shelves of blown glass artefacts in strong rainbow colours: transparent, opaque, iri-descent, matt; some of them perfect globes and others worked into fantastic shapes. A sturdy chair with high arms faced the kiln, flanked by piles of old newspapers and a wooden bucket full of water while, at the nearer end of the room, the space was taken up by a long workbench, a ceiling high cupboard and half a dozen or so large canvasses angled against the walls.

'Well, well,' said Buchanan, pausing on the threshold. 'They told us at the village shop that you worked with glass but I was thinking "stained glass" not something like this.' He wiped his rain-wet face with a folded hankie and then got out a business card and handed it across. 'This is my colleague, Ms Fitzpatrick. She and I are investigating the disappearance of Miss Lloyd and we wondered if you could help us.'

He narrowed his eyes on Buchanan's face, barely glancing at the card. 'Disappearance?'

'She's been missing for nearly a fortnight. The police are looking for her but Kerr asked Ms Fitzpatrick, who is an old friend of Irene's, to help.'

'Kerr? That's her partner, right?'

There was a short silence while both Fizz and Buchanan fell back and regrouped, then Fizz got her tongue working again and said,

'You didn't know her all that well, then?' He turned those big brown eyes on her and she near as dammit started giggling like the two old dears in the village shop. 'You see we only found you by sheer good luck. We don't know anything about you – even your name.'

'McVey. Graham McVey.' He walked down the room and collected the single chair which he placed for Fizz, saying as he did so, 'Sorry, I'm not organised for visitors yet. I've only been here since last Christmas and it's been, like, totally hideous, what with production deadlines plus all the refurbishment that's to be done, plus you name it, so I've had to concentrate on other priorities. However, the table's clean, Mr Buchanan, so – No? Well forgive me if I do. I've been hauling boxes since seven this morning and I could do with a rest.' He settled himself facing Buchanan and Fizz, fingered his silver earring, and regarded them both intently. 'So what's the story, and how can I help?'

His voice was a bit of a disappointment, actually. Fizz had, she now realised, expected it to be low-pitched and faintly resonant like Buchanan's one redeeming feature, but it was undeniably feeble in comparison and pitched just a decibel or two too high. Unfortunate, perhaps, but not a disaster.

'There's very little to tell,' she told him, finding herself somewhat surprised to discover just how true that was, even at this stage in the game. 'Irene appears, on the surface of things, to have walked out on Kerr but, unfortunately, a very valuable painting by Rubens disappeared at the same time. The police have been looking for both Irene and the painting for well over a week but – although there have been one or two unreliable leads, we still don't know for certain what's happened to her.'

He thought about that for a few seconds, grinning a little and shaking his head in apparent disbelief, then he said, 'Well, really! That's a turn-up for the books. I didn't know her all that well, of course but – Jesus! A Rubens? That's…that's…I mean, *wow*! Good for Irene.'

'There's still no incontrovertible proof that the theft of the painting and Irene's disappearance are linked,' Buchanan pointed out, 'and until they are, we have to proceed on the assumption that Irene could have been murdered in the course of the robbery. That's why we wanted to find you.'

Some of the animation drained from the guy's face. 'Me?' he said, waving his delicate hands about in an alarmed way. 'But I don't have anything to do with it. I haven't been within ten miles of Abbeyfield in my life. Like, I've only been here for a matter of months and I've hardly been over the doorstep in all that time.'

'There are things you can clarify for us nonetheless.' Buchanan stuck his hands in his trouser pockets and walked over to look out the window into the rain. 'It would be helpful if we knew, for instance, exactly what your relationship was with Irene.'

'Well, heavens, we hardly had any sort of relationship at all,' he carolled excitedly, his voice rising almost to a falsetto. 'She came in here, did her work, and – woosh! – she was off again. Always in a rush. Never once sat down and had a cup of tea and a chat. Simply wasn't interested in anything except getting on with her project and getting back to Abbeyfield. I was like: why not chill out a little, Irene, I'm not charging you by the minute, but she had one eye on her watch all the time.'

'I see,' said Buchanan, nodding gently as though he was adjusting to a new assessment of his witness as, reluctantly, was Fizz. 'Irene was renting studio space from you.'

'Right. She wanted to start this wood-and-glass project she'd been thinking about and a guy I knew told her I had the necessary gear and know-how. Here, look.'

He got up and pulled a dust cloth off a tall rectangular object that stood against the wall. Fizz got up for a closer view

and saw at once that it was the realisation of the sketches she'd
seen in Irene's studio: a celebration of light in all its forms.
The inks she'd used in her preliminary studies, even the acrylic
and gouache attempts she'd abandoned earlier were no preparation for the glorious exuberance of this still uncompleted
work. Worked on wood, it was as much a carving as a painting
and the shaped pieces of coloured glass and enamel that were
worked into its surface captured perfectly the effect she'd
been trying to achieve. The effect, Fizz realised, that she'd
been searching for in everything she'd produced since leaving
art school.

She looked over her shoulder at Buchanan. 'This meant a
lot to her,' she said, and he nodded.

'She didn't talk to you about Kerr?' he asked McVey.

'She didn't talk about nothing. Zip. I asked her if she had a
boyfriend and she said yes. I asked her where she stayed and
she said Abbeyfield. We talked once in a while about what it
was like living in a fancy place like that. That's about it.'

'And did she say she was happy at Abbeyfield?' Fizz wondered. 'Did she mention being worried about anything?'

'Nope.' He walked down the room to adjust the tempera-
ture of one of the cooling ovens and then came back, adding,
'She never talked about anything personal like that I'm telling
you, that woman could concentrate like a laser beam. When
she was working she didn't even know I was around. But, actually, I wouldn't be surprised if she was thinking of leaving.'

'She said that?' Fizz asked and he waved his hands at her as
though trying to back down.

'Maybe. I don't know. She must've said something like that
because I got the impression that...like...that one of these
days she'd be moving on.' He looked at both of them and got
the silent treatment which prompted him to dig a little deeper. This entailed cupping one hand under an elbow and laying
the other flat against his cheek while allowing his long eye-

lashes to droop most of the way down his eyeballs. This made him look a trifle brain-dead but after a moment it produced, 'With her boyfriend. That's what she wanted, I think, but he didn't want to leave. But, listen, it's not something I could swear to in a court of law. It was months ago and I can't remember exactly what was said. It's just – I mean, like I said, she wasn't much of a talker but I sort of got the impression that once she'd finished this project she was working on she'd be leaving the area.'

Fizz looked at her watch and gave Buchanan a nod. She had an appointment at twelve, back at the office, so further exploration of Graham McVey's memory banks would have to be postponed till a later date. 'You've been enormously helpful, Mr McVey. I do appreciate your giving us your time.'

'My pleasure.' He held onto her hand just long enough to dispel her faint doubts about his sexuality and switched on a glittery smile. 'It gets lonely out here sometimes so it's always nice to get a little company. If there's anything else you need to talk to me about just drop by.'

'Thanks. I may do that,' Fizz said, suffering a momentary pang of regret at the unfairness of life. Why did the best looking guys have to be the biggest tossers?

They thanked him and sprinted back to the car, Buchanan arriving there no mellower for another soaking.

'Well, at least that's one red herring eliminated,' he said bitterly, peeling off his suit jacket and hanging it on the hook in the back of the car to drip dry. 'I suppose we should be grateful that we didn't have to spend the entire morning hunting for him. Of course, he may have been lying about his relationship with Irene, but it didn't look like it to me. Everything tied in too neatly.'

Fizz took off her shoes and propped her feet up on the dashboard where the blast from the heater was at its maximum. 'Personally,' she said, 'I found it quite intriguing. He answered more questions than we asked him.'

'For instance?'

'Well, for a start, you only had to look at him to know why Irene was keeping her association with him a secret. It can't have escaped even your notice, *muchacho*, that the guy's sex on the half-shell. If Kerr had clapped eyes on him for one minute he'd have gone off like Vesuvius. Would he have been jealous? Bet your sweet ass he would. Would he – deliberately or inadvertently, take your pick – have made Irene suffer for every hour she spent alone with McVey? Would she have been mad to tell him the truth? Should she have turned down the chance to see her best creative ideas take shape? Did she do the only thing she could have done in the circumstances?' She looked at Buchanan's glum face and gave his knee a pat, wiping the resultant dampness off her fingers on the upholstery. 'I think we know the answer to all these questions, don't we?'

'We do,' he said, nosing out into the traffic, 'and it's nice to get that particular mystery cleared up. I'm just not sure that it was worth investing most of the morning to elucidate. It doesn't actually get us all that much further forward, does it?'

'Not directly, no, but it led us to Graham McVey and he's the only person who knew – or at least, the only person who admits to knowing – that Irene was keen to get the hell off the Abbeyfield estate. Had been for months. Don't you find that interesting? I do. Particularly as, if he's got it right, she wanted Kerr to leave with her.'

Buchanan drove in silence for a minute or two but, because he was obviously mulling things over in his mind, Fizz shut up and left him to get on with it. She needed time to do a bit of mulling of her own since much of her concentration over the past half hour or so had been focused on the chiselled features and tight buns of her host. Even now, in spite of his less than entrancing persona, it was none too easy to keep her thoughts on Irene's possible intentions or the causes that might have led up to them.

Ten years was a long time to stay in one place. Fizz had been in the same flat for nearly five years which was the longest she'd stayed put since she left Am Bealach to go to secondary school at the age of fourteen. Okay, she'd spent the long hols with Grampa and Auntie Duff, which broke the monotony a little, but she was still proud of herself for toughing it out for so long. Irene, however, had been at Abbeyfield for twice that length of time. How did that work out? Would you have passed through the pain barrier by then or would you be bouncing your head off the walls? Would Irene have been seriously unhappy? If so, why would Kerr balk at her idea of moving on? And if it were nothing but a passing fancy why would she have mentioned it to McVey?

'Nobody else thought to tell us that Irene wanted out.'

Buchanan's voice was so soft that, for a split second, she thought the words had come from inside her own head. 'What?' she said.

'This is the first intimation we've had from anyone that Irene wanted to leave Abbeyfield. Why has nobody thought to mention it before?'

'Maybe they didn't know,' Fizz proffered, and then thought about it. 'Well, of course, Kerr must have known – we must ask him about it – but there's no particular reason why she should have told anyone else.'

'She'd have told Eddie. Eddie was her confidant. If it was an idea that had been in her head for months I'm pretty convinced that she'd have discussed it with Eddie, and I'm just as sure that Eddie would have mentioned it to me.'

'Unless she had reasons of her own for keeping it from you,' Fizz mentioned, sending him a severe look that made him twitch. 'Or have you already eliminated her from our list of suspects?'

'No,' he said shortly, putting on his crab-apple face. 'I got

the impression she was happy to talk frankly about her relationship with Irene, that's all. However, you could be right.
She could have reasons for keeping certain information to herself.'

'Well, either Eddie was aware of Irene's intentions and isn't
telling or McVey's got it completely wrong. There's simply no
reason why Irene would hand out information that she was
keeping secret from her best friend on the estate to a guy she
barely knew. I just don't see it. No, either McVey's talking
codswallop or Kerr and Eddie have some reason for not telling
us. My money's on the codswallop theory.'

Buchanan sighed and wiped steam off the windscreen. 'I
think you're probably right, but we'll have to check it out. I'll
give Kerr and Eddie a ring this afternoon and see what they
have to say about it.'

That idea didn't grab Fizz at all. It was typical of the way
Buchanan eliminated all attractive women from his list of suspects. She said, 'Since when have you been in favour of tele-
phoning a suspect when you could question them face to
face?'

That surprised him into throwing a quick look at her. 'You
have your doubts about Kerr?'

'Why not? He certainly has motive, means and opportunity and, as I thought we had just established, we haven't any
proof of Eddie's innocence either.'

'It's been Kerr whose been setting the pace of this inquiry
all along,' he said, ignoring the E-word.

'Which means nothing, as you ought to know. Me, I want
to see his face when I hit him with the proposition that Irene
was unhappy at Abbeyfield. And that goes for Eddie too.'

He didn't like it, but there wasn't much he could do about it.
'Fine,' he said, grinding his teeth. 'We'll go together.'

The rain had stopped before they reached the outskirts of Edinburgh and by evening the blue skies were back on the job and the blackbirds were going at it hammer and tongs. Buchanan, as he drove once more to Abbeyfield, was moderately cheered by the turn in the weather although he would infinitely have preferred to be making the journey on his own. It was no fun communing with Eddie when Fizz was of the company. She clearly had not yet begun to suspect that there could be something between the head gardener and himself but she made him distinctly uneasy nonetheless and, with the best will in the world, she couldn't help but cramp his style.

He had telephoned Eddie during the course of the afternoon and laid the groundwork for a weekend rendezvous at a cosy little bistro he'd ferreted out a short drive from Abbeyfield but there were details to be confirmed so a little time alone with her was called for at some point in the next few hours. All he could hope for was that Fizz would fall for the "you-question-Kerr-and-I'll-talk-to-the-head-gardener" approach that had worked once already.

That being the case, he was less than delighted to encounter Kerr before they were halfway up the drive. He was accompanied by Victor Curzon and the Yorkshire terrier and the three of them were just turning into an overgrown little track that ran into the woods. Fizz stuck her head out of the car window and yoo-hooed them and they turned back to the driveway to await their approach.

'Where are you off to?' Fizz asked when they'd got rid of the preliminaries.

Kerr waved an arm towards the trees. 'Victor's just taking Indie for a walk but I'm heading up to the ice house. I left my bike there last week. Why don't you come with us? It's turned out a lovely evening.'

'Great idea,' said Fizz. 'I could do with stretching my legs.'

'Tell you what,' Buchanan said, spotting his chance, 'you go ahead and I'll just park the car and have a chat with Eddie while I'm waiting for you. It'll save time and we can —'

'We've plenty of time and anyway I want to talk to Eddie too. Come on, Buchanan, we both need the exercise.'

'Yes, but —'

'The path's dry,' Victor mentioned, 'and you get a good view of the house and grounds from the top of the hill. We'll probably be back here in less than half an hour.'

Obviously there was no way Buchanan could put up a fight without arousing suspicion so he had to bite the bullet and plunge into the thicket in his good shoes. It was cooler under the thick canopy of branches and, although the track was carpeted with leaves that had already dried out, the smell of wet loam lay, thick as treacle, on the still air. Indie went scurrying on ahead, busily investigating the undergrowth while, the path being barely two feet wide, the humans followed on in single file.

This was a part of the estate that Buchanan had not covered on his earlier exploration with Kerr and it was clear to him from the overgrown appearance of the path that it wasn't a frequently used route.

'The public obviously doesn't make much use of this part of the estate,' he commented and saw Kerr nod in affirmation.

'They're free to go where they want,' he said, 'but in practice most of them stick to the tarmac. There are plenty more inspiring places for hillwalkers in the area and even the ice house is so overgrown that you'd have difficulty finding it without a guide. I'd like to get it tidied up and open an easier way to it but with damn near thirty acres of woodland to attend to on my own I just don't have the time.'

'It must have been a virtually impossible task to search that acreage for Irene.'

'It was. Victor helped, of course, and so did Eddie but even at that we couldn't cover every square foot of ground. We had to stick more or less to the paths and just keep yelling and blowing whistles in the hope that, if Irene were some place where we couldn't see her, she was in a fit state to yell back.' He stopped and indicated the long slope ahead of them and to the right. 'I went back over all that area on my own, or as much of it as I could access on my mountain bike. Then I left my bike in the ice house and did the southern half on foot. Even at that, I can't be absolutely certain she's not lying in some hollow so I have to keep on going over the ground just to make sure.'

He turned to walk on but Buchanan held his ground, letting Fizz and Victor get further ahead and out of earshot. 'Irene wasn't entirely happy here, was she?' he asked, stopping Kerr in mid-stride.

His face, as he turned, was cool and closed. 'What makes you say that?'

'That's the impression I get from what I hear. Am I wrong?'

Kerr pushed his fists deep into the pockets of his cargo pants and laughed shortly, avoiding Buchanan's eyes. 'One of Grace's little tip-offs, no doubt?' Buchanan didn't answer. 'Well, whoever gave you that information, this time they've got it wrong. Irene may have had her reservations about life on the estate but she wasn't unhappy. She enjoyed her work and there was nothing wrong with our relationship – nothing we couldn't handle. Someone's just trying to make mischief.'

'Would she have considered moving elsewhere?' Buchanan asked carefully.

'I suppose so.' Kerr's eyes were still wandering erratically around. He was either embarrassed or trying to hide something. 'She gets a little restless sometimes and starts talking about making a new start somewhere down south or taking a job abroad. It's just a phase she goes through every so often.'

'Had she been talking about getting away from here before she disappeared?'

Kerr didn't answer immediately and in the silence Buchanan could hear a magpie's croaking call far away in the distance. Fizz and Victor had now stopped to wait for them at a turn in the path where a shaft of low sun spotlit them against the darkness of the woodland behind. Finally Kerr lifted his head and looked at Buchanan's face.

'Actually, yes, she had,' he said, with a sudden tensing of his jaw muscles that Buchanan was already learning to read as a danger signal. 'Why're you asking about that?'

'I'm just interested to know why you didn't mention it.'

'Well, obviously,' Kerr retorted, in a voice that rose abruptly in volume at every word, 'I didn't mention it because I didn't think it was significant. I still don't think it's significant. What it is, Tam, is a bloody side issue and nothing at all to do with Irene's disappearance, right? And frankly, it's nobody's business but —'

'Okay, cool it,' Buchanan snapped, reaching the end of his patience with an abruptness that caught him by surprise, over-riding his sympathy. 'I'm getting bored with your tantrums, Kerr. If you want Fizz and I to continue looking for a solution to this business I think the least we can expect from you is a little civility. Irene apparently chooses to let you get away with bad manners, that's her business. I don't so choose. I'd like you to remember that in future.'

It was evident from Kerr's stunned expression that he wasn't used to being slapped on the wrist. He was plainly unde-cided how to take the rebuke but before he could settle on the appropriate response there was a piercing whistle from up ahead that made him pause and look round.

'Is Indie with you?' Victor's voice floated down the path, sounding as if it were coming from much further away. He was standing in the underbrush at the edge of the trees with his hands on his hips and his head swinging from side to side as he scanned the terrain. As Buchanan and Kerr caught up with him Fizz stuck two fingers in her mouth and whistled again, loud enough to wake the dead and scare Indie into fleeing the country.

'Little bugger,' Victor said venomously. 'Where the hell's he got to? *INDIE!*'

'Where did you last see him?' Kerr asked.

'I don't know. I was talking to Fizz and I suddenly realised he wasn't here.'

Fizz pointed at a faint animal track that wound in among the trees. 'He was sniffing around there a minute ago as if he'd found something interesting. Maybe he followed a trail into the wood.'

'I'll kill him.' Victor plunged into the bushes followed by Kerr but they had gone no more than a dozen steps when one or the other of them muttered, 'What the hell…?' and there was something in the tone of the words that implied bad news.

When he caught up with them, beating Fizz into second place for once, Buchanan was immediately relieved not to see a body. What had caused the exclamation was, at first glance, nothing but a pile of cinders such as one might find anywhere in a forest where tree pruning was being carried out. Only the frozen attitudes of Kerr and Victor evidenced a deeper meaning that was not obvious to outsiders.

'What's up?' Fizz demanded.

Victor bent down and picked up Indie, who was rooting purposefully through the ashes. 'No one's done any work around here for years,' he said, glancing sideways at Kerr's grim face. 'And those are bits of material of some sort. Looks to me like someone's been burning clothes.'

Buchanan was immediately struck by the implications of this and his reaction was to look at Fizz to see how she was taking it. He needn't have worried. Fizz was good at treating Triumph and Disaster both the same, at least as far as anyone could tell. Nobody said anything for several seconds and then Kerr hunkered down and extended a finger to touch a blackened, gauze like web of material. 'That...it looks like...it could be Irene's scarf.'

'I don't think you should touch anything,' Buchanan cautioned him. 'It could be nothing to do with Irene's disappearance but the police will want to make sure of that. We should leave now before we contaminate the scene. Where's the nearest telephone?'

'Caitlin has one in the gatehouse,' Victor said, while Kerr remained crouched there, silent and immobile, as though he were unaware of what was going on around him. 'Let's go, mate. You're not going to find anything recognisable in that lot, it's much too charred, and there's no point in getting our knickers in a twist till we know what the police can make of it. It could be the bloody tinkers back again. Who knows?'

He stooped down and, with his free hand, hooked Kerr under the arm and pulled him to his feet. Kerr let himself be drawn away, walking like a zombie back to the track, but he remained deep in his own thoughts while the four of them walked back down the path to the gatehouse. Buchanan found the whole business deeply troubling. Kerr's all too obvious agony made him think of some mortally wounded animal, bleeding and writhing in front of him, and he knew there wasn't a damn thing in the world he could do or say to assuage it. For the moment some sort of natural anaesthetic seemed to be numbing Kerr's responses, at least enough to allow him to function, but he was bound to realise that the chances of the bonfire proving to be unimportant had to be slender.

They found Caitlin dressed, as she had been the evening before, in her green silk housecoat but minus the spliff. She seemed surprised and not a little displeased to receive uninvited visitors for the second night running.

'We need to use your phone,' Fizz told her, leading an incursion straight past her into the lounge. 'We just found a pile of burnt clothing up there in the woods and we have to phone the police.'

'You what?' Caitlin stepped back against the wall as the others pushed past and then followed them dazedly, checking to see if her modesty was sufficiently protected by her skimpy attire. 'I was just going to watch *Who Wants to be a Millionaire.*'

Buchanan explained the situation again in sufficient detail for Caitlin to comprehend the necessity of their intrusion and subsequently to produce the number of the man in charge of the police investigation: a certain Inspector Teesdale. While he waited to be connected he located the site of the fire on the large scale map of the estate above the desk and had the precise co-ordinates ready when the inspector came on the line.

'Typical!' The inspector's voice was deep and gritty with a pronounced Geordie accent. 'We only have two sections of that hill left to search, and that's one of them. We'd have found it ourselves tomorrow. I'll have a team over there within an hour but try to make sure nobody contaminates the scene before we get there.'

Buchanan hung up and took a few minutes longer to study the map, noting which areas Caitlin had marked as having been searched. It appeared that the police had already checked out all the low-lying sections apart from the two surrounding and immediately above the place where they'd found the fire so the chances of Irene's body being somewhere around that spot seemed fairly high.

Fizz had by then set her usual emergency procedures in operation by organizing the administration of alcohol all round. Kerr was the only one of them who was possibly in need of a stimulant but any excuse was enough for Fizz. Both

Victor and Kerr were getting speedily outside generous measures of whisky while Caitlin and Fizz were making inroads into a bottle of gin. Buchanan had to resist, as usual, not only because he was driving but because somebody had to stay sober enough to deal with the police.

He said, 'They'll be here within the hour. I told them the fire was in a fairly isolated spot but they want us to warn all the residents on the estate not to go near it. Do I use this phone to call the big house, Caitlin, or do you have an internal line?'

'You have to dial the number on the wall beside you there.'

Victor drained his glass. 'I'd better get back to Grace and let her know what's happened. What about you, Kerr? You going home or do you want to wait here?'

Kerr seemed to have difficulty making up his mind but Fizz answered for him. 'We'll stay with Kerr till the police get here. They'll want one of us to go back up the hill with them and Kerr's probably the one to do it. Sitting around worrying won't do him any good. I'll pop in and give Eddie the news on the way round.'

Buchanan, listening to the conversation over the sound of Sir Douglas's distraught mutterings, didn't feel moved to offer an argument about who'd talk to Eddie but he comforted himself with the thought that, whatever Fizz planned, there was oft a slip 'tween cup and lip. They all went out together, leaving Caitlin barring her door against further offensives, and walked round to the stable yard in the fading light.

'It'll be too dark by the time the police arrive for them to see what they're doing up there in the woods,' Victor said, tucking Indie under his arm like a parcel.

'They'll have floodlights,' Fizz opined. 'But I doubt if they'll do much except maybe secure the scene and take some forensic samples. We'll have to wait till tomorrow at least before we hear anything definite.'

'Why would somebody do that?' Kerr burst out suddenly, his voice hoarse with emotion.

'Do what, Kerr?' said Victor.

'If those clothes are Irene's…why would somebody set fire to them?'

Buchanan could think of only one reason but there was no way to phrase it without using the word 'murder' so he said nothing. However, Kerr was not so picky.

He threw a hand out in an uncontrolled gesture. 'If she's been murdered, why did her killer not bury her in her clothes? Why burn them separately?'

This was a question which had not occurred to Buchanan and he could deduce, from the length of time it took to attract speculation, that it hadn't occurred to the others either. The only explanation that presented itself to him was that the killer had taken steps to ensure all identification had been removed from Irene's body. However Kerr was quite capable of pursuing that thought to its conclusion and perhaps now was not the moment to present him with a picture of a shallow grave bearing a mutilated corpse, its teeth and facial bones smashed, fingerprints obliterated and heaven only knew what other horrors perpetrated in the cause of obfuscation.

Some twenty paces further down the path Victor said, 'That's a point, you know, Kerr. It could mean that the bonfire has nothing to do with Irene – just some idiot burning rubbish or…or maybe a burglar getting rid of stuff from a robbery.'

'It could have been there for months,' Fizz proffered, which although perfectly true as far as any of them could tell, failed to noticeably lighten the atmosphere. Given long enough they could probably, between them, come up with several alternative scenarios to account for burned clothing in a remote wood at least a mile from the public road but Buchanan for one found it difficult to release the conviction that what they'd just found had sinister implications.

When they got back to the stable yard Eddie, as luck would have it, was working in her front garden. She called out a cheerful 'Hello there' and waved but must have realized from their subdued response that all was not well. Dropping the trowel she was using, she hurried down her path to waylay them.

'Is something wrong?'

Kerr just shook his head irritably and kept going into his cottage, the other three stopped by the gate.

'Someone's been burning clothing in the woods, just below the ice house,' Victor said. 'It looks very much as though it might be Irene's.'

Eddie's eyes widened as she turned to look at Buchanan. 'What does this mean? Do you think she's been…that something bad has happened to her?'

'We're trying not to go down that road,' he answered. 'It could mean nothing but we've phoned the police and they're coming to take a look at it so we'll see what they have to say.'

She pressed her lips together and followed Kerr's retreating figure with her eyes. 'Poor Kerr. It must be terribly upsetting for him. God knows it's bad enough for the rest of us.'

Behind them the door of the Curzons' cottage opened and Grace came hurrying across the cobbles. 'What next?' she demanded as soon as her voice would carry to them and then listened to her husband's concise report with an expression of mingled censure and satisfaction.

'Well, there you are then,' she responded, her mean little eyes challenging each of them in turn. 'What more proof do you need? I said all along that Irene had to have helped the thieves – didn't I Victor? And once she'd played her part they obviously had no further use for her. They'll find her body next, mark my words.'

Fizz swung her head round to look at her, distaste writ large in her expression but, before she could say anything,

Eddie inserted placidly,

'Let's try not to leap to conclusions, Grace. God knows things are depressing enough without making them any worse.'

Grace's smile was a smirk. 'Stick your head in the sand if you like, Eddie, but it won't change anything. This business doesn't come as any surprise to me, I can tell you. I've been saying all along that that woman was too sweet to be wholesome.'

That did it for Fizz but Buchanan was ahead of her and grabbed her by the arm.

'We have to go,' he said, cutting across her opening syllables in a voice that told her there'd be trouble if she opposed him and she appeared, for once, to see the wisdom of discretion. 'I think Kerr is in need of some support right now. The police should be here in an hour or so but we'll hang around till then.'

He fancied he could feel Fizz shaking with fury as they crossed the yard but if she was upset by Grace's bitchiness she didn't vocalize it, just marched somewhat jerkily along beside him with her jaw clenched and her lips clamped shut. Buchanan sought for something calming to say but couldn't produce anything better than a companionable silence.

They found Kerr engaged, quite unaccountably, in a frenzy of house cleaning.

Fizz stood in the hall and watched him charging from room to room with his arms full of dirty clothes and sundry rubbish, and her rage abruptly gave way to concern.

'What on earth are you doing, Kerr?'

'Clearing up.' He disappeared into the kitchen from whence, presently, came the sound of the dish washer. Fizz looked at Buchanan. 'Has he flipped?'

'I reckon he's just keeping himself busy. Like you said, there's no point in sitting around worrying.'

Kerr came back and started to gather up all the photographs, which were still on the floor, and shove them anyhow back into the drawer.

'Need any help?' said Fizz and he straightened to look at her as if he had forgotten she was present.

'No thanks. I'd rather do it myself.'

'We'll go, then, shall we?' she said, stating the obvious. 'You wouldn't wants us to hang around till the police get here?'

'I don't think that's necessary, do you? From the police point of view, I mean?'

'No, but I thought you might be better with some company.'

'No, I'm fine, Fizz. Thanks anyway.'

He got to his feet with the clear intention of showing them out so they had little option but to go.

'Makes you feel like a spare prick at a party,' Fizz commented as they got into the car, clearly forgetting, for the moment, her decision to clean up her act.

Buchanan forbore to comment but felt tempted to agree.

Chapter Fourteen

The news, when Fizz started work at quarter to nine the following morning, was not good.

Failing in her attempt to contact Kerr by telephone, she got through to the estate office where she found Caitlin in a state of deep depression but only too willing to talk about it.

'Poor Kerr! He had to identify some little brass beads that they found in the ashes and, of course, they'd come from a scarf that Irene used to wear. I don't know how he's managing to hold together, I honestly don't, but he's up there with them now doing God only knows what. There are dozens of them here already, wandering about in those white overalls. A finger-tip search, his lordship says, and I think I heard a helicopter a minute ago. It's sounds like Dunkirk out there.'

Fizz had fought against pessimism all night but now felt it creep over her like a shroud. 'So, it's a full-blown murder enquiry?'

'I suppose so. Sir D says they'll be searching the big house and that means the staff quarters too, which is a bit of a bummer.'

Fizz could imagine it would be, particularly if you had a large stash of mary jane to flush down the cludgy. 'Okay. Will you ask Kerr, when you see him, to give me a ring straight away if anything transpires?'

'Sure, and if he doesn't, I will.'

Fizz thanked her, rang off, and immediately dialed Buchanan's home number, catching him as he was about to leave for the advocates' library. He was either half-asleep (not unusual at this stage in his day) or completely blasé regarding the development.

'I had a feeling this was what we'd wake up to,' he muttered. 'That detective inspector I spoke to on the phone last night seemed to be on the ball. At least we can honourably bow out now and leave things to the professionals.'

'Oh, I don't know about that.' Fizz said hastily. Irene had been a friend of hers and people did not mess with Fizz Fitzpatrick's friends and get away with it. 'We still have leads to pursue.'

'Have we? Oh, you mean, the "Save the Rubens" bunch? Well, I haven't time to start on that today but it's probably a stone that should be turned before we step down. Let me know how you get on. Must rush. Talk to you later.'

Fizz had suspected she might get landed with the thankless task of checking out the subscribers to the "Save the Rubens" fund so she wasn't too cast down at being handed it. She knew she was less pressed for time at the moment than was Buchanan but she could have done without being left with a morning's work on her hands without the least promise of satisfaction at the end of it.

After three solid hours of being put on hold, conversing with machines and listening to piped music she was ready to throw the telephone on the floor and stamp on it but at least she had established that the effort to keep Sir Douglas's Rubens in the UK was nothing more than an innocent collaboration of art lovers. As far as being a promising lead was concerned it was as dead as the Twist but checking it out had served a purpose nonetheless in giving her something practical to do at a point where she needed to feel she was fighting back. However, neither she nor Buchanan had any brilliant ideas on how to proceed from this point on so, in actual fact, the sensible thing to do was to take a couple of days off to see what might develop. Fizz, however, was in no mood to be thwarted. At the very least she could sit down with Buchanan and review the evidence they'd managed to put together. Sometimes you got too close to a case to focus properly and you had to stand back and see if any of the dots could be joined together to make a picture. It had worked before and there was no reason why it shouldn't work again. With this in mind she phoned Buchanan's office number and, finding him unavailable, left a message for him to say she'd be having dinner at his place. He wouldn't like it but she was pretty sure he didn't have anything more exciting on his agenda for the evening.

Both his moggies accompanied him to the door to greet her arrival, Pooky purring round her ankles and Selena plummeting off the ledge of the skylight in a doomed attempt to land on her shoulder – a little habit she'd learned as a kitten and one which had failed to endear her to those who were not accustomed to her ways.

'This is a nice surprise,' he said sardonically as she nimbly dodged Selena's suicide attack and trotted into the lounge. 'To what do I owe the pleasure of your company this evening?'

'We've reached a dead end: we have to talk things over. What's for dinner?'

He looked pained. 'If you'd given me more notice I'd have gone to the supermarket but I didn't get your message till twenty minutes ago. I'm not sure what's in the freezer.'

Nothing but junk food, Fizz was willing to bet, and she tried to avoid that nowadays even when someone else was paying for it. Scientists had been saying recently that junk food was addictive but that was no news to anybody. She could have saved them the research grant by citing her own experiences as an impoverished art student, at which point she'd developed a lust for fish fingers and ended up with a twenty-a-day habit not to mention a mushy pea dependency that had been the devil to kick.

'Let's take a look,' she said with determined optimism and made for the kitchen before he could put up an argument. It was a tip as usual, with dishes in the sink and the toaster, muesli packet and empty yogurt carton still on the table from breakfast-time. In all the time she'd known him she'd never seen his flat tidy. That came, of course, from being spoiled rotten all his life, first by his mother and then by his cleaning lady, Dolores, who he was still paying, in spite of his straitened circumstances, to muck out his flat twice a week.

'You tidy up, I'll cook,' she said, making a quick reconnaissance of the freezer and the fridge. 'There the makings of a Spanish omelette and if you want to nip down to the petrol station for a bottle of milk while I'm peeling these onions we can have cream of onion soup.'

He wrinkled his forehead doubtfully. 'Won't that take forever to be ready? I'm starving.'

'Half an hour max. On your bike.'

It took a little longer than the half hour, actually, but that was because she gave him the job of zizzing the milk, white sauce and boiled onions in the food processor and he couldn't even accomplish that without losing half of it on the floor. By the time they sat down to eat, however, the kitchen was tidy, the cats fed and the repast filling if not exactly cordon bleu.

'I've been half-expecting a phone-call from Kerr all day,' Fizz confessed. 'The CID has been all over the place like an army of ants since dawn this morning and I imagine they'll keep going as long as its light enough to see what they're doing. All the same, if Irene's body is around there you'd think they'd have found it by now.'

Buchanan glanced out at the sky which as yet showed no sign of approaching dusk. 'At this time of year they'd be in little danger of missing something till at least seven o'clock, even under the trees. When I went to bed at one this morning you could still pick out the ducks down there in the Water of Leith.'

'Yes, but a corpse can't be all that difficult to spot, even if it's well buried. You can't help thinking that, as the hours go by, the probability of finding a grave has to be diminishing.'

'I'd imagine so.' He fished an un-zizzed piece of onion out of his soup and chewed it with close concentration. 'It must be tough for Kerr, waiting for news, praying that they'll find nothing, that the clothes will be proved to be someone's rubbish, that he'll live to hope another day. Especially as he must know in his heart that Irene's dead. We should really take a run over there this evening and give him a little moral support, if nothing else. He can't keep on finding housework to do.'

Kerr's state of mind had not exercised Fizz to any great extent for quite a few days now. She knew she should be more sympathetic to the problems he was experiencing but it was difficult to worry about the mental health of someone who got up her nose quite as annoyingly as Kerr. Buchanan, on the other hand, was a total softie who could cite extenuating circumstances for Saddam Hussein. She was not in any doubt that he felt Kerr's distress quite keenly but she wasn't blind to the possibility that he had other, less philanthropic reasons for returning to Abbeyfield and, while determined to allow his romance to run its course, she felt very little compulsion to expedite such matters.

'I think we should give it a bye tonight,' she said, in a tone that brooked no argument. 'If the place is buzzing with coppers we won't be welcome and, anyway, Kerr has plenty of friends around him without our intervention. Don't you think it would be a more productive use of our time just to sit down and brainstorm for a couple of hours and maybe get things into a better perspective. Do you want more soup or will I put it in the fridge for tomorrow?'

'Tomorrow may never come,' he said, passing his plate. 'Are you sure we know enough for a brainstorming session? It seems to me that we've unearthed nothing constructive. We don't have a single suspect – not really, Fizz. I know you have your doubts about Kerr, maybe you always did, but surely, if he'd wanted to get rid of Irene he'd have found a better way of doing it. He must have known he was bound to be the prime suspect.'

'That in itself is not proof of his innocence,' Fizz mentioned. 'Anyway, he wasn't my prime suspect at first, if you remember. Sir Douglas was. Now I'm not so sure about either of them.' She split the remainder of the soup fifty-fifty, ignoring Buchanan's claim to the lion's share by right of the larger body mass he had to maintain, and filled the empty pot with water before she sat down again. 'The question is: who can we eliminate?'

Buchanan ate in meditative silence for a couple of minutes, then said, 'Grace, possibly. If you choose to assume that the person who killed Irene also killed Nanny I think that could be said to let her out. She's too heavily pregnant to be getting into a tussle, even with someone as frail as Nanny.'

'You think so?' Fizz wondered, by no means sure that she agreed with that estimation. 'I suppose she might *prefer* not to get physical but if she were hard pressed – as the killer must certainly have been to commit a second murder – I reckon she could manage it, as could any of the other estate residents. Kerr, Victor and Eddie would have no difficulty, nor would Caitlin, and either of the Fergussons could have tipped her over with an elbow.'

'Perhaps it would be more productive to ask which of them Nanny might have endangered.'

'Well any of them, surely, if she'd witnessed Irene's killing.'

'You think Nanny would keep silent for over a week if she'd witnessed a murder?'

Fizz hesitated. 'She would if the murderer were her precious Sir Douglas.'

'Sure. Or even Lady Marjory. But if Irene's murder is connected to the theft of the picture – and I'd stake my life on that being the case – that would eliminate both the Fergussons, wouldn't it? The only reason they could possibly have for stealing their own property would be for the insurance money and we've proved that to be a non-runner.' He looked at his empty plate which was so clean even the CID forensics department would have been hard pressed to say what he'd had on it. 'Will I serve the omelette?'

'No,' said Fizz without rationale, judging the tone of her

voice to be insult enough. The omelette was thick and succu-
lent, lightly smudged with golden brown on top, and bejew-
eled with shiny chunks of red and yellow peppers, carrot, and
courgette. It was one of the first things Grampa had taught
her to cook, during one of their frequent housekeeper-less
periods when she was at junior school, and it had taken plenty of practice to learn the trick of serving it in no more pieces
than there were mouths to be fed. Both moggies, having been
lucky with the spilled soup, were hanging around in the hope
of a second course and no way were they getting one.

'Scat!' she told them but they didn't know the meaning of
the word. 'Honest, Buchanan, you have those two spoiled rotten. I told you not to feed them tidbits. How can you put up
with having them trip you up at every turn?'

'I wouldn't *have* to put up with them if it weren't for you!'

'Me? How am I to blame? I never asked you to adopt either
of them!'

'You made it impossible not to.'

'Balls,' she said, knowing he'd cling to that justification till
the Last Trump rather than admit to being a sucker. She divid-
ed the omelette deftly between two plates and set them down
on the table. 'I don't suppose the Rubens could have been a
fake, could it?'

He lifted an eyebrow at her. 'How would that work out? I
can see where, if the original had been sold a long time ago and
replaced with a copy, Sir Douglas might try to claim the insurance money for the fake, but surely he'd remember to insure the
fake for its supposedly true value before he "stole" it? He could
have been hoping to pass a copy off as the real thing to this
American buyer of his – which would not be an easy thing to do
– but Irene would have spotted the imitation if no one else did.'

'Maybe she did spot it and that's why she was killed.'

He shook his head. 'Vassileiou wouldn't have parted with
mega-dollars without paying for an expert opinion of his own.

We're on the wrong track here. We're falling into the trap of believing what we want to believe – that, whatever happened, Irene played no willing part in the theft of the painting – whereas the phone-call Vassileiou received proves otherwise. She was the only person outside the family who knew the painting had a damaged area. You can't get away from that. There's only one estate resident other than she who could —'

The phone rang and he broke off to go and answer it, leaving the living room door open behind him. Fizz could hear him say, 'Buchanan...Yes, Kerr. What's happened?'

Hastily, she took another bite of omelette and rushed through to hear the rest, colliding with Selena who liked to keep her protector within line of sight.

'Yes, we heard that from Caitlin,' he was saying as she leaned her head close to his to catch the faint echo of Kerr's voice. 'Did they find anything? Nothing else? No disturbed ground? No evidence of...um...? Well, that's something.' He listened intently for a few seconds while Kerr rattled on indistinctly then clapped a hand over the mouthpiece and stared at Fizz as though he were about to tell her something but, instead he listened some more and exclaimed, 'That's crazy! How could she have...? Are they sure?'

'*What ?*' Fizz demanded, tugging at his sleeve. '*Who?*'

'Eddie,' he said tersely, and added into the mouthpiece, 'When was she taken in? ... Which station? ... But not charged? ... No, they can detain her for six hours under Section 14 of the Criminal Procedure Act but then they have to let her go. She could be home by eleven... Yes, I agree with you but we'll just have to wait and see... I don't think so, Kerr. It's too early to do that. Let's leave it till the morning and see if...Yes, you and I may believe that, but stranger things have happened. Would you like us to come over? Right. That's a good idea. Try to get some sleep and we'll talk in the morning.'

Fizz, seeing the conversation was at an end, returned to her meal and Buchanan joined her seconds later looking grim.

'Eddie's been taken in for questioning, right?' she said. 'On what grounds?'

Buchanan nodded, staring at his plate as though he had lost his appetite. Fizz rather hoped he had, since the omelette tasted as good as it looked.

'One of her gardening gloves was discovered near the fire.'

'Definitely hers?'

'Definitely. She identified it herself and in any case it was unmistakable because she buys particularly small ones from a catalogue. I daresay the forensic evidence could prove who'd been wearing it anyway.' He shook his head and forked absently at his food. 'It was found almost as soon as they started to examine the site of the bonfire, in the grass only a few feet away, together with a couple of used matches.'

'Wow. She's going to have a hard time talking her way out of that one.' Fizz leaned back in her chair and considered Eddie in the light of this new development. Eddie had not figured anywhere near the top of her list of suspects but apparently she should have: she was a smart cookie and quite capable of pulling the wool over anyone's eyes, particularly eyes as blinkered as Buchanan's. She also, one had to admit, appeared as capable of murder as any of the others. This new development was a bit of a slap in the face: a reminder that Fizz herself was not a real detective but only a bumbling, and possibly over confident amateur. However, every cloud had a silver lining. When you thought about it, there wasn't one of her suspects she'd rather see locked up than Buchanan's heart-throb.

'It's not anything like conclusive,' Buchanan was saying, but looking less optimistic than he sounded. 'The CID will have to come up with more than circumstantial evidence before they can charge her. I think they'll have to let her go and hope to uncover a convincing motive or solid forensic evidence that ties her to the actual killing. They don't even have a body yet for God's sake, so unless she goes mad and makes a full confession she'll be home this evening.'

'I wouldn't like to be her in any case,' Fizz stated, finishing her meal and eyeing Buchanan's. 'Even if they can't pin anything on her, imagine knowing that all your neighbours think you probably did it.'

'All but one.'

'True,' Fizz looked at him patiently, 'but only if she herself is not the guilty party. Are you going to eat that?'

'Yes.'

'Greedy swine. I bet you don't.'

Buchanan put a forkful in his mouth and chewed it aggressively. 'It's like sharing a Thomson's gazelle with a pack of hyenas, eating with you Fizz.'

'I just don't like to see food wasted.'

'Yeah. Right.'

'So, anyway, what was she doing with a working glove up in the woods? You don't need to wear gloves if all you're doing is putting a match to some clothes.'

'Maybe she used some branches to get the fire going.'

'Or maybe she was burying Irene there at the same time.' Fizz's mind shied away from the thought but she forced it back on track and added with an assumed callousness, 'It's a fair distance to transport a corpse but she's a strong woman. She also has instant access to corpse-burying implements: spades and picks, crowbars to move rocks, saws to cut through tree roots.'

'You'd know about that,' he said slyly, making reference to a certain incident in the not too distant past: one which she'd prefer forgotten. 'But, I don't think anyone would be stupid enough to leave evidence as visible as a bonfire anywhere close to where they'd disposed of the body. If Irene's buried in the woods it's not likely to be around that area.'

'Eddie was doing *something* with that glove, though, and

she's not saying what. The matches being found beside it would indicate that she took it off to light the fire.'

Buchanan was showing clear signs of being uncomfortable with the subject of this discussion. 'I don't doubt that's what the prosecution would submit but even that isn't going to get a conviction. They can't put her away for burning clothes and that, I need hardly point out to you, is all she's even suspected of so don't get too far ahead of yourself. There could be a dozen innocent explanations as to why that glove was there – it could have been planted in a deliberate attempt to frame her, for one thing. For another: Irene could, for some mysterious reason, have *asked* her to destroy her clothes. We don't really know *what's* been going on – do we? – so let's wait and hear what Eddie has to tell us when she's released.' He ate some more omelette and pointed to it with his fork, remarking, probably to annoy her, 'This is damn good, Fizz. Where'd you learn to cook like this? The kibbutz?'

'Tuh! They'd have thought they were at the Ritz! All those kibbutzniks ate was ratatouille. By the vat. I never want to look another aubergine in the face.'

Buchanan cleared his plate and then, no doubt because he felt the need of a little cold comfort, remembered he had a tub of ice cream in the freezer.

Fizz too was beginning to lose her confidence in Eddie's guilt. She said, 'Did I imagine it, or was Kerr finding it hard to accept that Eddie was involved?'

'He was. Or should I say, he appeared to be: it's difficult to be sure without seeing him face to face – not that one could be sure even then but you know what I'm saying. He wanted me to charge into the police station with all guns blazing and bust her out but even he must have realised that wasn't necessary.'

'What do you think, will they be giving her a rough time?'

Buchanan's eyes clouded. 'It won't be pleasant for her, I'm pretty sure of that. That sort of thing never is, particularly when one has no immediate way of proving one's innocence. It's a frightening situation to be in, no matter how sympathetic the questioning, but she's nobody's victim. I'm sure she'll give as good as she gets.'

Fizz was inclined to agree with that assessment. There was something about Eddie that was unlike other women Buchanan had singled out for attention in recent years: something adamantine, something resilient. Something, perhaps, that Fizz saw in herself and respected in others. Eddie was – there was no other word for it – grown-up, and the uncomfortable fact was that she'd probably be rather good for Buchanan. He needed someone to keep his feet on the ground, someone to remind him that he didn't live in a perfect world full of perfect people. She herself had toughened him up a little over the years but he still trusted everyone he met, still strove constantly on behalf of helpless ingrates, still fell for every sharp sister with a pretty face. She had saved him from a few of these in the past and had felt few qualms of conscience for so doing, but – bearing in mind that Eddie was innocent till proven guilty – what excuse did she have for trying to write her out of future installments?

Okay, yes, there was the idea that maybe she could keep him for herself. Only that was an extremely bad idea and it occurred to her only rarely and at times when she'd either had too much to drink or when she was suffering from sleep deprivation. She'd been a free spirit for too long to think of settling down and committing to one man and if she'd learned one thing about Buchanan it was that he was the committing kind. He wasn't just for Christmas, he was for life. In his case, you couldn't eat your cake without having it, and that was just too scary to contemplate.

So, if she didn't want him for herself, what excuse did she have for putting the skids under someone who did?

One day she'd sit down and think that one out.

Chapter Fifteen

Buchanan felt no clearer in his mind after his brainstorming session with Fizz than he had done before. This weighed on his spirits somewhat for most of the following day and it seemed to him that he had never before, at this stage in an investigation, been quite so clueless or so starved of possible leads. It made him question his original conviction that Irene had known her killer and, more specifically, that her killer had been someone from the estate. Certainly, Irene's existence had been largely circumscribed in recent years but it was at least possible that she had formed a relationship of some sort with a visiting member of the public or even that someone with a long held grudge had turned up out of her past. Neither scenario struck him as likely even now, but then, neither did the possibility of finding her killer among those she saw on a daily basis.

Fizz's contention was that if you knew what made people tick – their idiosyncrasies, their attitudes, their priorities in life – you could distinguish those who would kill, given the need, from those who wouldn't. She was happy to spend her time interacting with her suspects, hoping that sooner or later one of them would drop his or her guard and let out the single scrap of information that would allow her to see beneath the mask they presented to the world. That, of course, was a woman's way of working, circumspect and intuitive, but Buchanan invariably found it difficult to focus his concentration without a pencil in his hand. While Fizz followed her hunches – her *informed* hunches, as she claimed – Buchanan covered sheets of paper with lists of established facts, flow charts and cross-references. He knew there was merit in both approaches, he'd seen that established in the past, but, thus far into this particular inquiry, one had proved no more effective than the other.

The only way forward was to give Fizz her head. She was

bound to be worried by the way things were starting to look so if she thought there was anything to be gained by spending time at Abbeyfield, he was willing to go along with that till a more promising line of action presented itself. It was, after all, a strategy which held, if nothing else, the opportunity for further intercourse with Eddie – albeit of the social kind – and since that was the only kind he was likely to get in the near future he was inclined to go for it. It was not she but Kerr who phoned the following morning to report that she had been set at liberty after only a few hours spent helping the police with their inquiries, however Buchanan felt that her nasty experience was excuse enough to warrant another unsolicited visit. He was impatient to hear her rationalization for her glove being found close to the bonfire and with a bit of luck she might even need a shoulder to cry on.

He could not avoid the irritation of Fizz's presence at the tête-à-tête but that wasn't all that much of a drawback, as it turned out, because shoulders were not high on Eddie's immediate want-list. She was in an even worse humour than she'd been when last encountered.

'They are *so rude*!' she contended, angrily snapping over-enthusiastic shoots off Kerr's wisteria with a pair of long-handled pruning shears. 'I really don't see why I should have to put up with being treated like a common criminal – not to mention a compulsive *liar*! And why do they have to drag me off to Dunfermline police station to talk to me? Huh? Why can't they talk to me here as they've done before? I felt like a *felon*! All that was missing was the handcuffs!'

'They like to record that sort of interview,' Buchanan said, trying to sound soothing. 'I imagine they went over all the questions they'd asked you before, just to have your answers on record. It doesn't mean anything.'

'They kept me there for the entire evening, Tam! Half an hour – fine! It's a murder inquiry, I appreciate that, and I'm only too willing to be as helpful as I can but – *three hours?* There's a limit to the way decent people should be treated. I just think they have a damn cheek, that's all!'

'It does seem a little bit excessive,' Buchanan admitted.

'Well,' said Fizz, with no perceptible compassion, 'I suppose they have to get to the bottom of things any way they can. The fact that your glove was found at the bonfire site together with burnt matches – let's face it, Eddie – it may be circumstantial evidence but it's pretty suspicious.'

'Of course it's suspicious! I know it's suspicious, for God's sake, but I told them about sixteen times I'd no idea how they got there. They didn't have to go on and on about it all evening. Anyone on the estate could have told them I'm stupid about my gear. I could have left that damn thing anywhere. Any member of the public could have picked it up – God knows they nick everything that's not nailed down!'

'When did you realize you'd mislaid it?' Fizz asked.

Eddie held out both hands, displaying the neat suede gloves she was wearing. 'I have a dozen pairs, exactly like these. They get mislaid and turn up again all the time. All I can be sure about is that I never dropped one where they say it was found. I've walked up the ice house path from time to time but never in gardening gloves. Someone else must have used it.'

She lopped off a large, and surely unintentional, branch of wisteria and seemed a little aghast at the quantity that fell to the ground but the mishap did nothing to alleviate her bad temper. 'It's not that I'm a hostile witness,' she claimed, snipping a little less recklessly. 'I made no objection to having my house searched this morning, and nor did Kerr, but you should have witnessed the scene Grace made! Victor had to drag her away, in the end, to shut her up. You'd have thought she had a fortune in gold bullion buried under the floorboards.'

'You mean, they had search warrants?' Buchanan asked,

somewhat surprised.

Eddie shook her head, smiling without humour. 'Sir Douglas volunteered them a free run in the big house and was so loud in his assertions that we would all be busting a gut to do likewise that it would've looked suspicious not to go along with it. The local police had taken a quick look around when the Rubens was stolen – just to establish that it hadn't been shoved in a cupboard and forgotten, somebody said! – but this time they had a good old snoop into everything.'

'They would,' Fizz said. 'A search warrant would only allow them to search for whatever it was they allegedly hoped to find – the painting, for instance – but if you offer them the chance of a fishing trip they'll jump at it.' She sat down on the doorstep and tipped up her face to the sun. 'I don't suppose they'd tell anyone if they found anything of interest.'

'Probably not.' Eddie looked at her, stretched out in the warmth like a cat, and appeared to think she had the right idea. Her temper had by now simmered down slightly and she was able to prop her shears against the doorway and claim a section of the top step. 'I don't know. They might tell the Fergussons but if they do we'll be the next to know. Sir Douglas is good about keeping us informed.'

'What inspired Sir Douglas to invite them into the big house?' Buchanan asked.

'You know what he's like.' She pushed back her hair and gave Buchanan the first glimpse of her teeth he'd had in days. 'He has to be in the thick of things and they won't let him push his nose into anything else they're doing. I get the feeling he and Lady Marjory are secretly enjoying all the excitement. They can't talk about anything else – well, none of us can – even Victor, who's usually interested in nothing but football. He's been watching the outdoor search through his binoculars all day and giving us hour by hour bulletins.'

'How can they hope to find anything in all that area?' Fizz

asked, but got nothing but a pair of grunts in reply.

Buchanan could remember a similar search not so very long ago when Fizz had been the one to locate the corpse but her search area on that occasion had covered only bare rock, not acres of forest and scrubby moorland. He glanced at her, wondering if her thoughts were carrying her down the same road, and she smiled and nodded without bothering to vocalize her response.

Eddie stood up suddenly. 'Well, I have things to do,' she said briskly. 'Kerr should be back any minute now but if you —'

'I think I hear him now,' Fizz interrupted and, in the silence that settled like a blanket as soon as she stopped speaking, Buchanan could hear footsteps and voices coming from the direction of the greenhouses.

Presently Kerr appeared, accompanied by Sir Douglas, and walked quickly towards them.

'Hi! I wasn't expecting you this evening. Have you been waiting long?'

'Just a few minutes,' Fizz told him, grinning a hello at Sir Douglas – or perhaps expressing her opinion of his attire, which was a tribute to Marlon Brando in *On the Waterfront*. 'Eddie's been keeping us entertained.'

Kerr's eyes took in the mutilated creeper. 'So I see. I could have done that myself, Eddie.'

'I know, but you did ask me how to go about it and I felt like chopping something down.' She walked away without a farewell and without a glance at Buchanan, leaving her pruning shears lying where she'd propped them.

Sir Douglas removed his cap and shook hands with Fizz and Buchanan. 'Well, well. What do you make of this development, Tam? Dreadful business, isn't it? I was just saying to Kerr here, it's like something you see on television. *Midsomer Murders*, you know. *Prime Suspect*.'

Buchanan admitted it was rather. 'It must be very upsetting

for you and Lady Marjory.'

'Upsetting for everyone. And of course we've had to close our doors to the public and cancel the Camera Club dinner that was booked for Friday. Not,' he inserted hastily, 'that I should be complaining about that, with all the other tribulation we've had to suffer. In fact it's a blessing in disguise because Nanny's funeral is to be held that morning and the last thing any of us would want is to have all the brouhaha of a formal dinner in the evening.'

'Eddie tells me you all had to allow your homes to be searched this morning.'

'Indeed we did. Well, of course, we didn't exactly *have* to but, as I told the inspector, we all want to be as helpful as we possibly can. And, my goodness, but they were thorough. My sister was quite embarrassed to see how closely they examined every little space. We'd thought they were just looking for a body, you see, but no. There were two or three of them to a room and they opened every cupboard and drawer. Even rummaged around in the kitchen, would you believe? We were mightily intrigued, Marjory and I.' He giggled suddenly like a mischievous child. 'Complete waste of time, of course, but very interesting to watch. They turned up an old autograph album of my mother's I hadn't seen in years.'

'There seems to be neither rhyme nor reason to what they find interesting,' Kerr said, leaning against the doorpost in a weary slouch as if he were weighed down by his worries. 'They asked if they could take Irene's hairbrush away to see if the hairs matched up with some strands of hair they found on an old pair of my socks. What's all that about? I could have told them they matched just by looking at them but they said they wanted to make sure.'

Buchanan looked at him closely. 'Was there anything unusual about the hair they found?'

Kerr shrugged. 'There seemed to be quite a lot of it. They

asked me if I knew how it got onto my socks but I hadn't a clue. I might not have noticed it if they hadn't pointed it out.'

'And what about the outdoor search?' Fizz asked Sir Douglas. 'Have you heard if any further evidence has been found?'

Sir Douglas beamed down at her kindly, seemed about to give her cheek a pat, and thought better of it. 'Nothing at all, as far as I know, my dear. But they are a very different lot from the chaps who were here before, you know. This Inspector Herbison who's heading the investigation now, frankly, he's not a particularly sociable type. I could have been of considerable help to him in his search but he refused my offer – quite brusquely, actually – and went about the business in, to my mind, quite the wrong way.'

Buchanan avoided Fizz's hilarious eye and nodded his commiseration. 'They must, by this time, have covered all the ground they plan to search?'

'Not a bit of it. They're going to keep going till they've covered every square inch. All the chaps in overalls went off in their vans about an hour ago but they'll be back tomorrow to search the river and both banks. Caitlin knows all about it: she's been acting as liaison officer.'

He paused and cocked his head to listen to the purr of a car engine which had been growing steadily louder for the last few seconds. It was now just out of sight and slowing for the turn into the yard.

'More visitors this evening,' he said, straightening his shoulders self-consciously and raising a hand to adjust the turned-up collar of his tartan shirt. 'I wonder who this can be.'

It was the police: two plain-clothes detectives, youthful and unthreatening, who glanced placidly around the ring of faces and nodded a greeting.

'Good evening, officers,' Sir Douglas responded in a fruity baritone. 'Dare we hope there's been a development?'

The foremost of the two scanned the assembled cast as

he allowed his lordship to shake his hand, halting his gaze on Buchanan and again on Fizz, before letting it come to rest on Kerr.

'Could we have a word in private, Mr Gilfillan?'

A small tremor of unease ran through the group engendered, not by the words but by something coldly official in the way they were spoken. Kerr looked levelly at the detective for a moment and hesitated the way you would, Buchanan guessed, if you were postponing the delivery of unwelcome tidings. Finally he drew a deep breath and preceded the two detectives into the cottage.

After a moment Sir Douglas stepped away from the doorway, followed by Fizz and Buchanan, and moved across the yard till they were out of earshot of the murmur of voices.

'I have a nasty feeling about this,' Fizz commented in a subdued tone. 'That man had Bad News written all over him.'

'Perhaps they've found Irene's...er, found Irene,' said Sir Douglas. He slipped a hand inside the open front of his shirt and massaged his T-shirt as though to still the fluttering of a startled heart. 'Oh, dear. It's all too terribly tragic. Marjory and I had so hoped there might be a favourable – or at least a less painful end to this distressing business, but there's not much chance of that, is there, Tam? One way or another there will be heartache for us all.'

Buchanan tried to say something optimistic but knew that his insincerity would be apparent. Whatever the outcome, whoever was responsible for the theft of the Rubens and for the disappearance and probable murder of Irene, Abbeyfield would never again hold the same assurance of peace and security it had once promised its residents. He looked around him at the other cottages. Although the Curzons could not have been unaware that something was happening, they were keeping well out of it. Their door was closed against the world and their windows screened by nylon net but on the other side of the yard Eddie was standing hesitantly at the top of her pathway, evidently unsure whether to join the others or withdraw into her own space. Buchanan could understand her indecision, because he felt a trifle *de trop* himself, standing there in the audience, waiting to see the outcome of the detectives' visit. Decency would dictate a discreet withdrawal but, on the other hand, one should perhaps hang around in case Kerr might need some moral support when the two policemen had left.

While he dithered, Kerr's door opened and he came out, closely accompanied by the detectives. He was neither handcuffed nor even held by either of them but it was immediately obvious, by the swift way he was ushered into the back seat of the police car, that they were not off for a spin around the local beauty spots.

Sir Douglas uttered an exclamation of dismay and hurried forward to waylay the CID officers before they could drive away. Fizz would have followed him but Buchanan held her by the sleeve.

'Hang on, Fizz. Leave it to Sir Douglas.'

'But Kerr might…they look as if they're arresting him…he might need a lawyer…'

'If he needs a lawyer he knows where to find one. It's not your place to go rushing in when you don't even know if he's been charged with anything.'

She took that on board and they stood in silence, watching and waiting, while Sir Douglas continued in conversation, his voice audible but not quite loud enough to carry across the yard. Eddie came, almost willy-nilly, to stand beside them and the seconds ticked by. At last the car doors slammed and it pulled away, forcing them to move back against Eddie's garden hedge to give it room to make a U-turn in the enclosed space. As it passed by, Kerr's drawn face stared out at them, pale and expressionless, as though he were too stunned to register the concern that must have been manifest in their demeanor. Sir Douglas remained outside Kerr's cottage till the car had disappeared and then crossed the cobbles like an old man, shaky and bewildered.

'I don't like the sound of this…'

'The sound of what?' Fizz snapped impatiently, deferring to neither his mental state, his seniority nor his social position.

'They're taking Kerr in for questioning.' His voice trembled on the final word, making him pause momentarily to pull out a hanky and dab at the corners of his mouth. 'They won't say why, but Kerr is quite obviously very shocked and worried so I'm sure something nasty has turned up. Perhaps something they found in his house, I don't know. They won't tell me.' His eyes went from face to face, seeking reassurance. 'That young detective is very lacking in the social graces.'

'Questioning is only questioning, Sir Douglas,' Eddie said firmly. 'They're just doing to Kerr what they did to me. It doesn't mean anything.'

He shook his head miserably. 'This is serious. I could see it in Kerr's face. He looked…stunned. He wouldn't look at me when I spoke to him. He wouldn't answer me. He was like some stranger sitting there in the back of the car.'

'If they had anything substantial against him they'd have charged him,' Fizz said, but not as if she believed she was fooling anyone. They were all aware that that step could be just a few questions down the line and no one, it appeared, had any further palliatives to offer.

When the silence became awkward Eddie said, with a certain amount of militancy, 'I think we're going to have to accept that someone on the estate killed Irene. If it wasn't Kerr it was someone else we've lived and worked with for a long time, so it's going to be tough to face up to. Speaking personally, as Irene's close friend, it'll be a comfort of sorts to see justice done and I can't help but suspect that Kerr's as likely to be the guilty party as anyone else.' She straightened her shoulders and Buchanan could see by the bellicose light in her eye that she had recovered not at all from her earlier fit of pique. 'We all know what Kerr was like when he lost his temper and it's been obvious to me for a long time that he and Irene were going through a bad patch. There were rows every other week – violent rows – and, on top of that, I'm beginning to wonder if I left that gardening glove in Kerr's garden when I was dealing with the greenfly on his roses. Anyone could have found it there but, let's face it, who more likely than Kerr?'

Buchanan was somewhat surprised to hear her being so outspoken, Sir Douglas was plainly horrified, and Fizz was onto her like a hawk.

'You told the police you dropped the glove in Kerr's garden,' she said flatly, moving round to where she could get a better view of Eddie's face.

Eddie looked down her nose at her, hostility suddenly writ large on her features. 'And if I did? You expect me to sit there like a dumb ox while they tried to tie me in to Irene's murder?'

'No, I wouldn't expect that,' Fizz said, with a too-sweet-to-be-wholesome expression that Eddie clearly found insulting. 'I'd expect you to cover your own ass.'

'You've no conception of what its like,' choked Eddie, hot colour sweeping up from her throat and tinting her tanned face to the tones of a Cox's pippin. 'You've never been questioned by the police —'

'I have, actually.'

'Why does that not surprise me?'

'Th-the thing is,' said Buchanan, throwing himself, verbally if not physically, between the two, 'we could be reading a great deal too much into this incident. It could be that the guy conducting the inquiry is deliberately trying to give everyone a shake-up to see what comes out of it. He got more out of Eddie last night than she'd otherwise have given him, so now he's trying it on with Kerr. I really don't believe they are any-where near making an arrest – not unless they've found Irene's body and significant forensic evidence. If that were the case we'd know about it, so it's a bit early to be jumping to conclusions.'

'But he looked so stunned,' Sir Douglas muttered, shaking his head.

'Well, you can't blame him for that,' Eddie said, still boot-faced and breathing a little gustily. 'I was pretty stunned when they did it to me, I don't mind telling you. Anyway, right now I've had enough stress for one day. I'm off to bed. Goodnight.'

She turned and paced slowly up her pathway with her shoulders very straight and her head unnaturally high. Fizz watched her retreat and smiled her pussycat smile. Buchanan could have strangled her.

Dusk was bleeding the colours from the yard and turning the hedged gardens into blue pools of shadow. 'We must be on our way,' said Buchanan. 'Can we run you up the drive, Sir Douglas?'

He roused himself from a reverie to answer. 'Thank you, Tam. A kind thought, but I think I'll walk. It'll help to calm me down.'

They shook hands and saw him set off through the arch-way, hands in the pockets of his too-tight jeans and cap pulled low across his brow. Some of the swagger had gone out of his walk.

Chapter Sixteen

Fizz was invariably first into the office in the morning. She always woke early, winter and summer, and liked to complete the walk down the Mound and along Princes Street before shoppers and tourists started clogging the pavements. The fifteen or twenty minutes during which she had the office to herself were often the most productive of the day and they eased her into the flow of work in a gentle way that made it less of a chore. This morning, however, work was awaiting her on the doorstep, in the shape of a very glum and impatient Kerr.

She spotted him from across the road and her mind had already computed a dozen reasons for his being there before she got within range to say,

'Kerr? What are you doing here?'

'I need to speak to you.'

'What about? You could have phoned. When did they let you go?'

'Last night.' He jittered around while she unlocked the door, hissing through his teeth as though he were cold. 'I tried to get a hold of you at your flat about ten-thirty but you were obviously out.'

'You drove to Edinburgh to speak to me? What's the hurry?'

He jerked his head at the door, intimating that they could talk inside, and she led him upstairs with her mind a whirlpool of speculation. She had a horrible suspicion that, although the CID had evidently not, as yet, quite got its act together, he knew he was within an ace of being charged with Irene's murder. Just what he might expect her to do about it was a matter for speculation but she could only hope he wasn't going to burden her with a confession at this stage in the game. He paced up and down while she hung up her jacket and got them a couple of mugs of coffee, then she waved at him to sit down and said,

'Okay, Kerr, let's have it. What's eating you?'

'What's eating me,' he said tensely, 'is that somebody's playing silly buggers.'

Fizz drew a breath, relieved but still cautious. 'Somebody at Abbeyfield? How are they doing that?'

'Planting fake evidence.'

Fizz widened her eyes at him and reared back in her chair. 'You're sure?'

'Sure I'm bloody sure, I wouldn't be sitting here if I weren't sure.'

'So why *are* you sitting here, Kerr? If you can prove it you should be talking to the police, not me.'

He moved his mug in slow circles on the desk in front of him, smearing a drip around to make a shiny patch. 'I *can* prove it. I swear to you I can prove it, and I will if I have to, but it'll mean giving the CID information I don't want them to have. D'you understand?'

Fizz was afraid she understood only too well. She said, 'You mean you're not going to share your proof with me either? It's a trust-me-I'm-a-good-guy situation, right?'

There was a light in his eye that told her he was simmering underneath but for once he was keeping a cap on it. 'I can tell you a part of it, Fizz, but you'll have to trust me about the rest.'

'Great,' Fizz said. 'That sounds just dandy. Okay, go ahead. Try me.'

He pushed up the arms of his sweater and leaned towards her across the desk. 'That phone-call to Vassileiou? It had to be a fake.'

'You can prove that?'

He hesitated, glaring at her, then ground out, 'No, of course I can't prove it, but nobody's going to make me believe

Irene could have been aiding and abetting art thieves. You've got to know yourself, Fizz, that she'd never have done that.'

Fizz considered putting her head in her hands but thought she'd better not since Kerr was clearly losing the plot and would bear watching. 'I think it highly unlikely,' she said carefully and that seemed to satisfy him.

'Right. But as long as the police thought she was involved with the theft – and was probably somewhere in America – there was no way they'd be carrying out any investigations at Abbeyfield – which is the only way they're going to find out what's happened to her.' He took a second to gulp down some of his coffee, keeping his eyes on her face, presumably in case she showed any sign of disagreeing with that – highly problematical – conclusion. Fizz blinked at him blandly and kept her doubts to herself.

'Well,' he said, smothering a small burp with the side of his fist, 'I wasn't having that. Somebody at Abbeyfield is at the bottom of this thing, Fizz. I *know* it. I'm so sure of it I'd bet my soul on it. I mean that.'

Fizz looked at him, wondering if she really wanted to know what was coming next. 'So?'

'So, I decided to do something to focus the attention back on Abbeyfield.' He seemed to hesitate, letting his eyes wander for a second, then he said, 'I took some of Irene's old clothes and burned them in the wood.'

'Oh geez. Oh *bloody* geez!' Fizz leaned back in her chair as though she could distance herself from this information as easily as she could distance herself from Kerr. 'I wish you hadn't told me that, Kerr. Oh my God. You know how long you could get for wasting police time and interfering with evidence? Have you any idea how much that police search is costing the taxpayer? Have you gone mad?'

'You think I give a damn about that?' he said with a stone-faced and brutal intensity that shut her up faster than if he'd lost his temper. 'I'll do what I have to do to nail the bastard who killed Irene. Oh, don't act so shocked, Fizz! We both know we'd have heard something before now if she'd still been alive, so you don't have to pretend any more. I've finally accepted that she's gone from my life and now all I want is to see her killer suffer for what he did. There's not a goddam thing in this world that matters to me, not a thing or a person I wouldn't sacrifice to that end. They can put me in jail and throw away the key, for all I care. I'm in hell anyway.'

This time Fizz did put her head in her hands; she felt it was called for.

Kerr got up and tried to pace around in the restricted space available. There was so much angst roiling around inside him that it was almost visible but he was clearly determined to stay on top of it, which was something new.

'The point is, Fizz,' he said finally, 'that I was forced to do something and I did the only thing I could think of at the time. And it worked: you have to admit it worked.'

Fizz looked up through her fingers. 'The burned clothes...yes, it focused the attention on Abbeyfield, that's for sure. I can understand why you did that, but what was the point of planting Eddie's glove at the scene?'

'That wasn't me.'

She lifted her head and blinked at him as he picked up his mug and sank another gulp of coffee. 'You mean someone just happened to drop it there accidentally beside a pile of burned matches?'

He shook his head and met her gaze with eyes that were bright and possibly just a little deranged. 'Someone else put it there deliberately.'

Disbelief fizzled gradually into acceptance as Fizz thought about that. 'Who?' she said, confusedly. 'And why? And... how?'

'I don't know who did it. Not Eddie, one would assume,

not unless she's playing a very clever game, but it could have been any of the others. Why? Obviously to divert the increased police interest onto someone else. How? No problem. Everyone was informed about the bonfire a good hour before the police got here. You and Fizz were with me in my cottage for a while but the others had every opportunity to plant the glove where it would be found.'

Fizz was diverted for a moment by the thought that she'd have to tell Buchanan about this and he'd blow his top. Hard things would be said about her odd friends and the way they went about things but she thought she could probably bear it.

She said, 'You reckon somebody just happened upon Eddie's glove and decided she'd be as good a person as any to implicate?'

'Well, it's possible,' he said, speaking like a man who'd given the matter considerable thought. 'Whoever did it must have been aware that there wasn't time enough to be too choosy but, in fact, I'm pretty sure that the bastard was trying to focus suspicion on me.'

'On you? How come?'

He shrugged. 'Eddie told the police that the last time she remembered seeing that glove was a few days ago when she was spraying my roses. It's very possible that she left it lying there where she'd been working – she loses a lot of tools that way – and if I saw it I didn't register it. However, someone who was looking for something of mine to incriminate me with might very well have spotted it and would assume it belonged to me.'

Fizz wasn't entirely convinced but she said, 'It's possible.'

'It's more than possible,' Kerr retorted, 'it's almost certain because, when his first attempt to frame me went awry he tried the same trick a second time.' He sat down again, drawing his chair closer to the desk. 'When the police were searching my cottage yesterday morning they found a hank of hair –

not even a hank just a few dozen hairs – on a sock of mine in the dirty clothes basket. They were obviously Irene's, I told them that when they showed them to me, but they took them away to be tested along with Irene's hairbrush. I think I told you that, right? Well, when they came back yesterday evening they told me that the hair they'd found on the sock had not been cut off but *burned* off.'

He stopped and waited for Fizz to respond but she was unable to come up with anything better than, 'How could that have happened?'

'Well, obviously,' he said impatiently, 'the only way it could have happened is that Irene's killer put it there, knowing that the cottage was going to be searched.'

'Who knew that?'

'All of us. Sir Douglas told us that morning that he'd offered to let the CID loose in the big house and it was fairly clear to the rest of us that we'd be expected to be equally accommodating.'

'But someone would've had to get into your cottage without being seen. I know you don't lock your front door but anyone going in would surely be taking quite a risk of being spotted.'

'There's a back door,' Kerr admitted with a shortness that didn't quite hide his chagrin. 'It opens onto a sort of wired-in enclosure where we keep the big equipment like power mowers and trailers. We don't bother locking it during the day.'

Fizz shook her head in disgust and received a black look in return. 'Well, Kerr,' she said, trying to think positive, 'you've achieved one thing at least. You've more or less proved that somebody on the estate has it in for you. It could be the person behind Irene's…er, disappearance, or it could be someone who believes very strongly that *you're* the guilty party and is making sure the police investigate you thoroughly.'

The latter possibility appeared not to have occurred to

Kerr. 'I don't think it's personal,' he said uncertainly. 'It's somebody trying to lay a false trail.'

'You can't be sure of that,' Fizz insisted. 'Let's face it, Kerr, you have to be pretty high on everybody's list of suspects. They all know that you and Irene had your problems. They all heard that stand-up fight you had the night before she disappeared. They all know you're a bad tempered bastard. The miracle is that none of them were willing to shop you right away.'

She'd half expected a violent response to those home truths and, for a moment it looked as though she were going to get one, then Kerr dropped his eyes and nodded. 'I hear what you're saying and, of course, you're absolutely right, Fizz. We did have problems, and they were entirely my fault. I do have trouble keeping a grip on my temper but I don't believe it's as bad as you think it is. Sure we had our spats, Irene and I, and they were noisy, I'll admit that, but they weren't all that frequent – maybe once a year – and they were never serious. You're seeing me at my worst. I'm worried sick, I'm not sleeping, I'm raging at the way the police are dragging their feet. It's not easy to stay calm. But what the neighbours understand – and maybe you don't – is that Irene and I...' His voice broke and his already scowling face grew blacker. 'Everybody knew how we felt about each other so I don't believe anyone could really suspect I could have harmed her. I don't go along with that theory at all. What I proved is that someone on the estate has done away with Irene and, now that the police are doing what they should have been doing a fortnight ago, he or she is running scared.'

Fizz found herself somewhat attracted to that possibility since, from a purely selfish point of view, any destabilising of the situation seemed likely to offer the best chance of further leads, but she needed time to think about it.

'I'll get us another coffee,' she said, and receiving no

opposition from Kerr, took herself off for a few minutes quiet deliberation.

As she passed through the front office The Wonderful Beatrice caught her eye. She was obviously interested to know the business of Fizz's unscheduled visitor but was too proud to descend to a direct request for clarification.

'Tam was on the phone,' she said, peering over her glasses at a scribble on her notepad. 'I didn't disturb you as he said it wasn't urgent but I've to tell you...Kerr was allowed home last night and if you want to go over to Abbeyfield tonight it's okay with him.'

'Ah.' Fizz thought about that for a minute. 'Would you give him a ring for me, Beattie? Tell him I've got Kerr in the office right now and there's things we need to talk over before we go back to Abbeyfield. My place, six-thirty. Thanks, poppet, you're a real sweetheart, you know that?'

Beattie, who was anything but a poppet, gave her a basilisk stare, but Fizz went on her way convinced that she had brightened her day. As she spooned coffee into cups she considered what Kerr had told her and tried to estimate how much of it she would have to share with Buchanan. Pretty much all of it, she supposed, and it was obvious who he'd blame for involving him in a seriously iffy situation. If it ever came out that he – and she for that matter – had been aware of Kerr's finagling and kept their mouths shut there would be hell to pay.

And yet, at the back of her mind, beyond all the considerations of right or wrong, she had a feeling that things were looking up. Where, only a couple of days ago, she'd felt that the case was dead in the water, now something was at least stirring in the shadows. If you went along with Kerr's reasoning – and that was maybe not as crazy as she had at first supposed – you had to conclude that Irene's killer was still there at Abbeyfield, worried, jumpy, and willing to do something about it.

She hurried back to Kerr and found him standing with his

arms tightly folded across his chest, staring blindly at the rows of legal tomes that lined one wall.

'Kerr,' she said, sliding round behind the desk and pushing a mug across to him, 'do you think the same person could have pushed Nanny down the stairs?'

'Pushed?' he said in a tone that showed her the thought had never occurred to him. 'You think someone pushed her? Why, for God's sake?'

'Well, *I* don't know, Kerr. That's what I'm asking you. I was just thinking that the person who's trying to frame you must be feeling vulnerable. If it were me, I'd be making sure I'd covered all my traces, watching anyone who might be a danger to me, particularly if they knew something that might encourage the police to start taking a special interest in me. It was odd, the way Nanny's accident happened at this particular point in time. Okay, it could have happened any time but all the same it made me wonder if her sudden death might have been convenient for someone.'

His chest heaved as he drew a deep breath but he didn't answer straight away. For a minute or two he sat thinking, sometimes shaking his head slowly to himself, sometimes raising his brows as though willing himself to accept a possibility.

'God, Fizz,' he said at last, 'I don't know what to believe. I see what you mean about the coincidence of an accident like that happening within days of Irene's disappearance but the idea of someone having to silence Nanny – it's bizarre. Nanny scarcely knew what day it was. If she came out and told me she'd seen somebody carrying an unconscious woman across the lawn at midnight it's more than likely I'd just say, yes Nanny, don't let it worry you, and then put it out of my mind.'

'But if she was liable to say something to the police – even something she thought quite innocuous – she'd have been worth silencing. Try to remember if she was saying anything unusual before she died: anything that might have a bearing on the theft of the Rubens or on Irene's disappearance, anything strange about any of the residents.'

Kerr wrapped both hands around his coffee mug and stared into it as if he was consulting a crystal ball. It didn't look as if he were likely to remember anything much at all from recent conversations with Nanny but Fizz gave him time to think about it and got down a few notes on what he had told her. Just one thing bothered her about his account of burning Irene's clothes.

'It was Indie who found your bonfire in the woods,' she said, seeing he had given up on his cogitations. 'If he hadn't taken off like that into the bushes we'd never have stumbled across it. How were you planning to have Victor Curzon witness its discovery?'

Something approaching a smile twisted one corner of his mouth. 'That dog,' he said, 'is hooked on aniseed. I got myself a mouthful of the sort of sweets Grace feeds it all the time and simply spat a trail off the path and up to the edge of the cinders. I knew I'd have no problem getting Victor to take Indie on a walk in that direction, we've done it regularly together, but it was an added bonus to have you and Tam on hand to add a little extra credibility.'

Fizz had to smile a little herself at the thought of how pleased Buchanan would be to hear that he had been of service. It did occur to her that such duplicity marked Kerr as a cunning bastard who might be double-bluffing her all the way down the line but she shelved that thought for the moment. It was now after ten and she had work to do.

'Okay, Kerr. Now I have to do some thinking about what you've told me and see what I can make out of it. Leave it with me and I'll talk to you again tomorrow. Maybe Buchanan and I will take a run over to Abbeyfield in the evening.'

He made no move to get up and go. 'You think there's a

possibility of finding out who's doing this?'

No, would have been the honest answer to that one and Fizz didn't want to give Kerr false hopes but she had never been good at admitting defeat. She said, 'There's not a lot to go on in what you've told me, Kerr, there's no two ways about that, but I've made arrangements to talk it over with Buchanan tonight and, who knows, two heads may turn out to be better than one.'

'You don't want me to sit in on the discussion?'

'Not this time, no Kerr. We'll get back to you tomorrow – maybe sooner if we have a brainwave.'

'There may be things I've forgotten to tell you —'

'If so you can phone me. I'll be in the office till five o'clock.'

'Okay, but maybe I should hang around for a while in case —'

'Kerr,' she said. 'I have things to do. Go.'

Exit Kerr, pursued by doubts.

Chapter Seventeen

Fizz was looking very pretty when she opened the door to Buchanan. She had changed out of her hermaphroditic business suit into a pale greenish-blue sleeveless blouse and a short denim skirt that skimmed her knees in a flirty sort of way that drew the eye and gladdened the heart. She always got quite tanned early in the summer and already the pale gold of her hair was lightened at the tips, making the half curls looked like white capped waves in a smooth, corn-coloured sea. She stood waiting for him at the top of the stairs, the warm light of the evening sun from the staircase window lighting her like a blessing, and Buchanan was immediately swamped by misgiving. Fizz only ever looked this good when she had something to confess: usually something that she knew would make him very, very angry.

'Hi,' she said, compounding his anxiety by giving him a nice smile. 'I hope you're hungry. I've made three courses.'

Buchanan made no reply, partly because he'd run up the stairs and didn't want to pant, but she led the way into the kitchen/living room chattering brightly and pretending not to notice. The windows were opened to their fullest extent and a faint movement of air drifted in to flutter the corners of the tablecloth and the leaves of the parsley plant that grew in a pot on the window sill. There was beetroot and tomato soup (his favourite) simmering on the stove and the smell of something oniony drifting up from the oven and he could see a cheese board set out ready at the end of the working surface. It was enough to freeze a man's blood.

'You had a visit from Kerr this morning,' he said when she gave him an opening, in the hope of getting it over with. 'What brought that on?'

'Oh, it's a long story,' she said lightly, taking a carton of cream out of the fridge. 'I don't want to tell it in snatches.

Let's have our meal in peace, then we can discuss it later.'

He watched her morosely. Real cream tonight instead of the crème fraîche she usually gave him with beetroot and tomato soup. It must be worse than he'd thought.

'Nothing urgent, then?'

'No, nothing urgent. How was your interview at Saughton?'

Buchanan, in company with the prisoner's solicitor, had spent half the afternoon in H.M. Edinburgh prison in consultation with an alleged arsonist who was strenuously maintaining his innocence in the face of overwhelming evidence to the contrary. Larry the Bastard had left instructions for this matter to be cleared up one way or another before his return so it was currently demanding more than a little of Buchanan's time and concentration. The temptation to discuss the matter with Fizz, who sometimes brought a new and inspiring light to such issues, was too sweet to resist so they were at the biscuits and cheese stage before he was able to swing the conversation back to the topic of Kerr's visit.

'So, what did Kerr have to say to you this morning that was so important he had to drive in to Edinburgh instead of phoning? Did the police give him a hard time last night?'

She finished chewing a cube of Danish Blue before she answered, probably to give herself time to choose the right opening gambit. 'No, I don't think they were all that tough on him. If they were, he didn't say so, but there were one or two things that had been bothering him.'

Buchanan waited while she gathered up some crumbs on a licked fingertip and put them in her mouth. He could see that she was treading carefully and expecting trouble but he was determined that he wasn't going to lose his temper. Whatever she had to confess – he was sure it would be a confession – he would remain calm. Firm but calm.

'Uh-huh?'

'Well, he seems finally to have given up hope of finding Irene alive, so you can imagine how that's affecting him. On top of which, he reckons someone at Abbeyfield is trying to frame him by planting incriminating evidence.'

This was so far from what Buchanan had steeled himself to hear that he was momentarily confounded. 'Good God! Is he sure about that?'

'Yes, and I think he's probably right.'

'What evidence is he talking about?'

'Well actually,' she said with an airy wave of an oatcake, 'he's been up to a little jokery-pokery of his own. You know what he's like. Patience isn't exactly his long suit and —'

'What kind of jokery-pokery precisely?'

'Oh...it turns out that he got himself into a tizzy over the Vassileiou phone-call – which he never accepted as genuine, as you know. He was totally convinced that someone on the estate had to be the baddie and he knew the police would waste valuable time sussing out what he considered to be nothing more than a red herring so he felt more or less forced to do something to focus attention back on Abbeyfield. He was pretty much at the end of his tether, I imagine, and the idea that someone —'

'What did he do?' Buchanan asked, very calmly.

She regarded him warily. 'The bonfire in the woods. That was him.'

'Ah,' he said and looked out the window at the roofscape below.

There was a short silence while he reeled under the blow, his brain resolutely maintaining it's equilibrium by composing an assortment of remarks incorporating the words "shit" and "fan". He found it astonishing to reflect on how often his association with Fizz threw up these professionally embarrassing situations. Larry was already infuriated by the regularity with which Buchanan found himself at odds with the law, either due to his own lack of judgement or because events conspired to make escape impossible, and there was no denying that the last few years – ever since Fizz had invaded his hitherto peaceful existence – had seen their full share of compromising situations. Some had attracted the attention of the media and some, thank God, he had managed to keep relatively private, but Larry was unlikely to view another scandal with equanimity.

'We are required to inform the police,' he said flatly. 'We're not acting officially for Kerr so we can't make client confidentiality our excuse.'

'Don't worry. I told him not to tell anyone he'd mentioned it to me.'

'Fizz, if it comes out —'

'Why should it come out? You worry about such silly things.'

'I have a lot at stake,' he growled, knowing it was a waste of time. 'You, I dare say, could always fall back on pig-smuggling or dealing blackjack or one of your other talents but I'm bloody well committed to being respectable. God, why do your friends always take such chances with the law? They're a bunch of lunatics. They're a menace to society.'

Fizz looked as if she were about to take exception to that, as well she might because it wasn't exactly fair. Strictly speaking, those of her friends who'd transgressed in the past had done so only because she'd told them to.

'Anyway,' she said, with great restraint. 'Wait till you hear what else I have to tell you before you get your Y's in a twist. Burning Irene's clothes may have been a crazy thing to do but it at least got a response because somebody deliberately planted Eddie's gardening glove there, close to the fire, where it was bound to be found. Kerr's pretty certain that whoever did it found the glove in his garden, where Eddie last used it, and must have thought it belonged to Kerr. And when that plan failed, the same person got into his cottage and planted a hank of Irene's hair on a pair of dirty socks. Evidently that hair had been burned off, not cut off, and that's what the CID guys were questioning him about last night. He's now scared rigid about what this joker will try next.'

Buchanan, diverted for the moment from the contemplation of his own fate, felt a quickening of interest. 'Has he any idea who that joker might be?'

'Not a clue.'

'Have you?'

'No, but I've been thinking about it all day and I get the impression we're a step closer to finding out. I don't know exactly why, but I feel a lot more optimistic somehow. I feel there ought to be some way we can get a take on whoever's doing these things. That's why I wanted you to come over. We have to look at what we've got and see if we can scrape together enough to constitute a lead of sorts.'

She looked furiously determined, straining at the leash like a bloodhound, but Buchanan felt it would take more than motivation to shine any light through the Stygian gloom that faced them.

'What Kerr told you doesn't actually carry us much further forward, Fizz. All he has actually established is that the joker, as you call him or her, is someone who hangs around Abbeyfield.'

She held out a hand across the table and clenched it. 'But I can feel the bastard right here in my hand, Buchanan. We're that close, I swear it, if only we can focus our thoughts. I need you to put your mind to this.'

'Focus on what, Fizz? I wouldn't even know where to start.'

Her brows snapped down in irritation and she sprang up from the table and started to whisk dishes away into the sink. 'You're not trying! There must be some facts we can establish about this person other than that they're located at Abbeyfield. Can't we eliminate one or two of the residents? I *know* we can move forward on this, Buchanan, if you'll just concentrate.'

Flattered, in spite of himself, by this evidence of her belief in his cogitative powers, Buchanan made an effort to think about that while she clattered around, washing dishes and taking out her frustration on inanimate objects.

'You want a piece of paper and a pencil?' she asked, daring him to refuse.

He had nothing concrete to write down but he filled in a minute or two by listing all the residents and failing to find a good reason for eliminating any of them. Some appealed to him as suspects more than others but not for any reliable reason. Presently Fizz finished what she was doing, seated herself across the corner of the table from him and leaned over to see what he'd written.

'Okay, what next?'

Goaded into doing something, Buchanan drew a border around a column-shaped area of paper and labelled it "Joker: Known Facts". He said, 'What do we know about him?'

'Or her.'

'Him,' he said. 'I can't be bothered with all this him-or-her stuff. You can trust me to keep an open mind, I think.'

'Okay. What do we know about him? We know he's at Abbeyfield.'

Buchanan wrote "Abbeyfield" at the top of the column and then stared at the paper for a while. 'We know he's probably nervous.' He wrote that.

'We know,' said Fizz, 'that he wants to incriminate Kerr.'

That was added to the list. It was already longer than Buchanan had hoped but none of it seemed particularly illuminating.

'What else?' Fizz demanded as if he were some sort of clairvoyant.

Together they stared at the paper till it seemed to Buchanan as if the Joker were there on the white page staring back at him. The conviction took him that Fizz was right: they should already have information – if they could only grasp it – that they could use to move forward, if only a step at a time.

He wrote down "phone-call", drew a box round it, and stared at it.

'I suppose the Joker made the phone-call?' Fizz proffered.

'Presumably. In response to which,' he linked another box to the first, 'Kerr planted the burned clothes in the wood. That made the Joker nervous so,' another box was added, 'he planted the glove, accidentally framing the wrong person. Then he tries again.' He wrote "hair" in the final box and looked at the train of events, awaiting inspiration. 'What will happen next?'

'The ball's in Kerr's court,' Fizz said.

'God forbid!' Buchanan's brain reeled at the prospect. 'If he commits any more felonious acts I'm out of here.'

'He won't do anything without talking to me about it first,' Fizz assured him with what looked to Buchanan like totally misplaced confidence.

'I wish I could believe that, Fizz, but I have to say that in my view we can't trust Kerr to act rationally any more. Anyone who could deliberately waste police time and taxpayers money the way he did is dangerously out of control and neither you nor I can afford to be seen as accessories.' He found himself grinding his teeth and stopped while he still had something to chew with. 'You appreciate the position we're in, Fizz? This guy is running wild. He doesn't care what happens to him and he doesn't care what happens to anyone around him. We don't know what potentially damaging scheme he'll involve us in next and we should be taking steps to cover ourselves – probably by beating a hasty retreat!'

She met his furious glare with a steady, faintly saddened

regard. 'You don't mean that, Buchanan.'

'I do. We don't have a choice.'

'What's he going to do? He doesn't know, any better than we do ourselves, who the Joker is.'

'I'll tell you what he's going to do,' Buchanan retorted, plucking the answer straight out of his subconscious, 'he's going to try and lay a trap for him.'

Fizz fell abruptly silent, her eyes still on his face but not seeing him, her lips parted in thought. 'I bet you're right,' she murmured after a minute, and dropped her gaze to Buchanan's flow chart. 'That's the next carriage in your train of events.'

Buchanan pulled the paper towards him and added another square and then they sat and looked at it as though it were some sort of conduit into Kerr's subconscious. Fizz leaned closer, still focused on the paper even though there was nothing on it to inspire her, and the familiar smell of green apples drifted up from her hair.

'There's no way we can tell how he'd go about laying a trap,' she said.

'I don't know,' Buchanan muttered, his brain groping forward, blind as a mole, through the labyrinth. 'He doesn't have much of a choice open to him. How would you go about it?'

Fizz scowled at the line of boxes. 'I'd have to have something to bait it with.'

'You'd have to bait it with something the Joker wants.' Buchanan pointed his pencil at the list of known facts. 'What does he want?'

'He wants to incriminate Kerr.'

'Right. So that's the bait. What Kerr's going to do is offer him an opportunity to do just that.'

'He'd want to be able to prove that someone had planted fake evidence,' Fizz said. 'Or, preferably, catch the Joker actually doing so – red-handed, in front of witnesses.'

Minutes passed. The air seemed to Buchanan to buzz with electro-magnetic waves, or whatever it was that fuelled brain power. Finding the scent of Fizz's hair too distracting, he got up and looked out the window, leaning his hands on the sill and sticking his head out into the cool breeze.

'I'll tell you something else we know about him,' Fizz said suddenly, her voice charged with an animation that made him turn. 'He has access to Irene's corpse. He was able to lay his hands on that hank of hair when he needed it, wasn't he? That means that either she's not buried or that he dug her up to cut off the hair.'

She pulled the paper round and added "bio material" to the list.

'That's good,' said Buchanan, coming back to the table. 'If he used it once he'll almost certainly use it again. Not hair again, but skin or nail clippings, maybe. It's much more specific than anything else identifiable as Irene's – clothing, jewellery, or such like – and potentially much more damaging to Kerr. I think we'd be safe in assuming that the Joker will already be looking for an opportunity to plant it where it'll do most good so, if Kerr plans to have a trap waiting for him, he'd better move fast.'

Fizz thought about that for a while, then said, 'He has to offer the Joker an opportunity that's just too good to refuse. But, when you come down to practicalities, that's not as easy as it looks, is it? The police told all the residents to keep their doors locked in future so if Kerr were to go off leaving his door ajar the Joker would almost certainly smell a rat. We have to think of something cleverer that that.'

'Uh, hang on a minute,' Buchanan said. 'At what point did this become "we" and not "Kerr"?'

'But, of course we have to do it, Buchanan,' she claimed, blazing her eyes at him in what she clearly imagined was an intimidating manner. 'And we have to do it fast, before Kerr comes up with some harebrained and possibly illegal plan of his own.'

'Wrong.' Buchanan held up a determined palm against further argument. 'There is no "have to" about it, Fizz. I told you from the beginning that I'm staying strictly off-screen in this production and so, if you have any sense, will *you*.'

'Who's to know we're involved? Isn't it better to guide Kerr down a planned route than to have him do something that could get our faces in the paper again?'

Buchanan was painfully aware that there was probably some truth in that view of things. Personally he would have been in favour of simply getting on the phone to Kerr and putting the fear of death into him but, of course, when you were dealing with a nut like that there was no guarantee that such tactics would have any effect. One could only hope and pray that he had not already gone off half-cocked and made matters irretrievably worse than they already were.

'If the Joker can't plant incriminating evidence in Kerr's house,' Fizz went inexorably on, 'where can we get him to plant it?'

'Oh God, I dunno,' Buchanan said, starting to buckle under the strain. 'My brain's *bleeding*, Fizz. Let's have a break and a cup of coffee.'

'No,' she said, with her usual deep regard for another's pain, 'we're nearly there. Think, Buchanan.'

'It's impossible! Kerr doesn't have any place of his own outside his cottage. He doesn't have an office or even a studio like Irene's, and leaving something to be found where he usually hangs out – like in the woods – just isn't going to pinpoint him alone. We need some equipment that no one can get at other than Kerr…or…or something that's specifically *his*.'

'We could get him to leave something unguarded…something like a big kitchen knife…in the garden, maybe.'

Buchanan pinched the bridge of his nose between his fingers

and squeezed his eyes shut. 'We're dealing with a person who's too smart to fall for something obvious, Fizz. We'll have to do better than that.'

'Okay, we have to put something in a place where the police are going to find it which means one of the sections they haven't searched yet.' She commandeered the pencil and drew an ornate frame around each of the boxes. Having accomplished that without clarifying matters any she then sketched a wall of trees penetrated by a rough path. 'Some place in the woods.'

Buchanan massaged his temples and tried to visualise the map above Caitlin's desk. 'They've already covered all the low lying areas except the upper slope of the hill where we found the bonfire and they'll probably have finished that by tomorrow. We'd have to set our trap further afield.'

'There's an ice house up there in the woods somewhere,' Fizz said thoughtfully. 'Kerr told us he'd left his mountain bike there, remember that?'

'Uh-huh.' Her words settled gently into Buchanan's brain and took time to take root. He said, 'It's quite high up. I saw it on the map.' He sat up. 'Who else knows it's there?'

She frowned and bit the end of the pencil. 'Victor knows. He was planning to walk at least part of the way with Kerr. In fact, Kerr had arranged the whole thing so that Victor would be a witness to the finding of the clothes. He'd laid a scent trail that he knew Indie would follow.'

Buchanan nodded, storing that away to think about later, but he couldn't afford to be deflected right now. 'It's possible some of the others also know the bike's there,' he said, 'but if we're going to lay a trap we have to make sure everyone has the chance to see the bait. We'd have to tell each of them separately that Kerr's bike is lying up there in the ice house completely unguarded.' He turned the possibilities over in his mind, unwilling to accept that so unsophisticated a scheme had a chance of success. 'Is it too simple?'

'The best plans are always simple,' said Fizz bracingly, blessing him with a satisfied smile. 'We'll be going to Nanny's funeral tomorrow afternoon so there's bound to be an opportunity to speak to everyone. You see? I told you we could do it.'

'Do I get my coffee now?'

'You do. With cream and sugar. To hell with unclogged arteries.' She got up and put the kettle on. 'One of us had better phone Kerr and tell him to hold his hand till we work out the details.'

Buchanan was not willing to be the one to descend the hundred steps to the nearest phone booth, not if he was expected to ascend them again, so he said nothing in the hope that Fizz would show her gratitude for his mental effort by volunteering. He sat watching her pottering about and considered the practicalities of the entrapment they were about to perpetrate. Obviously, it would have to be very carefully orchestrated, particularly if they wanted it to produce facts that might be required to stand up in court. In itself, what they would be doing was not illegal but he wanted to be sure that his own ass was well and truly covered, and Fizz's too, if that could be achieved. One could never quite be prepared for what might occur – not when dealing with Fizz and her friends – but still, as Fizz herself would argue, there was certainly something to be said for living dangerously.

Chapter Eighteen

Fizz was not greatly in favour of funerals, especially the traditional variety which, it turned out, was what the Fergussons had considered appropriate for their aged retainer. She herself had left instructions that, when her own time came, she was to be thrown on the nearest compost heap but, failing that, she could only hope that any rites considered proper by her friends would centre on celebrating her life – or even in celebrating getting rid of her – rather than simply depressing all concerned.

Only about sixteen people gathered to give Nanny a good send-off, all of them connected in some way with the estate, and if it didn't seem much of a fan base to show for seventy-eight years on earth, at least it could be said that most of those who'd turned up appeared to be genuinely saddened by the old lady's demise. Even before the onset of the melancholy organ music and the gloomy sermonising of the priest it was clear that anyone turning up without a long face and a hushed voice would stand out from the crowd like a drag queen. During the service even Buchanan appeared affected, but then he was one of those people peculiarly susceptible to organ music and had only to hear a passage played in a minor key to start contemplating the brevity of life. In another age he could have made a good living as a professional mourner.

Both he and Fizz had been up half the night working out the practicalities of their planned entrapment and had parted in something less than the best of terms due to Buchanan's interminable nit-picking. He was determined that, if Irene's killer did actually fall into the trap, the ensuing media spotlight would catch neither him nor Fizz in its beam and, while that was fine with Fizz, she was pretty choked off when she realised that she did not figure personally in his plans for the final scene. He had actually gone ahead and engaged Joe, one of their private investigators, as an independent witness and it was to be he and Kerr who were to have the fun of concealing themselves close to the ice house and witnessing the springing of the trap. This was, of course, outrageous but neither reasoning, threats nor foul language could budge Buchanan one inch and Fizz was wary about risking a total breakdown of diplomatic relations by defying him since she might need him for something in the future. That did not mean she had any intention of submitting to his authority, of course, but the situation would require deft handling if she were to have her own way.

'They all look so ordinary,' he said as they watched the rest of the Abbeyfield contingent leave the graveside. 'So innocent, every one of them. Makes you wonder if we're barking up the wrong tree. Or just plain barking.'

'One of them could look a lot different to us by tomorrow morning.'

'With a bit of luck. At which point we're going to have to decide what to do with our findings.'

Fizz tipped down her sunglasses to look at him over the rims. 'We tell the police, surely?'

'That would be one choice of action but not, I think, a good one. Our trap won't catch us the murderer, you know. All it'll catch is the person who's been planting the false trail. The chances are that the two are the same person but the worst crime he could be charged with would be interfering with the course of justice and that's the last thing we want.' He took her by the elbow and headed for the car park ahead of the other mourners who were still milling around, talking to Nanny's parish priest and to each other. 'No. Our little scheme is fine, as far as it goes, but all it can be expected to achieve is to pinpoint the person we should be concentrating our attention on.'

'Yes, of course.' Fizz nodded as though she had accepted

that fact all along but actually it came as a bit of a blow. She'd
been so chuffed with the success of their brainstorming the
night before that she'd envisaged a speedy conclusion to the
case. Now it appeared likely to drag on and on, and with Larry
the Bastard due back at his desk in two days time, guess who'd
be carrying the heavy end of the investigation on her own.

'The next bit's crucial,' Buchanan was saying when next she
paid attention to him. 'Just remember to pick a good time to
do your party piece. If they all hear it at once that would be
ideal but if you can't achieve that it's not the end of the world,
we can do it piecemeal. But make sure you don't wait too long
in case some of them leave early.'

'Buchanan...what are you on about? You know I'm much
better at this sort of thing than you are. Relax, for God's sake.'

'Right. Sorry. Just making sure, that's all.'

It was interesting to see that he was verging on the jittery,
Fizz reflected as they got into the car. He usually managed to
preserve at least an outward appearance of sanguinity, whatever the situation, but it looked like he felt more hopeful than
he pretended to be that the end was in sight.

The Fergussons had laid on a rather generous buffet and,
after a meandering, maudlin and unnecessarily lengthy speech
from Sir Douglas, the assembled mourners got into the food
and booze with a noticeable eat-drink-and-be-merry gusto.
The drawing room had seemed large to Fizz on her last visit
but today, with the buffet table taking up almost the entire
end wall and the grand piano claiming its own considerable
space, it felt quite cramped. People split up into bunches,
Buchanan quickly forming a small group of two with Eddie,
but Fizz was cornered by Lady Marjory.

'Let me top up your glass, my dear. What's that you're
drinking? Tonic?'

'No, really, I'm fine,' Fizz laid a hand across the top of her
glass. She could imagine how much gin she'd get if she let

Lady Marjory do the pouring.

'You'll have something from the buffet, then?'

'I will, certainly, in a few minutes. It looks very tempting.'

'All Mrs Oliver's work, really. She's been working very hard. Nanny was very special to us all, you know, and we wanted to give her a good send off.' Her eyes drifted round her guests with what appeared to be genuine affection. 'We're a very close-knit – a very loving little group, you know. As Douglas says, these people are the only family we have now.'

Fizz wondered if she were deluding herself or if she thought she was deluding her audience. Probably the former, judging from her face, which just went to show how easy it was to believe what you wanted to believe. It made her think of Larry the Bastard who, according to Buchanan, was convinced that his staff held him in the utmost reverence. "You'll find me firm but fair," he apparently told every new recruit. "I believe in letting my staff know where they stand and they respect me for it. Am I right, chaps?" The chaps loathed him to a man but like the Abbeyfield staff, they knew what side their bread was buttered on so his self-deception persisted.

Unable to think of a more intelligent rejoinder, she said, 'I can understand how close you must have been to Nanny after sharing a roof with her all these years.'

'Yes, indeed, she's a part of all my best memories.' She turned her head and looked at the photographs on the piano beside her. 'Here is a staff photograph taken when my parents were alive – that's them sitting at the front, that's Douglas there beside my father, and that's me in my riding breeches with my little sister, Agnes. You wouldn't recognise Nanny but there she is, in the back row.'

Fizz looked obediently and counted thirteen of a staff which didn't seem excessive considering the standards they were expected to keep up both indoors and out. Nanny's face was a slightly over-exposed blur.

'We had to let most of them go after my parents died,' Lady Marjory said, fingering the frame as though reluctant to put it down, 'but Nanny stayed on – to take care of us, as she used to put it.'

'She was quite a character.'

'Indeed she was. She used to keep us all going with her reminiscences.'

'And her ghost stories, yes.'

Lady Marjory ducked her head attentively. 'Ghost stories?'

'I'm told Nanny liked to tell ghost stories. Doesn't Abbeyfield have a ghost?'

She laughed, shaking her iron-grey head. 'If we do, it never revealed itself to anyone but Nanny. But then, half the stories she told about the old days were pure invention also. I wouldn't be surprised if, these last few years, the dividing line between remembered facts and what were actually incidents she'd read in books became a little blurred.' She set the staff photograph back on the piano and sorted out a further selection of snapshots for Fizz's delectation. 'My grandmother as a debutante. Douglas in the south of France – dear me, what a heart-throb he was! Another of Douglas looking every inch the man about town, don't you think?'

In fact, fully three-quarters of the photographs were of Douglas in a variety of poses but wearing the same, slightly batty but supremely smug expression that had, in middle age, become habitual. At some stages in his life he had been quite passable but at no point had he merited such adulation as Lady Marjory's. Fizz was more interested in the occasional appearance, in the more recent pictures, of current members of staff. There were a couple of rigidly posed groups showing familiar faces wreathed in less familiar smiles but the same faces showed up in a variety of snapshots and in more casual, more revealing poses. It was intriguing to see Eddie, for instance, playing tennis with Sir Douglas and Victor wheeling the late –

and hugely fat – Lady Audrey in a wheelchair.

'But now I insist that you have something to eat,' declared Lady Marjory, just as Fizz was getting interested. 'Caitlin, dear, come and look after Miss Fitzpatrick. I'm depending on you young things to see that we're not left with all this food. We don't want Mrs Oliver's hard work to go to waste, do we? And, as Douglas says, it doesn't fry up very well for breakfast.'

With a bray of laughter she strode off to where Victor and Sir Douglas were laying waste to the drinks table and started chivvying them to come and eat. Kerr was hovering, stiff faced and pallid, by the fireplace while Buchanan and Eddie were now discretely installed in a window bay, out of Lady Marjory's line of sight, and seemed to be getting on together like a house on fire. Eddie was all pouting and dimples and smiles and Buchanan was clearly lapping it up with a readiness that did nothing for Fizz's appetite. She filled her plate however, under Caitlin's supervision, and concentrated on double checking what she already knew about the progress of the police search.

'So, the police must have covered all the grounds by this time, I suppose?'

Caitlin bit the end off a pastry and examined the stuffing. 'Just about. They still have the section from the ice house to the top of the hill to finish – they're doing that tomorrow – and then they'll be moving on to the outlying sections, and God knows how long they'll take to complete those. Nobody could claim they're not thorough.'

'I can't imagine they'll find anything now, can you? Not a body, anyway. I mean, why lug a body all the way up a hill when you could bury it closer to home?'

'That's what Inspector Herbison thinks, if you ask me, but with all the media interest associated with the theft of the Rubens they have to go the whole hog. Otherwise I reckon they'd have searched the woods, maybe, but nothing further.'

Fizz found herself wondering if Caitlin would be the one who'd appear radically different in the light of tonight's revelations. She could see neither guile nor nervousness in the woman's eyes and she appeared more interested in her food than in anything else but then, so did everyone else in the room, with the possible exception of Buchanan and Eddie.

As she looked across at them Buchanan glanced round and caught her eye. He turned away immediately but a moment later he glanced round again, as she'd known he would, and she sent him a half smile. He was obviously somewhat discomfited by her regard and she should have done the decent thing and turned her back on him but it was too much fun to see him constantly having to check on her to see if she was still looking.

Presently Eddie discerned that she had less than his full attention and, in what looked like mild vexation, headed for the buffet, leaving him to trail after her with a face like thunder. Fizz continued her conversation with Caitlin but her mind was awake to the main purpose of her presence at the feast: namely to establish in everyone's mind the unguarded availability of Kerr's mountain bike. Ideally, she needed all the suspects to be within earshot and now, with the arrival of Eddie and Buchanan, every one of the Abbeyfield residents was grouped quite closely around the eats table. Kerr was the most distant, still leaning against the mantelpiece, but that was all to the good since she could, in addressing him, raise her voice to a level that would be heard over the background hum of conversation.

Judging that she wouldn't get a better chance than this, she took a deep breath and said,

'Kerr, could I borrow your mountain bike sometime? I've a notion to take a spin down the river bank and see how far it goes.'

The words were intrusive enough to halt the conversation

for a few seconds. One or two heads turned momentarily in her direction, some swung round to take in Kerr's reaction as he said,

'Sure. You're welcome to use it but I'm afraid it's still lying up at the ice house where I left it when I was looking for Irene. I'll probably take a walk up there and collect it tomorrow morning.'

'Great. I'm not in any rush; tomorrow afternoon will be just fine.'

Sir Douglas and Victor both entered the discussion at this point, extolling the beauty of the river path and the merits of the estate's game fishing, and the general level of conversation took up where it had left off. Nobody, as far as Fizz could estimate, had shown any particular interest in the exchange but at least their little performance had gone every bit as well as it had in rehearsal and if it didn't have the effect they hoped for, no blame could be laid at the door of either of the actors.

Their cunning plan was a long shot, she accepted that, but it gave the illusion, if nothing else, that they were moving ahead and that was good for all of them. It gave Kerr something to focus on, it satisfied Fizz's need to be proactive, and it undoubtedly provided Buchanan with a soupçon of excitement that, whether he realised it or not, had been singularly lacking in his recent past. Hope was a potent drug. Whatever the odds against catching the guilty party in their trap, the very possibility of actually doing so filled her with optimism. With a bit of luck they could not only identify Irene's killer but get enough evidence to nail him and that was about the best conclusion to this depressing episode that any of them could hope for.

The three of them: herself, Buchanan and Kerr, were the first to leave the reception. They'd worked out, earlier in the day, that Kerr would have to be at the ice house before any of the suspects were in a position to see him go and, although he knew that their tame detective Joe was already there, he was impatient to set off up the path before darkness fell.

Buchanan gave him a lift down the deserted driveway as far as the turn off to the stable yard. From there he walked through the trees to the ice house path while Buchanan and Fizz parked the Saab outside his cottage and holed up there for the next few hours in order to give the impression that he was in there with him.

It was a long evening. They played Scrabble for a while but Fizz was trying, at the same time, to figure out a way of having a front seat when their trap was sprung so Buchanan won three games out of three and couldn't quite disguise his jubilation. It was well after ten by that time and, although not fully dark, they both felt they'd done enough to establish Kerr's presence in the house. The lights had already gone out in the Curzons' house and Eddie's windows remained as blank as they had done all evening. Whether there was anyone inside her cottage or not was anybody's guess and Buchanan refused to be drawn into a discussion on the matter since, he insisted, it made no difference. If Eddie was up at the ice house causing mischief they'd know soon enough.

He looked at his watch. 'We'll give it another ten minutes and then make our noisy exit.'

The idea of making any kind of exit at this point was doing Fizz's head in but she still had not come up with any way either of getting shot of Buchanan's supervision or of talking him into sticking around for the denouement. She didn't like leaving the crucial bit to someone else, she didn't trust Kerr to play his part according to the script, and she really, really hated doing the Cinderella thing while everyone else was at the ball.

'I don't know about you,' she said, taking her shoes off and wiggling her cramped toes, 'but I'm starting to worry about Kerr.'

His head jerked round. 'Oh great. Now she tells me.'

'Not that he's the baddie. I don't think that. Well, not seriously. What bothers me, though, is what he'll do when he sees who it is planting the evidence. He looked so jumpy tonight. When I see him thirsting for revenge the way he does I start to wonder if he'll be able to sit tight and let Irene's killer walk away from the ice house. Maybe we should stick around and keep a watch on him.'

Buchanan shook his head. 'Not necessary. I already thought of that. In fact, that's why I chose Joe to be our independent witness. I warned him to be ready to stop Kerr doing something silly and if he can't do that, neither could we. Joe was fifteen years in the police force before he started his PI business and he's heavier than Kerr. Besides, I spent an hour briefing Kerr last night, making sure he understands the legal aspects of the case and the importance of doing everything by the book. I think he'll be okay.'

So much for that little plan, Fizz thought, peering through a chink in the curtains at the shadowed yard. 'So, what do you envisage happening after the evidence is planted?'

He was getting ready to leave, putting his jacket on and looking for his car keys. 'I told Kerr to phone me first thing in the morning. We can decide then what to do with the evidence we have.'

'No, I mean, what will the baddie do after planting the evidence?'

'Come home and go to bed, I imagine.'

'Yes, but Kerr announced that he was going to go and get the bike first thing in the morning. The Joker's going to be asking himself: what if he gets to it before the police search? There's no point in planting evidence on the bike unless the police find it for themselves.'

Buchanan paused with a hand on the door handle. 'The search will be starting again at first light.'

'Yes, but Kerr is an early bird. He's often out and about at crack of dawn. If it were me I wouldn't take the chance of Kerr making an early start, would you? I'll lay you any money that the Joker will make sure that Kerr's diverted early tomorrow morning – prevented, somehow or other, from going up the hill till the police have a chance of finding the bike.'

Buchanan's hand fell to his side. 'Hell, you could be right there, Fizz. We should have thought that through.' He came back and leaned against the table, thinking. 'Does it matter? Kerr could simply go along with it and let himself be sidetracked.'

'It depends what methods are used to side-track him,' Fizz said, looking, she hoped, extremely worried. 'I think, at the very least, that Kerr ought to be prepared for what might happen. He might be in serious danger.'

'I don't think anyone would go to those lengths, to be honest, but I'll leave him a note just to be on the safe side.'

'That's not sure enough.' Fizz said, thinking hard. 'What if someone comes in and sees it? What if someone gets to him before he reaches home? Breaks his leg? Sets his house on fire?'

'Now you're being paranoid, Fizz,' Buchanan said, but she could see he was concerned.

'I think I'll have to stay the night,' she said, 'so that I can be here when he gets back.'

'Surely that's not necessary?'

'I think it is, Buchanan. I wouldn't feel right just hoping for the best. It could be dangerous.'

He jiggled his car keys impatiently. 'It's not a good idea for you to stay here alone. Besides, we have to be seen to leave.'

'That's no problem. We can drive off in the car and then I'll walk back up the drive and come in by the back door.'

He turned and slid a look at her along his shoulder and for a minute she thought he'd rumbled her but, if he did, it still didn't stop him worrying about leaving Kerr unprepared for what could happen in the morning. His face was drawn as he said,

'Dammit, I know this is unnecessary, but I suppose we shouldn't take chances at this stage in the game. If I'd thought about it earlier I could have asked Joe to stick around unobtrusively for a few hours. Now, we'll both have to stay.'

'Uh – why both of us? I'll be fine on my own.'

He gave her one of his looks. 'I doubt that, Fizz.'

'What's that supposed to mean?'

'You expect me to believe that you wouldn't be up that track like a roe deer the minute my back was turned?' He laughed, shortly and unappealingly, and shook his head. 'Sorry, Fizz, but this is one case that's not going to reflect badly on either of us. We're keeping a low profile whether you like it or not and if that means I have to keep an eye on you for the next eight hours, so be it.' He walked to the door and held it open, waiting for her. 'We'll have to leave the car somewhere off the estate and walk back.'

Fizz was too sleepy to enjoy a hike but she was willing to suffer a little more discomfort if it meant hanging on to the possibility of being in on the action and, for the moment, she had no option but to play for time.

They left a lamp on as they left to give the impression, to anyone who saw the front door open and close, that Kerr was still inside and then drove sedately down the drive, past the start of the ice house path, past the dark and soundless gatehouse, and a good mile and a half along the empty road. Buchanan was sombre and uncommunicative and Fizz was absorbed in her own thoughts. If the gods were on their side, someone on the estate was, right at this minute, getting ready to move: maybe visiting Irene's corpse, maybe already leaving their house and moving quietly through the trees towards the ice house. Kerr and Joe would be in position and she could imagine the tension they'd be under, ears and eyes strained for the first footfall, the first movement of shadow on shadow, that would herald the killer's arrival.

'This'll do nicely.' Buchanan turned the car into a farm track and crawled it forward, careful of its paintwork, till it was out of sight of the road behind a tall pile of hay bales. 'If it rains tonight we'll have trouble getting out in the morning but we'll have to chance that.'

'It won't rain,' Fizz said, looking at the thick cumulus above them. 'It's still enough down here but those clouds are on the move. They'll be gone in a couple of hours.'

'You're probably right. So, someone who wants to reach the ice house under cover of darkness would be well advised to get moving now, before the sky clears and the moon comes out. Maybe we'll see some early action after all.'

Fizz was inclined to agree with that conjecture and the prospect goaded her back along the road like a cattle probe. It was difficult to see how she could witness the finale now, since it would be foolish to risk running into the perpetrator en route to the ice house, but impatience nagged at her nonetheless and, in spite of Buchanan's protests, they were back at the gatehouse within thirty-five minutes.

It was by that time on the devil's side of midnight and the place was silent as the grave as they picked their way through the rhododendron bushes that lined the drive. It was impossible to be totally silent but Fizz was in no hurry to be indoors and she made frequent pauses, not only to listen for the approach of other footfalls, but to play for time while she thought of more delaying tactics. Buchanan had to know she was swinging it but he made no complaint, just stood in the shadows, patiently waiting, every time she raised a warning hand. City bred, he wasn't much of a tracker, but at least he knew his limitations and invariably followed Fizz's lead in situations like this. In truth, Fizz had no real expectation of running into anyone: she was more concerned with inventing an

excuse to go up the hill, but during one of her pauses it suddenly came to her that she could hear breathing.

She grabbed Buchanan's arm and dug her nails in, drawing
him carefully deeper into the gloom. For several seconds she
froze like that, raking the darkness with her eyes, and then the
laboured panting was joined by another sound, the pad-pad-
pad of feet on the grassy verge. And then, in a blur of shad-
owy movement, a figure took shape, hurried past, and was lost
again in the dark tunnel of trees: a stooped and bulky figure,
darkly clad, furtive, that crossed their path at right angles on
a course that could lead only to the ice house.

Their quarry. Irene's murderer.

Sir Douglas.

Chapter Nineteen

It was twenty to three when Kerr got back and by that time Buchanan was ready to jump out of his skin with impatience. Fizz had been asleep for well over two hours, curled up in an armchair with her hands under one flushed cheek and her lips a little apart, pale pink and curved like the petals on a rose. If she would just stay like that, Buchanan thought, fascinated by the sight – not necessarily asleep but placid and trusting, smilingly content, the picture of purity and vulnerability. Anyone seeing her right now for the first time would never guess what devastation she could cause when she was awake. As he tucked his jacket round her she stirred a little, squeezing up her eyes against the light, so he put the lamp on the floor where it was less obtrusive and then just sat there watching her breathe and trying to figure out their next move.

Three hours after their discovery that Sir Douglas was their man, the truth was only just beginning to sink in. Of course, he had considered his lordship as a suspect, and at some length, but in the absence of any substantial evidence his instincts had tended towards someone with considerably more chutzpah than Sir Douglas. Caitlin, perhaps, or even Lady Marjory. Sir Douglas's bumbling benevolence, which still struck him as totally genuine, scarcely tied in with the picture he'd previously formed of a calculating and single-minded killer and he now found himself questioning his assumption that the theft of the Rubens had to have something to do with Irene's disappearance. There could be no logical reason for Sir Douglas to steal his own picture and the idea that Nanny's death might also be laid at his door seemed totally ludicrous. For the first time he now felt – if not actually glad – at least content that he had agreed to setting a trap for the killer. If they hadn't achieved this breakthrough they could have wandered around in circles for ever, basing their investigations on a set of spurious assumptions.

The question now was: how to go about securing evidence that would tie Sir Douglas firmly to Irene's murder, and the answer to that one was proving particularly elusive. Left to his own devices, Kerr would stop at nothing to get at the truth and, although Buchanan felt fairly confident that he could, for the moment, maintain some sort of control over him, that control would evaporate as soon as they ceased to move quickly and confidently towards a conclusion. At best – at *very* best – he had twenty-four hours to nail Sir Douglas, after that he couldn't guarantee he'd be able to hold Kerr back, and the consequences could be horrific for all concerned. Even now it could be too late. Joe, big and fit as he was, might have found it impossible to keep Kerr still and silent when he came face to face with his woman's murderer. Buchanan had taken great pains to explain the necessity of doing things the smart way but would that sort of conditioning hold when push came to shove?

Apparently the answer to that was yes because just as Buchanan was starting to doze off he felt a cool draught on the back of his neck and Kerr was standing there, wired and wide-eyed, in the kitchen doorway.

'Tam,' he said breathlessly, his chest heaving from what must have been a speedy descent from the hill, 'You're not going to believe this.'

'I am,' Buchanan told him. 'We saw him start up the path last night. Sir Douglas.'

'You've been here all night? I thought —'

'We realised there are things we should have discussed.'

At which point Fizz woke up and started bitching about not having been wakened sooner and demanding to know what she'd missed.

'I just got back this minute,' Kerr snapped back at her and, tearing off his jacket, fell into a chair. 'God, what a night! I hope I never have to live through that again.' He fingered a swollen cheekbone. 'I don't know where you dug up that heavy of yours, Tam, but he's a violent bastard. Slugged me when I wasn't looking.'

'I told him to control you any way he could,' Fizz told him calmly. 'I wasn't planning on knocking my pan out to make this thing work and then having you louse it up at the last minute. Joe wasn't just there as an independent witness, he was there to stop you doing something stupid – which you were obviously about to do or he wouldn't have hit you. Just tell me you didn't blow the whole thing.'

Kerr clenched his teeth over what was perceptibly an abusive retort and shook his head. 'No. Sir Douglas was inside the ice house at that point.'

'You'd better tell us what happened,' Buchanan said. 'Right from the beginning.'

Kerr gestured hopelessly as though he felt unable to convey the drama of the preceding hours in mere words but, once started there was no stopping him. Stripped of it's descriptive passages, his report held no surprises. Basically it told them no more than they could have guessed: that Sir Douglas had spent a matter of a few minutes in the ice house, emerged wearing surgical gloves, and rushed back down the path to the big house. Neither Kerr nor Joe had gone into the ice house but the detective had placed an invisible seal across the doorway to preserve the integrity of the forensic evidence and then settled down to await the arrival of the police search party.

When he finished Buchanan stood up and stretched his stiff shoulders. There was now a line of sunshine between the floor and the door leading into the kitchen and he knew he'd have to go soon or risk being seen as he left the estate. He said, 'We've been trying to figure out what Sir Douglas's next move is likely to be and it seems probable that he'll try to keep you busy this morning. He'll want to make sure you don't go up and collect your mountain bike before the police find it so

I think you should prepare yourself for seeing him again in an hour or two.'

Kerr looked sick and his hands momentarily gripped the arms of his chair like claws but he managed, for the first few words, to keep his voice steady. 'Yes, you're probably right. We've been talking all week about building a groin for the salmon fishing down at the bridge pool. He'll make that his excuse. *God!*' he burst out then, clapping both hands to his face. 'I don't know that I can do this, Tam! How do I keep my hands off the bastard, tell me that?'

'Because Fizz and I will be with you,' Buchanan told him, and saw Fizz's head jerk in his direction. 'You can spin him some excuse about showing us the river. He knows I'm interested in salmon fishing so it won't sound too unlikely. It means we'll have to walk back and pick up the car, maybe kill some time having breakfast somewhere, and then drive back here as though we were just arriving. If we time our arrival at about eight-thirty that should be early enough.'

'Both of us?' Fizz put in. 'Do we both have to go? Couldn't I hang around and talk to Caitlin or something? I mean, we have to get a quick result on this thing so I don't feel like wasting what could turn out to be an entire morning listening to fishermen's tales. There's things I could do here.'

'Like what?' said Buchanan, just checking.

'Well, I'd have to think about it, obviously, but I'm sure I could find a more productive use for my time than walking the river bank.'

She seemed genuinely not to have any specific plans for the morning but Buchanan was reluctant to leave her behind where she could work her black arts on Eddie or get into serious trouble talking to the wrong people. One would have thought she'd want to focus in on Sir Douglas and give what she called her intuition full play but clearly that idea didn't grab her at the present time.

'We'll talk about it on the way,' he said. 'Let's get moving before people start to wake up.'

'You go,' she said, yawning widely. 'There's no need for both of us to walk all that way. I'll start down the drive in half an hour and you can pick me up round the corner from the gatehouse.'

Buchanan demurred, for no better reason than that he wanted her under his eye, but she looked so worn out that he couldn't bring himself to insist. 'Okay,' he said, 'but don't be late. I can't hang around in the car so you'll have to be there before me.'

'I will be,' She waved him away with a lazy hand. 'Go. Go.'

He took a long look at her, wondering what she could be up to, but could do nothing but go.

Fizz waited till she was sure he wasn't popping back for any reason then she leaned back in her chair and looked at Kerr.

'What?' he said with his usual glower.

Fizz glowered back. How Irene had put up with this bloke for ten years was the mystery of the century. 'Is there anything you'd like to tell me at this point, Kerr?'

'Such as?'

'Such as: if we're to accept that the person who's been planting the false evidence is the person who stole the Rubens – and I think we must – then why would Sir Douglas want to steal his own painting?'

His eyes clearly wanted to dance away sideways but he tried not to let them. 'How would I know? He's obviously deranged.'

Fizz looked pointedly at the clock. 'I don't have time for this, Kerr. That question's been annoying me for the last three hours and the only answer I've come up with is that he didn't steal it. You did. You stole it to make the police get their fingers out and start looking for Irene. Am I right?'

As she waited for him to answer she couldn't help hoping

that, miraculously, there might be some other explanation, but that was pie in the sky. He didn't even try to dissemble, just looked her belligerently in the eye and said, 'Yes. And I'd do it again tomorrow. If I hadn't done it they'd still be palming me off with, "We're looking into it, Mr Gilfillan. As soon as we have any information we'll let you know." I knew from day one Irene wasn't okay. Was I to sit there and twiddle my thumbs while there was a chance of finding her alive?'

'Oh hell,' she muttered. 'Oh, bloody *hell*, Kerr. If this comes out Buchanan and I could find ourselves in a position to be charged as accessories. He'll have my guts for garters – and Larry will have his.' This didn't appear to have the depressing effect on Kerr's spirits that one might have hoped for, so she added, 'You'll have to put it back PDQ.'

'It's my ace card, Fizz,' he said coldly. 'I'm not going to throw it away without buying some advantage with it.'

'What are you planning to do with it?'

'I don't know yet, but if it starts to look as if Sir Douglas is going to get off scot free I may be able to pin the theft on him. Add a charge of theft to one of interfering with the course of justice and the CID will have to suspect him of doing away with Irene too. They'll stay on his back till they uncover something that'll put him behind bars for the rest of his life.'

Fizz had a certain sympathy with this way of thinking. It might not be entirely moral but you could hardly expect the guy to stand by and let his wife's murderer get off with a slap-on-the-wrist sentence. She said, 'If that's your plan, Kerr, you'd better be bloody careful. It'll have to be found some-where that doesn't incriminate an innocent party.'

'You don't have to tell me that.'

'Where have you hidden it?'

He answered her only with a come-*on* look but, in any case, she'd decided as soon as she said it that she didn't really want to know. Wherever it was, it was presumably somewhere inaccessible to the CID and for as long as it stayed there they were reasonably safe. With a bit of luck no one but herself and Kerr need know the truth.

'Just promise me one thing, Kerr,' she said. 'Promise me you'll never let anyone know you took the Rubens. Specifically Buchanan. If there's any question of his being charged as an accessory after the fact his boss will go apeshit.'

'It's not the sort of thing I'd particularly want to come out.'

'Is that a promise, then?'

'Sure, Fizz.' He laughed, softly and painfully, as though he had a broken rib. 'It's a promise.'

She looked at him from the corners of her eyes, noting the way his fists kept clenching and unclenching on the arms of the chair, and she could see he was getting himself totally wound up about coming face to face with Sir Douglas again. There was sweat on his brow and on his top lip and the muscles at each side of his mouth kept bulging in and out as he clenched his teeth. The omens for the next few hours were looking extremely bad unless a way could be found to channel his aggression and give him something to work towards. Obviously, the best way forward would be to find Irene's body, but she had to be careful how to put that to him.

'Now that we know who's responsible for Irene's disappearance,' she said, 'have you had any better ideas about where we could look for her?'

'I haven't been thinking along those lines,' he said. 'Should I have been?'

'Well, I don't know. I just thought – you know – where would Sir Douglas have hidden her? She's evidently not in the big house and she's not in the grounds, otherwise the police would have found her by now. That means she's not on the estate but, Sir Douglas almost never goes off the estate, does he? Can you think of any place he does go, or has gone in the past, where he might have hidden her?'

Kerr was silent for a long time, so long that Fizz's thoughts had moved on to what she might persuade Buchanan to buy her for breakfast. Then he said,

'I could count on my fingers the times he's been off the estate in all the time I've been here and they've all been occasions like yesterday – funerals, visiting his wife in hospital, that sort of thing – and either Victor or I had to drive him every time. I really don't see how he could manage to transport Irene any great distance.'

'But she must be somewhere, Kerr – and somewhere reasonably accessible since he appears able to put his hands on… on biological material any time he chooses.'

Fizz suddenly realised that she wasn't just channelling Kerr's thoughts into a more positive direction, she was talking sense. She sat forward in her chair and fixed Kerr with a hard look.

'Think, Kerr. There must be some place the CID wouldn't think of looking.'

'There isn't. They've been all over the grounds, into all our houses, through everything with a fine-toothed comb.'

'They missed her,' Fizz told him flatly.

'That's not possible, Fizz. I saw how they went about it and they simply —'

'Listen to me, Kerr. She *has* to be here on the estate. That's the premise you have to start from, no matter how unlikely it may seem. If Sir Douglas is responsible for her disappearance – and we know he is – she's within a mile of the big house – and you're the best person to find her. You know Sir Douglas. You know his habits and you know his mind. Where could he hide her?'

Kerr lurched clumsily out of his chair and started to walk aimlessly around the room, looking at nothing and mumbling incoherently as he thought. From the occasional word Fizz could pick out she deduced that he was reviewing the various outbuildings around the property but she was certain that was a waste of time since they'd already been examined closely enough to rule out any possibility of hideyholes or unsuspected basements. Besides, since Sir Douglas couldn't have transported a body any distance from the main centre of activity around the big house, he'd have had to motivate Irene to go to his chosen locus on her own two feet and murder her there. Not impossible but, to Fizz, the likelihood of that decreased in direct ratio to the distance from the big house and its immediate environs.

'There aren't any old buildings that the police might have missed?' she prompted, not too optimistically. 'Any that Sir Douglas might know about...maybe fallen down...maybe half finished...'

'The police would have found anything like that,' he said irritably. 'They went round all of Sir Graham's constructions before they even started on anything else. There's the old chapel...Sir Douglas's father did some conservation work there – just stabilising the old walls, I think. But the CID searched that place thoroughly – I saw them myself – and if there had been a...a grave there, they'd have found it.'

'I suppose so.' The clock was now spurring Fizz to leave but she wanted to give Kerr something to think about while she was gone, something that might prevent him from taking matters into his own hands. She said, 'However, it's something well worth checking out. The chapel's handy to the big house – in fact, there may be some way Sir Douglas could have got Irene there without going through the grounds. Also, it can't have been easy for the police to search, not with all that fallen masonry piled up everywhere. I reckon I'll take a good look around there while you and Buchanan are keeping Sir Douglas out of the way.'

'You won't find anything,' Kerr said morosely, but he halted his pacing to look at her and there was an unwilling hope behind his eyes.

Fizz pulled on her Doc Martens and started to lace them up. 'It's the logical place to look,' she said. 'In fact, Kerr, it's the only place to look. I really can't imagine where else Sir Douglas could have buried Irene but by all means keep thinking about it. You may come up with another possibility by the time I get back but, if you don't, I'll give it the whole morning if necessary.'

'You're that optimistic?'

'You bet.'

Now, that was a very large porky-pie, but Fizz was not shy of bending the truth in a good cause. If Kerr was going to get through the morning he needed a hope to cling to and the thought that she had even a faint chance of making a break-through would surely help him to keep a lid on his emotions. It was also quite possible that, if she couldn't arrange a more productive use for her morning, she might even fulfil her promise and take a quick look around the ruins. In a case like this, when one had only a single lead, one could do nothing but follow it and hope for a miracle.

Chapter Twenty

By the time they got back to Kerr's place at eight-thirty, after picking up the car and killing an hour over breakfast, Sir Douglas had already contacted Kerr. Just as predicted, he had suggested an exploratory outing to the bridge pool to discuss the practicalities of constructing an artificial salmon lie. They found Kerr fairly vibrating with tension and making frequent trips to the bathroom from whence the sound of retching emerged to dismay his listeners.

'This isn't going to work,' Buchanan told Fizz as they waited for him to emerge. 'There's no way he's going to be able to keep his cool when he sees Sir Douglas.'

'He'll be fine when the time comes,' she said confidently, supplementing her already adequate breakfast with the yoghurt Kerr had found himself unable to face. 'It's the hanging around waiting that's getting to him. Once he gets out into the fresh air and starts having to think about driving, or whatever, he'll calm down. Just keep him busy.'

Buchanan had no idea how to go about keeping Kerr busy but, for the fifteen minutes or so before they set forth to meet Sir Douglas, he appeared to have plenty to do: loading spades and various other bits and pieces into the back of the Land Rover and attending to various projects around the place that had to be serviced before he could leave. By the time he indicated he was ready Buchanan himself was feeling a bit on the jumpy side, oppressed by the thought of how easily the whole thing could go pear-shaped and unhappy about what Fizz could get up to on her own.

'If you're going to go snooping around the ruins,' he told her while Kerr started the Land Rover, 'you'd better make sure you have permission first: if not from Lady Marjory, at least from Caitlin.'

'Oh, I probably won't bother looking there,' she said airily.

'I only said that to keep Kerr happy. Sir Graham may have done some work around there but the chances of the CID missing anything like that are practically zilch. I'll probably just have a nice cosy chat with Caitlin or Eddie.'

Buchanan halted and looked at her to see if she was intentionally winding him up but she merely opened her eyes at him inquiringly.

'Fizz,' he said, experiencing a rush of anxiety that amounted almost to desperation, 'would you mind leaving Eddie to me? There are things I want to discuss with her.'

'What things?'

'Personal things.'

She looked highly entertained. 'You mean, Cupid's been firing his little golden arrows at last, Buchanan? And here I thought you were a confirmed bachelor.'

'Apparently not,' he said recklessly. 'So I'd appreciate it if you'd concentrate your efforts elsewhere for the time being and leave me a clear field.'

'Ooooh, absolutely. Let me not to the marriage of true minds admit impediment, and all that crap.' She grinned impishly and gave him a little push towards the waiting Land Rover. 'I'll await developments with beating heart. See you later.'

Buchanan felt immeasurably cheered by her reaction. It was manifestly obvious that his suspicion of her bona fides had been totally groundless and, although her insouciance was perhaps a tad less than flattering when you came to think about it, his prospects of getting together with Eddie now appeared to him to be rosier than he had imagined. She could be a little touchy at times – witness her inexplicable peevishness yesterday afternoon – but a bunch of flowers would sort that out and, hopefully, pave the way for a return to the *entiente cordiale* that had pertained last week, back in the Bavarian summerhouse: an occasion that was still technicolorbright in his memory.

Just let us get through this morning without any major disasters, he prayed silently as they jolted down the rough track that led to the river and, for the moment at least, he could feel justified in permitting himself a certain tentative optimism on that front as well. Kerr seemed to have settled down into a sort of grim impassivity. He made only the briefest of replies to Buchanan's attempts at conversation and drove the Land Rover like an automaton, but that was likely to be less noticeable to his boss than his earlier erratic behaviour and, if the explanation for this improvement could be traced in the faint scent of whisky detectable on his breath that too was all to the good. In his current situation, he had, after all, every excuse for having a hangover and if Sir Douglas didn't immediately assume his taciturnity to be a result of that, he could be encouraged to do so.

They were first to arrive at the bridge pool, a deep, slow-roiling basin downstream from the stretch of fast water where Sir Douglas proposed to build his salmon lie. The river wasn't, to Buchanan's eye, a patch on the Stronach river at Am Bealach where he did most of his salmon fishing, but the occasional day ticket might provide some reasonable sport at the right time of year. He tried to pick Kerr's brains about that but received only monosyllabic answers because his whole attention was focused on watching for the approach of Sir Douglas.

They had only a couple of minutes to wait before he came charging along the path beaming with health and vigour. Such was his expression of honest bonhomie that Buchanan recoiled inwardly, swept by a wave of revulsion. He could barely return the man's greeting and it was only the need to camouflage the almost palpable aura of malevolence surrounding Kerr that spurred him to pull his lips back in what must have been a travesty of a smile.

'Well, well, well. This is nice, Tam. Glad you could come with us this morning. Not a bad wee river, eh? We'll not be all that long sorting out what we have to do here so we can take a walk up to the falls and let you have a look at some of our other runs.' He turned to Kerr who was staring, stiff-faced, into the pool as though wondering if it were deep enough to drown a man. 'I was thinking in my bed last night, Kerr, that another place that could benefit from a groin would be the bend below the yellow rocks. You know where I mean? Near where the Butter Burn comes in? Would that be feasible?'

Kerr's grunt could have been taken as an indication that it was worth considering and Sir Douglas apparently took it as such. 'Well, we can take a look anyway and show Tam the pick of the beats on the way down. You're not in a rush, I hope, Tam?'

'No rush at all,' Buchanan said, making an effort to insert a semblance of enthusiasm into his tone. 'I'd be very interested in seeing how you manage a river like this.'

'Oh, we don't do as much as we should, I'm afraid – don't have the resources any more – but we try to cut back the trees where we can and keep the path clear. Got to do that, you know, to keep the business coming. And if we get these groins built before the start of next season it should be worth the effort. What d'you think, then, Kerr? See where that little runnel comes down by the bank on this side? Looks promising to me.'

Kerr, his back firmly turned to his lordship, waded into the river till the water lapped the top of his green wellies and executed a series of exploratory swipes with his spade. 'Too gravelly. We'd have difficulty getting a firm base.'

'Try a bit further up.'

While they wandered up and down, prospecting for the ideal site, Buchanan walked over to the bridge and leaned on the wooden rail, watching them and marvelling at Kerr's sudden assumption of self-control. He was still, quite clearly, not himself, and even Sir Douglas must have noticed that, but considering the stress he was under, he was managing to appear comparatively calm. Maybe Fizz's – totally reprehensible –

promises were somehow giving him the strength to hang on, virtually from minute to minute.

Even from Buchanan's point of view, the tension was excruciating. Not only was he scared stiff about what Kerr might do, he was seriously concerned about the thought that Fizz might be rummaging around in the precarious environment of the ruined chapel. She was never the most level-headed of women and he just wished he could be certain that she wouldn't allow their desperation for a breakthrough to goad her into doing something harebrained.

Twenty minutes after Buchanan and Kerr had left in the Land Rover Fizz was peering over the fence that surrounded the ancient chapel. She had actually considered, for a second or two, dropping in on Caitlin but it was not yet nine o'clock and there was a limit to how far even Scottish hospitality could be expected to stretch.

The building itself turned out to be completely invisible from the public part of the grounds but when one climbed over the locked gate with the 'Strictly Private' notice on it and picked one's way through a stand of prickly burdock, it revealed itself to be not at all as ruinous as one had been led to imagine. The stonework was black with age and many of the window embrasures were without glass but apart from a certain amount of damage to the roof, through which the blue sky appeared in several places, it looked pretty salvageable.

Inside, it was gloomy, even on a summer morning, and looking up at the rotting timbers above her head, Fizz was disinclined to hang about. She took a quick look around, purely for conscience's sake, but could see nothing of any interest apart from a vase of day lilies on the altar which appeared to indicate that either Sir Douglas or Lady Marjory still worshipped here – though not very regularly, she guessed, since the blooms had been dead for some time.

Behind the altar was a flight of narrow stone steps leading downward. They were not hidden from sight in any way, so presumably the area they led to had already been scrutinised. She took off her sunglasses and dawdled on the top step, vacillating between curiosity and laziness and bending down to see what was beneath,. It was creepy down there and it was also a waste of time but, hell, she had nothing else to do anyway till Buchanan got back.

The treads were slippy beneath her feet as she went down and she had to trail a hand, for balance, across the slimy wall at her shoulder in case she took a header into the gloom below. But when she reached the bottom she found that quite a bit of light managed to filter through from above, enough at least to let her see that it was one unbroken space, equal in area to the chapel above. It appeared empty apart from a collection of vast marble sarcophagi spaced along the walls, all of them empty – and visibly so, since the lids had been levered askew, possibly by the police searchers. Beyond them, against the furthest wall, lay the remains of a damaged sarcophagus, more elaborately carved than the others but smashed into a mound of recently scattered pieces.

Wondering which of Sir Douglas's ancestors had been buried here, Fizz moved forward to look at the skewed covers. They had once carried information about their one-time occupants but what was visible was too worn to yield more than the occasional tantalising syllable. One part-discovery teased her towards the next till she had worked her way, almost without being aware of it, to the heap of smashed marble at the rear of the area. It was darker there but the carving on the chunks of lid was deeper cut and she could almost trace the outline of the letters with her fingers.

L...A...D...Y...C...A...R...she was half reading, half feeling, when a sound behind her made her spin round, gasping at the sight of a bulky silhouette against the light.

'Well now,' said a familiar voice. 'I wonder what you're doing.'

Fizz had nothing to be afraid of other than, at worst a ticking-off for trespassing, but that didn't stop her heart bouncing around like a ping-pong ball. The faceless figure loomed impossibly large above her and there was something almost nightmarish about the way it had covered the whole length of the crypt without making a sound. She had to snatch a couple of quick breaths before she could say,

'I hope you don't mind, Lady Marjory. I'm afraid my curiosity got the better of me.'

The faceless figure moved closer, almost blotting out the light from the opening. 'Curiosity? About what, may I ask?'

Fizz waved a hand at the coffins. 'I just wondered who was buried here. Some of your ancestors, I imagine?'

Now she could see the expression on the big, strong-boned face above her and it wasn't nice. There was, in fact, a peculiar intensity in the gaze that made her wonder if all that stuff about in-breeding causing madness was actually true. She tried to edge round a little to open a line of escape but Lady Marjory wasn't having any.

'You must have missed the Strictly Private sign,' she said, with a silky intonation that disappeared abruptly as she added, 'as you climbed – oh, so nimbly – over the gate.'

'You saw me?' Fizz tried for a light laugh but it came out like a strangled sob. 'That was naughty, I suppose. Obv-obviously the walls are quite dangerous in parts, but I've been very careful. Actually, I was just leaving.'

'Were you?' said Lady Marjory, not pleasantly, still standing her ground between Fizz and the steps like something carved out of Mount Rushmore.

Fizz leaned back against the broken sarcophagus and tried to get a grip on a handy lump of marble. If Lady Marjory started to get physical – and it looked like that was on the cards – she was certainly going to need some sort of equaliser. She'd held her own, before now, against an assailant of Lady Marjory's height and weight, but this time she didn't have the advantage of surprise, and Lady Marjory didn't have balls.

'Tam Buchanan will be waiting for me outside by now,' she lied, still groping unsuccessfully. 'I told him I'd only be a few minutes.'

'I don't think so. He's gone down the river with my brother this morning, hasn't he? But what's one lie among so many, Miss Fitzpatrick? You really are quite a stranger to the truth, aren't you?' She straightened, sliding both hands into the pockets of her shapeless cardigan. 'You're a foolish young woman, Miss Fitzpatrick. Foolish and arrogant: a very dangerous combination. You should remember that when you start poking your nose into matters which don't concern you.' She bent down to push her meaty face close to Fizz's. 'You and your young man have been upsetting my brother for too long. Worming your way into our private business, asking questions, stirring up trouble. I'm afraid you'll have to be stopped.'

Fizz couldn't see Lady Marjory's hands but with her senses working on all cylinders she suddenly knew, maybe from the movement of the woman's shoulders, that her hands were coming out of her pockets and – whatever they held – it boded her no good. Without pausing to think she lunged upwards and rammed her head hard into Lady Marjory's face and, as she staggered back, followed up with two thumbs to the eyes backed by all the power she could muster.

For a couple of seconds the way to the stairs was clear and she dived for it, knowing that speed was her only weapon. Rubble churned under her feet as she ran, coffins appeared to slide sideways to get in her way. Slipping and stumbling in the half dark she had gone no more than a half dozen strides when something like an armoured car walloped her in the back and she went down, flattened beneath a colossal weight that squashed every last cc of air from her lungs.

Annihilated even beyond the reach of her adrenaline, she barely registered the stabbing pain in her neck and when the blackness began to creep in around the edge of her vision and the sensation in her arms and legs began to disappear she simply concluded she was dying.

Chapter Twenty-One

As the sun rose in the sky Buchanan's fears became lulled by the idyllic scene around him. The warmth, the scent of trampled grass, the drone of bees in the gorse had a soporific effect and the calm, steady flow of the river soon slowed his fevered thoughts to their own pace. He leaned on the balustrade and watched Sir Douglas and Kerr splashing about in the shallows and gradually he found himself concentrating less on his immediate problems and more on planning his next move.

There had to be some way of tying Sir Douglas to Irene's killing. If time were not such a problem they could possibly have contrived another trap, one which would have forced the man to re-visit Irene's body only, this time, in front of hidden witnesses. No doubt Fizz would presently be expecting some sort of creative input from him along these lines but inspiration was dragging its heels somewhat and the thought of all the work he had to catch up with before Larry's return didn't help any.

'That should do it, Kerr,' he heard Sir Douglas saying. 'We can use some of that old masonry that's lying around outside the chapel. It's nothing but an eyesore where it is so we'll be killing two birds with one stone.'

He reached a hand to help Kerr up the bank but Kerr ignored it and hauled himself out of the water with the help of his spade, pushing past his boss without a glance. Sir Douglas drew back in some surprise and threw an enquiring glance at Buchanan, who forged a grimace. Behind Kerr's back he raised an imaginary glass to his lips and clasped his forehead, bringing a half-amused, half-sympathetic smile to his lordship's face.

'Not feeling quite the thing this morning, eh?' He closed in and clasped Kerr's shoulder in a fatherly manner. 'One too many last night?'

Kerr froze and his hand tensed on the handle of his spade

but, with an effort Buchanan could only guess at, he resisted shaking off his lordship's touch and grunted an affirmation.

'Well, well. Can't say I blame you, old son. Not a happy time for any of us but we just have to grin and bear it, don't we? Chuck that spade in the back of the Land Rover and we'll take a nice easy stroll up to the falls.'

He came to the end of the bridge and tried to make meaningful eye contact with Buchanan as Kerr walked away. 'Damn sorry for the lad, and all that,' he said quietly. 'Must be a strain on him, not knowing what's happened to Irene, but drink's not the way to handle it. Keep busy, that's the answer. That's what my father did after my mother died, and it's what's got me through these last few weeks.'

'Your father kept busy by building things, I'm told,' Buchanan said, detecting what could be a profitable line of discussion.

'Indeed he did. We'll pass one of his projects on our way to the falls. A fisherman's rest: one of his early attempts but still standing after nearly fifty years. He did quite a bit of work in the grounds after my mother passed on.'

With Fizz's current whereabouts in the forefront of his mind Buchanan was moved to murmur, 'And in the chapel.'

Sir Douglas paused, his eyes serenely following the flight of a pair of crows high overhead. He looked as innocent as ever but Buchanan experienced a faint, inexplicable chill of uneasiness. What was so interesting about a pair of crows?

'The chapel? No. He didn't build anything there.'

'Just conservation work?'

'A little.' He turned at looked round at Kerr who was taking his time, clattering things about in the back of the Land Rover and probably psyching himself up for a return to the fray. 'Ready, Kerr? Let's go, then.'

He set off down the path and Kerr fell in behind him, pale as the meadow sweet on the bank below, his jaw working with repressed hatred.

Buchanan hesitated. He'd had a bad feeling all morning about leaving Fizz to her own devices and now it was really bugging him. His eyes were drawn to the Land Rover and, for a moment, he was tempted to jump in and rush back to the big house to make sure she was okay. It would take him a scant five minutes to reach her but he knew, even as he toyed with the idea, that it was out of the question.

Fizz *might* have gone to the chapel: that was a possibility. But if he left Kerr alone with Sir Douglas all hell would break loose: that was a certainty.

Really, he didn't have a choice.

The fact that Irene was sponging her face with water came as no surprise to Fizz. She was not aware of having been unconscious and she was not alarmed at finding herself in unfamiliar surroundings nor by her apparent inability to move her limbs. She registered, with no more interest than a stranger passing by, that Irene was crying and heard the words she was sobbing out without attaching to them the least shred of meaning.

She felt utterly relaxed and at peace, content to lie there and to let Irene or anyone else do with her as they willed, but slowly – infinitely slowly – formed thoughts began to coalesce from the mist of vague sensations in her head and she began, quite nonchalantly, to wonder if she'd missed a bit.

'Stop,' she croaked, becoming abruptly oppressed by the sound of Irene's weeping but Irene, misunderstanding the demand, abandoned the face sponging and wept all the louder.

'I'm so sorry...' she kept spluttering over and over. 'Oh, God, I'm so sorry this has happened...'

Finally Fizz was forced to push her weakly aside and lever herself up onto an elbow. 'Someone put something in my G&T,' she said, experiencing a wash of indignation, but it came out as a jumble of meaningless syllables.

Irene put an arm round her shoulders and held a glass of water to her lips. 'Drink a little of this, Fizz. It'll help to clear your head.'

Fizz discovered she was parched with thirst and emptied the glass.

'You're not hurt, are you?' Irene said.

The question barely registered in the sludge that was left of Fizz's mind but she became aware of a throbbing pain in both shins and, when she investigated, discovered bruising and scraped skin from knee to ankle. She looked at Irene's bleary face. 'Wha'…wha' happ'ned?'

'Lady Marjory dragged you down the stairs.'

Fizz looked where she was pointing and saw a delicate iron staircase against one wall. Another wall was lined with the shelves of canisters, a third was covered with metal storage cupboards and a fourth was hidden behind what looked like a shower compartment, a water boiler, and a network of pipes and conduits. It was a biggish room, probably twenty feet square or more, and was furnished more like a bed-sitter than anything else, with two sets of bunk beds and a collection of quite nice chairs and tables but something about it gave Fizz the creeps.

At the third attempt she managed to mumble, 'What th' hell is this place?'

Irene eyed her warily. 'It's a fall-out shelter.'

Fizz was, for a moment, too dazed to fix a meaning to the term, then she found herself picturing the local landowner back at Am Bealach who had, long before she was born, been suspected of constructing a fall-out shelter somewhere on his land. Nobody knew where it was and old Ewan Cameron had been too wise to tell, knowing that, if the dreaded four-minute warning ever rang out, plenty of his tenants would be desperate enough to fight their way in.

The first cold ripples of dismay started to disturb the placid surface of her thoughts as the truth sank in.

'You've been here...in this place...for...for...?'

'For two weeks,' Irene nodded, stoically wiping her eyes. 'It could be worse. I've everything I need: food, warmth, a shower and toilet. There's even books and tapes, drawing and painting stuff...if I wanted to make use of them.' Her voice wavered as she added, 'A family of four could exist down here for thirty years.'

Fizz's head had now cleared enough for her to suffer a jolt of panic at this revelation. She sat up and swung her legs to the floor. 'He...abandoned you down here?'

'No, no, it wasn't Sir Douglas, it was Lady Marjory. His lordship was furious with her and he comes to see me every day.' She pushed back her long hair distractedly. 'It was all a horrible mistake. I'm as much to blame as his lordship. He's just a very silly, very deluded, very pathetic person who made some terrible mistakes and didn't know how to retrieve the situation. The poor man's been going mad for the last fortnight.'

'Irene...' Fizz looked at her in amazement, only now beginning to recognise the miracle of her presence here beside her. 'We thought you were dead. We thought Sir Douglas had done away with you.'

Irene burst into fresh tears and threw her arms around her, hugging her so tightly that she began to feel dizzy again.

'I knew you'd look for me, Fizz...I knew you and Kerr would never give up...and that's what kept me sane. I don't deserve a friend like you.'

Fizz struggled free and got woozily to her feet. Her head felt three-quarters full of sleep but there was an autopilot at work in there and it was telling her she had to make an effort to wake up. 'I could murder a mug of coffee.'

'Sure...sure.'

While she messed about using a small hand-pump to fill an electric kettle Fizz took a closer look at the room, opening the cupboards she could reach to reveal stacks of new clothing in sealed plastic bags, boxes of old fashioned drugs and antibiotics, spare parts for a variety of appliances: stacks and stacks of every conceivable necessity plus sundry luxury items like board games and playing cards. Old Sir Graham had followed the construction manual to the letter, obviously, but there wasn't a lot of comfort to be found in that discovery.

She shuffled across to Irene and leaned on the work surface beside her. If she took deep breaths and concentrated closely the fog seemed to recede a little. 'Do you know whereabouts on the estate we are?'

Irene shook her head. 'One minute I was sitting in my studio, the next I woke up on that bed, same as you did. At a wild guess, I'd say we're not far from the old chapel. I saw a couple of burs on Sir Douglas's trousers one day and there are burdocks growing around the ruins.'

Fizz looked up at the high ceiling. The thought of being trapped underground should have scared her rigid but she merely registered the fact and passed on. There were nebulous memories floating at the back of her head like under-developed snapshots and she thought she recognised the old chapel among the images. She nodded. 'I think that's where I was when Lady Marjory jumped me.'

Irene followed her gaze for a moment, then handed her a coffee and moved across to sink down onto one of the chairs in the sitting area. She seemed almost resigned to her confinement but Fizz could feel an imperious need shake off the residual dregs of whatever it was that had been pumped into her system and start finding a way out. She looked around the walls and said,

'You have tried to escape, I imagine?'

'Of course. But look at this place, Fizz. It's built to withstand a siege. We're obviously underground and the cover at the top of the ladder is made of something that doesn't even scratch when I batter it with a length of iron plumbing. I tried yelling up the air vent for days at a time, because I knew old Nanny still comes to pray in the chapel every day and I thought she might hear me, but she never did.'

That revelation re-opened a file in Fizz's memory. Nanny's ghost stories. Could Nanny have heard something and concluded the place was haunted? If she'd confided as much to Sir Douglas – or, more likely, Lady Marjory – that could account for her opportune descent of the servants' staircase. She started to share this conclusion with Irene but stopped herself just in time to avoid giving her an excuse to start blubbing again. She needed her focused.

'So, it's Lady Marjory who's behind this business?' She discovered that she was slumped almost at full length and managed to haul herself into a more upright position. Her mind seemed to be clearing a little but there was no strength in her arms and legs and her head kept lolling around against the back of her chair. 'How did you fall foul of her?'

Irene shook her head, making her long hair fall about her face the way it used to do when she was a scruffy student. 'I didn't fall foul of her: she thinks I'm some sort of paragon. Something between an angel and an earth mother. Oh, God, it all sounds so stupid, Fizz. I can't believe how it all got so out of hand.'

'What? She's not a lesbian, is she?'

'No! It was Sir Douglas who fell for me – months ago. Oh, I should have told him to go and see a shrink, I know that now, but – you must have met him, Fizz. You know what an old sweetie he is, and I...I just couldn't bring myself to slap him down. I tried to make a joke of it, laugh at his ridiculous advances but – it was awful! I just couldn't make him see the whole idea was ridiculous. He thinks he's irresistible, you see.

Lady Marjory dotes on him – to an insane degree – and old Nanny keeps telling him he's a god, and by and by he's come to believe it. He couldn't begin to accept that I simply didn't go for him.' She looked hard at Fizz and shook her head. 'You don't understand that, do you, Fizz? You've always known exactly who you are, but who did he have to compare himself with? He's not the only person in the world who believes what he sees in the mirror his friends hold up to him, is he? Don't we all do that to some extent?'

'You should have told Kerr.'

'Oh sure,' Irene retorted with some asperity. 'And watch him knock the daylights out of the poor old duffer and probably face charges for it? We're not rich, you know Fizz: we both need to keep our jobs here or – at the very least – to make sure we have good references when we leave. I tried a dozen times to talk Kerr into looking for a new billet but it only caused arguments.'

Fizz nodded, seeing the difficulties. It wasn't entirely surprising that Sir Douglas had mistaken Irene's natural warmth for affection and, while she herself would have nipped things in the bud PDQ and to hell with hurting his feelings, she knew Irene to have the kinder heart and, possibly, the softer brain.

'So, what brought things to a head?'

'Lady Marjory did.' Irene moved a regretful hand. 'I didn't realise she knew what was going on but Sir Douglas tells me she was miserably unhappy – for his sake – and, apparently, had been for years, ever since Lady Audrey started to go down the hill.'

'Heart trouble, somebody said.'

'Eventually, yes, but what caused her heart problem was her overeating. In the end, she was well over twenty stone and could barely get around. I think it made Sir Douglas very unhappy and, from what I've pieced together, it would appear that Lady Marjory couldn't stand to see him like that – tied to an unattractive wife who had been unable to secure the succession of the title by giving him an heir. So, when Sir Douglas suddenly found what he imagined to be the love of his life, Lady Marjory decided he must get what he wanted.'

Fizz waited for what was to come but Irene had gone all quiet on her and just sat there combing her hair with her fingers till prompted with an impatient,

'So?'

'So, she got it into her head that if his wife were out of the way I'd fall into Sir Douglas's arms like a ripe plum.'

'She offed her?' Fizz said, delighted to hear that her unwillingly discarded suspicions had in fact been on the ball.

'Apparently,' Irene nodded, a small censorious frown between her brows. 'Lady Audrey was a lovely person, actually Fizz, and I was upset when she died but, more than that, I was shocked. There was – I don't know how to explain this – but there was something about Lady Marjory's manner when she gave me the news...something smug...something...*satisfied* that scared the life out of me. I thought I was being silly. It's not an easy thing to believe, that someone you know could take a life, so I tried not to think about it. But, Sir Douglas started to come on strong, sitting in my studio half the day, talking as though it were only a matter of waiting a decent length of time before we announced our engagement. It was bizarre! I couldn't see any way out.' She stared at Fizz, her eyes wide and despairing. 'What should I have done? What would you have done, Fizz?'

Fizz would have told the guy to get stuffed and bugger the consequences but there seemed no point in saying that now. 'Tough call,' she said. 'What did *you* do?'

'Nothing. Oh, I tried to tell him I loved Kerr and wanted to stay with him but he couldn't accept that. He kept looking for other reasons that might be forcing me to reject him: the class difference, my need for independence, anything but the one reason that mattered: that I found him totally unappealing as a man. Then, one day – a fortnight ago – he started to talk about how our love was obviously meant to be: how opportune it was that his wife had passed on when she did and – Fizz – I *knew* they'd killed her! I saw it in his face. So unmistakable I nearly fainted. Literally. I staggered. He must have seen how it hit me and he knew I'd go to the police.'

'You didn't say anything, surely?'

'No, I'm not stupid, Fizz! I went home determined to make myself believe it wasn't true, that I didn't need to tell Kerr about what had been going on. I tried again, that evening, to make him promise to look for another job but we had a furious row about it. I lay awake all night trying to decide whether to cause endless trouble by taking my – possibly groundless – suspicions to the police or whether to keep my mouth shut and hope to talk Kerr into leaving. In the morning I went into work early, planning to think it over for a while and maybe phone some friends in the medical profession. I thought I might find someone to talk to, someone who could help me decide whether Lady Audrey's heart attack could have been induced.'

'What made you think that could have been the case?' Fizz inserted, sipping her coffee and trying to ignore the first twinges of panic, like small electric shocks, that were starting to break through her lethargy.

'She had a problem called sleep apnea, something quite common in very overweight people. What it boils down to is that they can simply stop breathing in their sleep. Normally they don't sleep all that soundly so they wake up when their oxygen cuts off but, if they don't, they can suffer brain damage or a heart attack, as Lady Audrey did. However, it would be very easy to slip her a couple of sleeping tablets to make sure she didn't wake up when her breathing halted.'

'You think Lady Marjory would do that?'

Irene looked down into her empty mug. 'I know she used sleeping pills herself from time to time. She'd had them for years – old fashioned Temazepan tablets – like the "jellies" that guy used to push at the students' union, remember? She gave me one a while back when I had toothache and couldn't get to the dentist till morning. I've been thinking about it and I reckon she could have used the same stuff to knock me out that morning in my studio – and you too, Fizz. You could split the capsules open and draw up the contents into a syringe – much quicker and twice as powerful. I suspect she would have killed me outright if Sir Douglas hadn't prevented it.'

'She got you before you had a chance to talk to the police, obviously. How did she do it?'

Irene shook her head. 'I can't remember a thing about it, but I guess she just walked in and slipped it to me while my head was bent over the desk. If we're right about this place being somewhere in the region of the old chapel she'd have found it quite easy to get me out, and down the back stairs before any of the staff came on duty and there's a door in what used to be the laundry that opens on that side. Maybe Sir Douglas helped her, but she could have carried me without his help. She's a strong woman.'

'You think he was in on the plan?'

The words hung in the air for a few seconds while Irene chewed her lip and ran a forefinger studiously around the rim of her mug. 'I think he had to be, Fizz, to some extent. He tries to blame it all on her ladyship but he's so full of excuses he must feel at least partly to blame. I truly believe he thought it would only be temporary – just till I "came to my senses" as he put it. For the first few days I'm sure he actually believed he could talk me round. He never admitted being aware of how Lady Audrey met her end but when he realised I knew what had happened he switched to going on about our having our whole life ahead of us and how we could forget the past and live happily ever after. And then, as time went on he began to realise the whole thing had been a pipe dream and he was now riding a tiger.'

Fizz rubbed her eyes, trying to shake off the lethargy that still plagued her. 'Didn't you try going along with his ideas? Maybe if you'd made out that you were actually madly in love with him – had sex with him, even – he might have fallen for it and let you out.'

'That was one of the first things I tried,' Irene retorted with an impatient gesture. 'And it was working – I'm sure it was, though I hadn't reached the point of offering sexual favours – but that scheme collapsed when he discovered I'd been shouting through the air vent. You and Kerr were my only hope but at least I knew you were doing everything possible to find me.'

'You *hoped* we were.'

'No, I knew it as soon as Sir Douglas told me the Rubens had been stolen. When I thought about it, it seemed like one of your ideas.'

Fizz hauled her head up. 'He told you about that?'

'Sure. It never occurred to him that anyone other than an art thief could have taken it. He actually expected me to feel sympathy for him because the police were going to be poking around looking for it. Lady Marjory was going to inject me to keep me quiet while the area was being searched but Sir Douglas wouldn't have it. He tied me up and gagged me instead.'

'Heart of gold, that man,' Fizz muttered, prompting another of Irene's frowns.

'He's not an evil man, Fizz.'

'Right.' Fizz knew it was a waste of time talking to her because she'd find a way to forgive anybody, no matter what they did to her. She and Buchanan would make a fine pair. As

far as she herself was concerned Sir Douglas deserved everything the Law could throw at him, and then some, no matter
whether it was he or his sister who set the whole mad escapade
in motion. And she was going to make sure they both regretted every bit of it: especially the mistake of meddling with
Fizz Fitzpatrick.

'Okay, Irene,' she said, hauling herself out of her chair like
a sack of potatoes. 'Let's see about getting ourselves the hell
out of this dump.'

Buchanan had managed to put Fizz's whereabouts to the back of his mind well before they reached the falls. Kerr had helped him enormously in this endeavour by starting to twitch uncontrollably and by refusing to look at Sir Douglas, even when his back was turned. With his concentration focused almost entirely in making sure he was between the two of them at all times, Buchanan could barely keep up his end of a seriously one-sided conversation and it was left to Sir Douglas himself to fill what would otherwise have been an awkward silence.

Fortunately, he didn't find that a problem. He knew every inch of his river: every pool and run, every hidden lie, and had a story to tell about every stretch.

'This has always been called the Dominie's Pool – well, for a couple of hundred years at least – but don't ask me who the dominie was or where he taught. There was a Miss Annie Lawson, a distant cousin of my great grandfather's, who took a thirty-eight pounder out of it in 1835. Funny how often you hear of women landing big fish, isn't it? Something in the pheromones, somebody once told me. The fish pick up on it and come running. Pity they can't bottle it – eh? – and sell it in the tackle shops. These trees are becoming a bit of a nuisance, Kerr. Need to get them cut back. And there's the fishermen's rest, I was telling you about, Tam. Not exactly an architectural gem, I don't suppose, but damn handy when you need to sit out a shower or want to eat your picnic lunch out of the wind. Take a look inside.'

Buchanan obediently ducked in at the low doorway and, as he did so, he heard Sir Douglas say, 'Come on, old chap, cheer up, for God's sake.'

'Get your filthy hands off me!' Kerr's snarl jerked Buchanan around like a marionette but his exit was blocked by

Sir Douglas's bulky body and as he jostled his way past he was just in time to see the flash of Kerr's fist as it connected with his lordship's cheekbone.

'*Kerr, NO!*' he yelled, lunging for him, but the blow took Sir Douglas with all the force that had been building in Kerr for the last six hours and it threw him sideways, crashing him into Buchanan and knocking them both to the ground.

The bank was steep just there, and slippery, and for a couple of seconds Buchanan thought he was headed for the pool below. He managed to stop his slide in time but, in those same seconds, Kerr had grabbed his lordship by the throat and hurled him into the river. By some lucky chance he landed a pace or two from the pool's edge, in something like four feet of fast moving current, thrashing wildly and clawing for purchase on the nearest boulder. Kerr was on top of him in an instant and by the time Buchanan scrambled up the bank he had both hands round Sir Douglas's neck and, roaring like a mad bull, was holding his head under the water.

Having tried diplomacy, Buchanan had no choice but to join the fray and from that point on all hell broke loose. Kerr was a big man, heavier if not taller than Buchanan, and he was in the grip of a rage that had turned him into a wild animal, lusting for blood. His face was contorted and suffused with blood and his body, as Buchanan's shoulder hit it square on, was as rigid and unyielding as bedrock.

Nothing short of a tyre wrench was going to break the grip he had on his boss. In a maelstrom of white water, yelling and roaring, he and Buchanan wrestled for control. At one moment Sir Douglas's head would be a foot under water, the next, Buchanan would drag it forth long enough for the man to snatch a breath, but a moment later Kerr would regain the upper hand and it would disappear again in the foam.

This deadlock continued for what seemed like hours. Buchanan could not summon the strength to overpower Kerr

completely any more than Kerr could shake off his interfer-
ence but, in the meantime, Sir Douglas was going downhill
fast. The effort of staggering about, fighting the thrust of the
torrent, never mind wrestling with the supercharged maniac
that was Kerr, was taking it's toll on Buchanan too. If he could
have snatched a spare second to grab a rock and stun Kerr
with it he'd have done so – he doubted his ability to land a
decisive punch – but in a ding-dong battle like this one spare
seconds were hard to come by.

He hung on grimly, longer than he'd have believed possible, with his shoulder and thigh muscles screaming and his
breath rasping holes in his lungs, and he must have been within a heartbeat of defeat when he realised that Kerr was weak-
ening too. That discovery gave him a sudden boost of adrenaline and, in desperation, he loosed his grasp on his lordship's
collar and, with all his remaining strength, rammed his shoulder into Kerr's side. Kerr's feet slipped from under him and he
went down like a felled oak, disappearing in a fountain of
spray, and Buchanan managed to grab the sinking Sir Douglas
and start hauling him towards the bank.

Exhaustion made everything appear to happen in slow
motion. The bank grew no nearer as Buchanan staggered
towards it. Kerr rose from the water with the slow majesty of
a whale's tail and started after him like some nightmarish figure, enraged and inexorable. Sir Douglas's still windmilling
arms and churning legs slowed them even further and, when
they at last reached the river's edge, the bank reared above
them, impossible to scale in the time available. Buchanan
could only push Sir Douglas against the slope and get in front
of him to halt Kerr's charge.

'Get away from him!' Kerr grated, coming at them like an
armoured car.

'No, Kerr,' Buchanan said, with Sir Douglas choking and
spluttering in his ear. 'This won't solve anything.'

'He killed Irene. He's going to die.'

'No, he's not. We're doing this my way.'

Kerr's hand landed on Buchanan's shoulder and wrenched him half aside. 'Move, Tam!'

Leaning back against Sir Douglas, Buchanan got a foot up against Kerr's middle and catapulted him back into the torrent, but in a moment he was up again, shaking the water from his eyes, twice as mad. He said nothing as he fought his way back but he looked less than human and Buchanan's guardian angel was begging him to cut and run, now, while he still had the chance.

'Don't do this, Kerr,' he was starting to say when his brain suddenly translated the gibberish in his ear into plain English.

'Not dead...no, no...wouldn't kill her...'

'*Not dead*?' He spun round to stare at the drowned face behind him, holding Kerr off with a stiff arm and shouting again, '*Not dead*? Kerr! He's saying she's not dead!'

Kerr pushed him away with more strength than Buchanan had guessed he had left and dropped his big hands on Sir Douglas's shoulders, half-lifting him from the bank.

'What? What d'you mean, not dead, you bastard?'

'She's alive...'

'Where?'

'Up...up at the house...I'll show you...'

Kerr let him drop and, turning aside, put both hands and then his forehead against the bank as though to hold himself upright. For a moment they all stood there in a silence that contrasted conspicuously, in Buchanan's mind, with the pandemonium of a moment ago. He put a hand on Kerr's back for a second and then decided he'd better get Sir Douglas out of the river while he had the opportunity. It wasn't easy on his own, but a minute later all three of them were sprawled on the grass like haddock tipped from a seine net, with water running from them like a flood.

Kerr got to his knees and stooped over Sir Douglas. 'Where have you got her, you pathetic turd?'

'Up at the house,' Sir Douglas whimpered twitching away from him as though he expected further violence at any moment. 'It wasn't me, Kerr, it was Marjory. I wouldn't have hurt a hair of —'

'Where in the big house?'

'Not...not *in* the house...in...in, ah, the old fall-out shelter my father built...ah...under the chapel.'

'You bastard —!'

Kerr's hands shot out towards his neck but Buchanan was ready for him and swatted them away. 'For God's sake, get a grip, Kerr! You could have killed him back there and where would Irene be then? Locked up in a fall-out shelter for bloody life, that's where, with nobody knowing she was there. When are you going to start using your head?'

Kerr shivered and sat back on his heels, still staring hate at his lordship but starting to get a grip on himself. Sir Douglas pushed himself backwards with his hands and feet, putting distance between them, and sat there slobbering and wiping drips and phlegm from his moustache. His eyes were bright red and his bouffant hairstyle had collapsed, exposing a wide bald patch on the crown of his head.

'Okay,' said Buchanan, striving for a semblance of calm although something akin to dread was already taking hold of him. Two elements he did not like the sound of had made their way into the scenario, namely: the abbey and Lady Marjory, and his imagination was beginning to run out of control. 'Do we head back for the Land Rover or press on on foot?'

'Land Rover,' Kerr said shortly and grabbing Sir Douglas by an arm, jerked him to his feet and gave him a shove that sent him staggering down the path. It had taken them well over an hour to walk up from the bridge pool but they were back there in thirty-five minutes: jogging, running, goading

Sir Douglas when he slowed down, dragging him when they
had to. Kerr harangued him mercilessly all the way and
Buchanan didn't intervene, even when the man was reduced to
tears, concluding that Kerr needed some outlet for his anger if
he were not to kill Sir Douglas outright.

Another five minutes and they were outside the chapel.
There was no sign of Fizz, either in the immediate surroundings or in the part of the grounds they had passed through on
the way there. That didn't mean anything, he tried to tell himself, she could have spent the morning with Caitlin. So why
was he getting that shrinking feeling in his guts?

Sir Douglas got a bunch of keys out of his trouser pocket
and started to unlock the gate but Kerr snatched them from
him and did it himself, dragging his boss by a handful of jacket as he sprinted across the rough ground to the doorway.

'Where? Where?'

'Downstairs...behind the altar there.'

They clattered down into the half dark, Buchanan now in
the lead – though what good he thought he might do there he
couldn't have said. Sir Douglas stopped at the foot, probably
unable to see his way forward, but Kerr kept shouting in his
face.

'Get on! What are you waiting for?'

Huge white sarcophagi and catafalques littered their route
to the back wall where his lordship fell to his knees in front of
a pile of smashed marble. Crouching beside him, Buchanan
put out a hand to steady himself and felt glass beneath his fingers. Curious, he picked up the object and brought it closer to
his eyes to see what it was and found himself looking at Fizz's
sunglasses.

He couldn't speak, but the breath went out of him with a
rush and he heard himself moan with the pain, the sound covered by the rattle of stones as Sir Douglas pushed aside some
large blocks. With Kerr screaming at him like a drill sergeant

he fumbled some sort of key out of his pocket – a long flanged spike of metal – inserting it into what must have been an opening low down in the pile. There was a soft *clunk* and the pile moved a few inches to the side allowing a shaft of light to fan up into the gloom.

Immediately, Kerr grabbed him and dragged him aside, but Buchanan was in the better position to reach the opening first. No matter that Kerr's need was greater than his: no matter that he'd been worried longer or was more deeply involved with the woman he needed so desperately to see: Buchanan was through that opening like a ferret down a rabbit hole.

Below him was a bright light, a steep iron stepladder, a square of concrete flooring. Precipitating himself down the steps, his head had not yet cleared the opening when he heard Fizz scream.

'*No Buchanan! No-ooooooooooo!*'

And, at that second, he found himself standing on air with the concrete floor swooping up to swallow him.

Later, when the doctors had finished X-raying him and setting his fractured femur and the nurses had tucked him tidily into a hospital bed, it occurred to him that it would have been a good idea to look before he leaped. If he'd had time for a few minutes' calm reflection between realising that Fizz was trapped below and actually rushing to her rescue he'd have at least considered the possibility that she wouldn't be taking her imprisonment sitting down. Anyone who knew her would have realised that she'd be planning her escape within minutes of the trap door closing above her, and only a fool would have scooted down that ladder without checking the treads.

He slept for a while, with the assistance of a couple of painkillers, and awoke with the arrival of the evening visitors, worried people with cheerful faces who sat close to their loved ones and held hands on the coverlet and spoke in intimate whispers. He hadn't expected a visitor of his own since Fizz hated hospitals and he hadn't felt it necessary to inform any of his friends or family of his accident. However, just as he was about to doze off again, he looked up and there was Eddie walking up the ward.

'Well, hello you,' he said, grinning like a lottery winner.

She leaned over with a waft of spicy perfume and planted a kiss on his brow, just below the bandage. 'How're you feeling?'

'Not too bad, actually. In fact, now that you're here, pretty damn good.'

'I'm sure your leg hurts.' She pulled the chair closer to the bed and sat down, putting a couple of magazines and a bottle of grape juice on top of his locker without comment. He started to thank her but she shook her head. 'How long do you think they'll keep you in?'

'Not long, I don't think. They say there's possible concussion and some internal bruising so they just want to keep an eye on me overnight. I'm afraid it rather knocks our date on the head, though.'

She pushed a hand through her hair and let it fall, not looking at him. 'I saw Irene this afternoon,' she said. 'She's pretty shaken up by the whole experience, I think. But Kerr's talking about taking her away for a long, lazy holiday somewhere before they start looking for new jobs and, really, they both look so happy just to be together that I'm sure they'll soon put it all behind them.'

'What about the Fergussons?'

'We haven't heard anything yet but I don't think we'll be seeing either of them for a long number of years, do you? There's no shortage of evidence against them and even if Lady Marjory takes the blame for Nanny's and Lady Audrey's murders, Sir Douglas is bound to be implicated. He was certainly an accessory after the fact and now that the Rubens has been found he —'

'The Rubens? It turned up?'

She lifted her head. 'Yes – but of course you'd left in the ambulance by that time. It turned up in the fall-out shelter, so there's not much point in their denying knowledge of its whereabouts. Whatever could have inspired them to do such a foolish thing?'

Buchanan wasn't willing to hazard a guess. He was just enormously glad the whole business was behind him and he could get back to an ordered existence with a clear conscience and little damage to his reputation. He could explain away his broken leg without having to tell Larry which stairs he fell down and, with a bit of luck, he'd be allowed home tomorrow in time to finish off the briefs he'd been entrusted with before the great man got back on Monday. It had been a hectic fortnight but it couldn't be said to have brought no rewards, and one of them was sitting by his bed right now.

He held out his hand to her and, after a slight hesitation, she dropped hers into it and looked at him with a strange expression. For a moment he thought she was about to speak but she just sat there and waited for him to make the next move.

'What about next weekend, then? I should be back on my feet by then – on at least one foot, anyway, so we'll have something to celebrate. Do you like seafood? We could eat at Poseidon and then go to Georgio's for a few drinks then, if you like, we could go back to my place and continue with what we started back in the Bavarian summerhouse last week. Would that be nice?' He waited for her enthusiastic response and then added, 'Or an itinerary of your choice. I'm amenable to persuasion.'

He was prepared for almost anything other than,
'I don't think so.'

'Uh…sorry?' Buchanan said. 'You don't think what?'

She looked at him directly then, her eyes very blue. 'I don't think we have a future, Tam.'

For a moment words deserted him. He could not believe the way this woman blew hot and cold. One minute she was practically ripping the pants off him, the next she was acting like she couldn't stand the sight of him.

'Why not?' he said at last.

She slipped her hand out of his, drew back from him, and spoke very softly. 'Frankly, Tam, I'm not in the market for a quick fling. I'm thirty-six. I've done all that, and it was fun at the time, but now I'm looking for a stable relationship. Not to put too fine a point on it, my biological clock is ticking and I don't think you're the man I'm looking for.'

It struck Buchanan that she had come to that conclusion rather suddenly and he said so. 'You're not giving our relationship much time to develop, are you? A quick fling wasn't exactly what I had in mind either, Eddie. I thought – I still think – that we could be onto something good here and, believe me, that doesn't happen to me too often. You must have thought that too, at one point, so what happened to change your mind?'

A corner of her mouth lifted, creasing her brown cheek into a fan of threadlike wrinkles. 'I opened my eyes, Tam, and saw what I should have seen earlier. A few years back I'd have gone along for the ride but not at this stage in my life. I'm not in the market for a man who's in love with another woman.'

'What other woman, for heaven's sake, Eddie?' Buchanan gave a snort of laughter. 'Fizz? If you're talking about Fizz, you're way off target. She'd be horrified if she heard you say that.'

'Really? But you aren't, are you, Tam?'

He stopped like he'd been stiff-armed and, for a space of a few seconds, they stared at each other, separated by an arm's length and an insurmountable lack of understanding.

He moved a hand in a jerky, meaningless gesture. 'Fizz and

I are colleagues, that's all. Well, perhaps a little more than colleagues. Friends. But platonic friends. To be honest with you,
she drives me crazy most of the time and I know I drive her
crazy too. There's never going to be anything between Fizz
and I.'

'Well, I'm sorry to hear that, Tam, because it's quite clear to
me that you're in love with her. You hardly speak a sentence
that doesn't have her name in it, your eyes are on her all the
time she's in the room. You think I don't see the little secret
messages you pass from one to the other with your eyes? The
private jokes? The way you consider her comfort and conven-
ience all the time? The way you rush to her side the moment
you even suspect she could be in trouble?'

She tipped her head to one side and waited for him to
make some reply but it took him a moment to find the words.

'No, you're quite wrong, Eddie,' he said finally. 'You don't
know Fizz. She's – yes, I'll admit she can be…you might call
it stimulating as a friend, and certainly we've been thrown
together a lot in recent years, but she's…I don't like to say
this, but she's poison ivy. It would take me all night to tell you
the trouble she's caused me in my career and now that I'm
investing everything in becoming an advocate I'd actually be
better off not knowing her at all. The last thing I need is a
woman who gets me a name for the sort of underhand dealing
she goes in for on a regular basis.'

'Wrong answer, Tam,' she said, giving him a rather wistful
little smile. 'Not what I was hoping to hear, I'm afraid. The
fact that she's not a suitable mate for an ambitious young
lawyer is very sad but it doesn't change the way you feel about
her, does it? So, I'm truly sorry, Tam, but I'm not interested in
being a substitute. If you'd lied to me, told me she was like a
sister to you, that she was boring as hell, that she had bad
breath and no sex-appeal, I might have been tempted to do
something stupid like say, okay, let's give it ago. But you

couldn't say those things, could you?' She pushed her chair back and stood up. 'Maybe there's some way you can work it out: either marry her or get her out of your system, but if you can't offer me a whole man, there's no future for us.'

He caught her hand and held on to it for a second or two, disposed to dig his heels in, but suddenly knew there was nothing he could say to convince her. Seeing it in his face, she dropped a soft kiss on his cheek and turned quickly away.

'Goodbye, Eddie,' he said. 'I hope you find someone.'

'And you. But I think you've found her.'

He watched her walk quickly to the door, her feet silent on the rubberised flooring, and wondered if it was really all over or if she'd change her mind when she'd thought about it for a couple of days. Maybe he'd give her a ring in a week or so and see if, by that time, she'd realised what rot she'd been talking. Where did women get their ideas from anyway?

His eyes were still on the door when it swung open again and Fizz walked in, scanning the beds for him and toting an armful of tatty paperbacks. She was wearing her denim skirt and a white T-shirt with a picture of the Loch Ness Monster on the front. Scarcely what the young lawyer about town was wearing this season.

'Hi,' she said laconically, dropping into the chair Eddie had just vacated. 'Feeling better?'

'Much.'

'Good.'

He waited.

She said, 'You're mad at me, right?'

'Mad at you? Why would I be mad at you?'

She shrugged. 'No reason, actually, because if you hadn't been coming down those stairs too damn fast altogether you'd have heard me telling you to stop. But that's okay. Blame me if it makes you feel any better. I'll even apologise, if you like. I'm sorry. There. Does that take the pain away?'

Buchanan blinked at her, realising that, however badly phrased, he'd just had an apology. She must be feeling seriously guilty, which would be a whole new experience for her. 'That's fine, Fizz. We'll forget the whole business. Just one thing, though.'

She looked at him warily.

'Don't get me into any more of your escapades, huh? It's high time we grew up, the pair of us, and started to act like rational human beings. If any more of your friends – or even clients – get kidnapped, or murdered, or indeed seriously discommoded in any way, count me out. Right? Would you do that for me?'

'Damn tootin', old buddy. Couldn't have phrased it better myself. From now on I'm doing something more practical with my time. Bingo, maybe. Hooked rugs. Gardening.'

'You don't have a garden.'

'I could knock together a window box.'

'Sure.'

She drew in a breath, wrinkling her nose with distaste at the pervasive smell of disinfectant. 'So what else is new?'

'Eddie's just gone,' he told her, looking for a change in her expression, but she showed no glimmer of interest. 'She tells me the Rubens was discovered in the fall-out shelter.'

'Uh-huh.'

'Has anybody any idea what motive the Fergussons might have had for stealing their own picture?'

'Not so far. I dare say it'll all come out in the wash.'

'You don't seem wildly curious about it,' he said.

'Frankly, I don't feel much like worrying about it this evening. We've done what we set out to do and I'm happy just to leave it like that.'

He gave her a look that was meant to illustrate how atypical he found her lack of interest but she didn't seem to notice.

'Must dash,' she said, checking the time on the clock

behind her with a concern that struck him as remarkably sudden. 'I'm going to the library on the way home. Give me a buzz at the office if you need anything.'

She leaned over, patted him on the head and whisked away down the ward leaving, on the still and sterile air, the merest whiff of brimstone.